Twisted Fate

Samantha Ford

Cover Credit
Photography by: Neil Tally
Cover Design by: Jessica Bruzdzinski
Title Design by: Rachel Blackwelder

©2014 Samantha Ford
All rights reserved. No part of this publication may be reproduced, distributed, or transmitted in any form or by any means, including photocopying, recording, or other electronic or mechanical methods, without the prior permission of the publisher.

ISBN: 1499791828
ISBN 13: 9781499791822
Library of Congress Control Number: 2014916045
CreateSpace Independent Publishing Platform
North Charleston, South Carolina

Dedicated to my family and friends who have supported me throughout this process. I couldn't have done it without your love and encouragement. Also to Dalton Barrett McKee never give up on your writing or anything else you want to do and remember I'm always in your corner.

Acknowledgments

Many people, in multiple ways, have been instrumental in making *Twisted Fate* a reality and not just a vision in my mind. I want to acknowledge the help and encouragement each of you have given me. At the top of my list is my family. Dale Blackwelder you're a wonderful father to our children and for that I am thankful. Speaking of children, Paige, TJ, and Megan, you three are the motivation for everything I do in my life. Thank you for the few quiet hours I stole to write while you were sleeping. To my mom Cindy without your support I wouldn't be where I am now in my life's journey, and for that I will always be grateful. My dad, Tim Ford, you are not only my father, you are my friend and I know you will always be there, so thank you. Jessica Bruzdzinski, my pain-in-the-butt little sister; we fight...we argue but I know you always have my back and I will always have yours.

Several women have directly helped me with *Twisted Fate* by reading chapters as I wrote them. Ashley Jenkins, Kelly Russ, Rachel Blackwelder, Sally Hinson, and Haley Albertson, you have no idea how much you helped me by sharing your ideas as you read my drafts. I will always be thankful for the time you spent reading and the honesty each you showed me when you gave your thoughts and ideas about what you read.

Book cover models, Chelsea Ford, my sister, and Chris Hale, thank you for allowing me to use your beautiful picture to bring Presley and Luca to life. Your dedication to helping me make sure everything was perfect is why I love you both. Amy Rodgers (Simply Stylin'), you did an amazing job with hair and make-up for the cover. Of course, you work is always amazing, so thank you for doing what you do, and doing it great. Neil Talley thank you for taking such wonderful pictures. You made my job of picking just one very hard.

Quinn Loftis, author of *The Grey Wolf Series*, I would never have had the courage to write *Twisted Fate* had your books not inspired me so much. Reading your books has reignited the passion I had to write, which had been buried for far too long... thank you so much.

There are two more people who helped me with this book, but also in every stage of my life, Grandma Pat (Ford) and Grammie (Cynthia Barrett). Grandma Pat, not only did you read as I wrote, but most importantly you kept me motivated throughout this whole process. You can raise my spirit, you make me laugh when I want to cry...sometimes I laugh so hard I cry anyway! Grammie, you used your spelling and grammar skills to edit *Twisted Fate*. You make me believe in myself because you believe in me. You pushed me to reach my potential and made me challenge myself. I am blessed to have two wonderful grandmothers. Your faith in me and your love for me gives me the strength and courage I need to put myself "out there" and do this. I love you so much and I thank God for you every day.

Prologue

At 3:00 PM the last bell of her junior year finally rang. Presley could barely contain her excitement about the upcoming summer. She had one week of cheer camp and her boyfriend, Eric, had only two weeks of football camp. Either camp could interfere with the amazing summer they had planned. Fortunately, neither camp started till early August. First on their agenda was a week at Myrtle Beach with friends, many who were now officially high school graduates. It was a tradition at their school for graduates and their friends to spend an after graduation week at Myrtle Beach. This trip would be one last chance to be childish and make stupid decisions before beginning to plan for their future lives.

She was excited as she exited Mr. Hall's bio class into a crowded hallway filled with loud and boisterous teenagers ready to totally enjoy the freedom summer always brought. Suddenly she felt two big muscular arms wrapping around her tiny waist and pulling her against an equally muscular chest. Presley felt Eric's warm breath against her sun kissed skin as he moved her long blonde hair to the side and placed a gentle kiss on her neck.

"Hey, beautiful are you ready to blow this place?" he asked Presley.

She turned to him and looked into his sparkling green eyes with her beautiful baby blue eyes. He had blonde hair that he kept tousled and messy. He looked like a typical all American jock.

"About a week ago, babe" she smirked. Then, making sure no one was looking, she placed a quick kiss on his lips. At the same time she slipped her hand in his and intertwined their fingers.

They made their way through the crowded halls to the front doors. When Eric opened the heavy doors Presley felt her lungs fill with fresh air as the bright sun of a June afternoon in North Carolina warmed her skin. Once again her thoughts were on the upcoming summer and how wonderful it promised to be.

They walked through the front yard of the school heading towards Eric's red Ford F150. Presley saw Becca's brown pony tail bouncing as she quickly walked toward them with her new flavor of the week, Joey. Becca never seemed to have the same boyfriend for more than a week or two. She liked to tease Eric and Presley about being like an old married couple. They had been together for almost two years. The two of them were rarely more than 10 feet from each other when they were not in class. Becca believed long term relationships were best left for after college so those relationships would not interfere with the fun of being teenagers with no responsibilities. However, truth be told, if Caleb Howser decided he was ready to commit to her she would throw that belief out the window!

"Alright, Mr. and Mrs. Clever are you ready to party?" she asked as she threw her arms around Presley's shoulders. Eric looked down at Presley with a smile on his boyish face as he said, "Presley in a bikini with no parental supervision. I've been ready for this since middle school." Presley blushed hearing the desire in his deep voice. She just rolled her eyes hoping no one noticed the pink in her cheeks.

"Alright, well Joey and I will probably just meet you at the hotel," Becca said as she walked away giggling.

After Becca and Joey left Presley and Eric hopped into Eric's truck. Presley slid to her normal place in the truck. Sliding across the passenger seat, stopping when she was sitting next to Eric in the middle of the bench style seat. One of the reasons she loved the truck so much was that she could be close to Eric. After a quick ten minute drive they pulled into Presley's driveway. Presley's home was the typical upper middle class house. She lived in a four bedroom house that had a simple elegance. It was always clean and neat. The yard had a simple landscape with one tree in the center that still held the wooden swing she sat on as a young girl. There were small flower beds on each side of the front door.

"Alright I will be back at about six to get you. You and your cute little tush better be packed and ready to go," Eric said with a smile on his face. He reached down, put his hand on the back of her neck and pulled her lips to his. The kiss started gently at first but deepened quickly.

"I thought you wanted me to hurry up and get ready" she said breathlessly as she pulled away. "We have a minute" he said, pulling her back into the kiss. She pushed away from him again and opened the passenger side door. "I love you baby and I will be ready," she giggled as she jumped down from the truck closing the door when her feet hit the driveway. "Love you too," Eric shouted through his open window as Presley opened the front door to her house.

When Presley entered her house she was thinking about how great it was that even though she and Eric had been dating almost two years whenever she saw him she felt the flutter of butterfly wings in her stomach. Every time they kissed it felt like the very first time. Becca didn't know what she was missing!

Her parents were still at work so she headed upstairs to finish packing and change. She went to her closet and took out a lavender tank top and a pair of light denim shorts with strategically placed tears. She quickly pulled her hair into a messy bun on the top of her head and began gathering the stuff she would need for a week at the beach. Since she had already packed her clothes, she simply needed to get together the necessities she had used getting ready for school that morning. After going through her mental check list she was sure she had everything and was ready to go.

It was only 5:30 so she decided she had time for a quick snack and to pack a small cooler for the four hour drive. She had just finished her PB&J sandwich and started packing the cooler when she heard the front door open. As she was placing the last bottle of water in the cooler her dad entered the kitchen.

"Hey, baby girl, I see you are already to go," he said as he pulled her in for a hug. "I'm not sure how I feel about this Pres."

"It'll be okay Dad, I promise to TRY not to do anything stupid" she giggled as she emphasized the word try.

"UGH….you're a smart girl please, don't let the salt in the air make you forget it," her dad replied.

"I won't Daddy," she told him. She was smiling and batting her lashes as she lifted herself to her toes to kiss his cheek. Just as she lowered herself back down her father rolled his deep brown eyes when he heard the doorbell chimed.

"And that would be the other thing I am worried may make you lose your good sense." Presley's dad liked Eric but wasn't sure how he felt about the intensity of their relationship.

Presley let Eric into the house. After chatting with her father for a couple minutes about their plans and who would be with them at Myrtle Beach Presley and her dad said their goodbyes and I love yous. As she headed to the door Presley turned to her father and hugged him.

"Tell mom I love her and I will call when we get there."

"Okay, please be careful. Oh, and Eric," he paused turning to face Eric. "If she doesn't come back in the exact same condition she is now I will ring your neck," he chuckled.

"Um....yes sir" Eric said knowing that although Mr. Kluttz was laughing he was also dead serious.

Presley and Eric climbed into his truck. Presley, as usual, took her place in the center of the seat. They pulled out of the driveway and headed out for what promised to be the greatest week of their lives. When they reached the corner and stopped at the red light Presley turned her big blue eyes up to look at Eric. "I love you baby," she whispered when he looked down to meet her gaze. He placed a finger under her chin and tilting her face up gently placed a kiss on her lips. "I love you, too," he said. She laid her head back on his arm and they both looked at the road ahead. The light turned green and as Eric pulled forward Presley heard the most God awful sound coming out of her own mouth as she saw the Ford Explorer running the red light. She squeezed her eyes shut when she heard the sound of crunching metal and felt her body being violently thrown left to right. She smelled the odor of burning rubber. She felt small slivers and chunks of glass embedding in her skin. She thought the truck must have flipped at least twenty times as she was tossed about like a rag doll. Then she sensed nothing but darkness.

Chapter One

9 Months Later

Kevin sat in the back booth of the Waffle House waiting for his friend's arrival. He was dressed in a hunter green polo with loose fitting jeans. His work boots had obviously never seen a day of manual labor. His light brown hair was cut short and his freshly shaven face held a look of total boredom. Stephanie showed up just as he was beginning to be frustrated by the fact that she was almost always late. She came in smiling as usual. Her auburn hair was cut just above her shoulders. The mischievous look in her green eyes told him she was up to something. She was wearing a long white sweater with black leggings and black Ugg boots.

"Hey, Kev, is Pres coming tonight?" she asked as she lowered herself into the booth.

"Yeah, why?" he asked cocking one eyebrow almost afraid to hear the answer.

"Well, Marcus is bringing this guy who started working with him last week and he's starting school tomorrow ...soooo... I thought maybe we could do some match making," she said smiling very pleased with herself.

"Steph, you know she is going to kill you right? You can't push her into something she isn't ready for," he sighed knowing this could be bad very, very bad.

"I'm not saying she has to run off and elope with the guy. After everything she's been through I think she is due for some fun. If there is a little romance involved all the better."

"I guess," was all Kevin had to say.

"Is she talking to her mother yet?"

"Nope. She still pretty much refuses to be in the house with her." He said shaking his head while playing with the straw in his soda.

"Can you blame her? I mean first her boyfriend dies. Then she finds out her dad is not her dad. Both of those life altering events happened in a 24 hour time frame. I mean seriously, she is handling it better than I would. I probably would have already killed somebody."

"What time are Marcus and Romeo coming?"

"First, his name is Luca and, secondly, I would guess they should get here in about 20 minutes."

The waitress approached their table with a glass of sweet tea Stephanie hadn't even ordered.

"Here you go, sweetie, when is the rest of the brat pack getting here?" Sarah asked handing Stephanie the glass.

"Thank you. They should be here in a minute. Can I get a bacon egg and cheese sandwich?"

"David's already started it," Sarah told her.

"God, we come here too much!" Kevin laughed.

Sarah was laughing with him as she walked away from the table.

Presley entered the restaurant and headed straight to the back where she and her friends always sat. She looked awesome in her skinny jeans, black ankle boots, red tank top and short black leather jacket. Her long blonde hair now had cherry red streaks. Her appearance, as well as with her life, had experienced a drastic change since she lost Eric. Her once bubbly, friendly attitude, as well as her appearance, now seemed dark, gloomy and jaded. She was still friendly but it was obvious to her friends her once cheery outlook on life was now weighted down by deep sadness.

"What's up, guys?" she asked as she took her normal seat next to Kevin.

"Hey babe," he said as he kissed her cheek.

"Are you going to tell her, or am I? " he asked, looking over to Stephanie. At that moment Stephanie suddenly doubted her brilliant idea.

"What is going on?" Presley asked, preparing herself for an answer she didn't want to hear.

"Okay don't get mad, but Marcus is bringing a guy from work and..."

Presley cut her off mid-sentence. "Seriously Steph, when are you going to stop this?" Presley sighed as Sarah brought Stephanie's sandwich. Even though Presley had not ordered a cup of coffee, Sarah had one for her.

"You're a mind reader, Sarah!" Presley said reaching for the sugar for her coffee.

"You guys make it too easy," she said while heading back to the counter.

Now Presley focused her attention back to Stephanie. "Alright spill!"

"Well his name is Luca, he's 18, and he just moved here from Virginia and, oh yeah, he is gorgeous." She said while taking a bite of her sandwich.

Kevin just sat back and waited for the fireworks.

"Does he THINK he is coming here to meet me?"

Stephanie finished chewing and then answered, "Well no. When he saw a picture of you and me on Marcus's phone he said you were very pretty. He doesn't know you are going to be here." She took another bite of her sandwich.

"Did you know about this?" Presley darted her glare to Kevin.

He raised his hands in surrender, "Just found out about it, I promise!"

Their banter went back and forth for a couple more minutes but it was interrupted when they saw Marcus and Luca enter the restaurant. Presley's eyes widened at the sight of Luca. Stephanie had so lied to her. He was not just gorgeous he was handsome, almost unnaturally beautiful. His dark, almost black, hair was short on the side and slightly longer on the top. His eyes were royal blue. His body seemed too muscular to be a teenager. Even his face was flawless...a perfectly shaped nose, strong chin and full lips. The smile spreading across his handsome face led Presley to believe he was pleasantly surprised to see her there.

Marcus took his spot next to Stephanie and kissed her quickly. "Hey babe, miss me?"

"You wish," she said grinning slyly.

Luca took a chair from the table across from them. Turning it backwards and putting one leg on each side he sat at the end of the table between Presley and Marcus. Presley caught a whiff of Luca's cologne. ***Oh dear God, he even smells heavenly. Okay, maybe I won't kill Stephanie yet***...Presley thought. Instantly she was taken back by the smug smile that crossed Luca's lips. ***Did I say that out loud?*** She looked around the table and realized that none of her friends were laughing uncontrollably and no one had a look of shock on their face. No, she hadn't said that out loud. Looking back over at Luca she noticed that smug smile was gone.

"Pres. this is Luca Davenport and Luca this is Presley Kluttz," Marcus said pointing his finger between the two of them.

"Nice to meet you Presley, I have heard a lot about you."

"Should I be worried?"

"No it was all good I promise," he said winking.

Presley immediately felt heat rise to her cheeks so she quickly turned to Kevin to change the subject. Hearing Stephanie let out a little chuckle she shot a meaningful glare at her. Her friend decided it would probably in her best interest to shut up. Turning her attention back to Kevin she successfully changed the subject. "You staying at my house tonight?" she asked. As the question came out of her mouth she couldn't help but notice the obvious look of disappointment on Luca's face. She decided to ignore it because it was probably her imagination.

"You know I will if you want but you are going to have to stop using me a shield for your mom."

"She won't be there she is working third tonight so maybe I just want to hang with my bestie."

"Okay," he said, rolling his eyes.

"So are you two like together?" Luca asked feeling very confused. He would have thought Marcus would have told him if Presley had had a boyfriend when he asked about her.

The whole table burst out laughing and choking on drinks. Presley was the one who finally answered.

"No he is my very best friend. My very gay best friend!"

"Oh, okay," Luca said feeling a little better that maybe he still had a chance with this beautiful blonde.

"So, Luca, who do you have for homeroom?" Stephanie asked

"Mrs. Farmer," he answered.

"Oh, me too. Why don't you meet me in front of the school? I can be your tour guide," Presley said without thinking. She saw the smile spread across not only his face but Stephanie's, too. ***Oh smooth*** she thought.

"That would be good. What time?"

"7:45."

"Good it's date," as he winked at her. ***He has to quit doing that or I am going to pass out right here. What the hell is wrong with you girl? Get it together, he is just a guy!*** Luca let out a little chuckle almost in response to her inner bantering. She looked at him oddly which caused him to look away and shut up.

The group continued to inform Luca about the ins and outs of the new school he would be attending. Luca sat back and watched as they all sat around joking and picking on each other. He had a feeling he hadn't had in a long time the feeling he was just a normal teenage boy with real friends. He did keep a close eye and ear on Presley. Her spunk and wit intrigued him a lot. He hadn't been so immediately drawn to anybody like he was to her...not ever. There was something in her that seemed to be calling to him. There was something going on and he was going to figure out what it was.

About 10:00 the group parted ways to head home. "Don't forget about me," Luca whispered in Presley's ear from behind her. When she turned to face him he gave her that wink he knew she really liked. Then without another word he headed toward his blue Mustang. He jumped in and drove home.

"I am guessing we will be talking about that fine piece of masculinity tonight," Kevin said watching Luca pull away.

"You know it!" Presley said watching the tail lights of the Mustang as it drove away.

Chapter Two

Presley entered her dark house about 15 minutes after she had left the Waffle House. Her mind still clouded with confusion over her attraction to this boy she didn't even know. She couldn't wait for Kevin to get there. She needed to confide in the person she trusted the most. She had known Kevin since the third grade but they didn't get close until after the accident. He had lost his sister in the sixth grade when she drowned in their family's pool. When Presley lost Eric Kevin was there for her. He knew how she felt. He knew that telling her everything would be okay was not only useless but also a big fat lie. Because of that he became her best friend and only confidante.

Presley paced the dark living room going over in her head exactly what she wanted to talk to Kevin about. She felt a sense of relief wash over her when lights from Kevin's car illuminated the darkened room.

"About time you showed up!" she joked as she quickly opened the door.

"I got here as quickly as I could. You do know I can't fly... right?" He asked as he quickly kissed Presley on the cheek.

"Aw, babe you can do anything you put your mind to!" she replied with a wink.

Still laughing the two of them headed upstairs to Presley's room. "When is your mom getting home?"

"She probably won't be home till after we leave for school," Presley quickly answered.

"So, where are we going to start? I think we have two things we need to talk about. The hot new guy, or me telling you that you are going to have to talk to your mother sooner or later... for your sake as much as hers. What are we going to discuss first?"

"Okay Dr. Phil, I do realize sooner or later I'm going to have to get past this stuff with my mom but really she lied to me and to my dad for 17 years. Now because of her lie my dad can't even look at me. So a couple months of silent treatment is the least she deserves," Presley told him with a very decisive tone to her voice.

Looking at her with love and concern Kevin said to his friend, "I'm worried about you. You just said you've lost your dad, your brother lives eight hours away and you're not speaking to your mom. You need your family, honey, Y'all were so close there is no way you are okay with this."

"I'M NOT OK WITH IT!" she yelled as Kevin stepped toward her, wrapped his toned arms around her and pulled her close. The tears began to fall as she continued, "Look, I still talk to Brandon like once a week. I think I am going to visit him over summer break. Plus, I do have the two best Grandmas in the world. I usually talk to each of them at least twice a week. So, you see, I still have family, not to mention I have you."

"Pres, look at me" he said tilting her head up to look at him. "That is not what I mean. You need to talk to your mother. You are hurting yourself as much if not more then you are hurting her. You need to clear the air and salvage some type of relationship with her before it's too late. I promise she is waiting for you to make the first move and she is praying every day it will be the day you let her back into your life."

Presley began wiping the tears from her eyes. "I will think about it. Now to a nicer subject. What do you think about Luca?" she said as she pulled from his embrace.

"Well, he is defiantly hot and seems to be nice. He appears to be infatuated with you and, that feeling seems to be mutual, I must say."

"You think he likes me?" She couldn't help but smile. Her smile quickly faded when she said, "It doesn't matter, I can't..."

"First, yes, he most definitely likes you. Second, why not? I mean you don't have to jump in with both feet but you could at least get to know him and see what happens."

She plopped herself on the bed letting out a deep breath as she hit the soft full sized bed covered with her signature red comforter with black pillows and black sheets.

"I don't know I still feel like I would be cheating on Eric. I know in my head that it's not true but my heart just doesn't get that. Plus, how would it be fair to Luca for me to even think about getting involved with him when my heart still belongs to Eric?" The tears once again started to fill her eyes. These days Kevin was the only person she ever let see her cry.

"Aw, Pres, come on. A piece of your heart will always belong to Eric but that doesn't mean you should shut it off to everybody else, including your mother. Eric wouldn't want that for you. He would want you to be happy," he gently told his dear friend.

"Just had to throw that mom thing in didn't you? It's weird I mean I am talking about this guy like I already have feelings for him and I just met him two hours ago. What is that? I mean seriously," she said sounding disgusted with herself.

"Look if he had looked at me the way he was looking at you tonight I would be picking out wedding rings!" he laughed as he plopped down next to Presley. He propped his elbow up and rested his head on his hand.

"You aren't right you know that don't you?" Presley said with a laugh.

"I know that's why you love me."

"You are right about that. Hey, I'll make you a deal," she said with a sly smile forming on her lips.

"Okay, now I'm scared, but let's hear it."

"I will keep an open mind about Luca if you call Jimmy and work out your mess. You never know maybe we can double date to prom," she laughed. Jimmy and Kevin started seeing each other last summer but in August when Jimmy left to go to school at North Carolina State University Kevin started pulling away.

"Okay, let's amend that a little. You keep an open mind about Luca and I will call Jimmy. However, if you want me to even consider going to prom you have to talk to your mother," her friend said with authority.

"You are such a pain in my butt," Presley moaned.

"Again that's why you love me!"

The two settled down for the night, turned on the TV and drifted to sleep.

The next morning Presley's alarm clock went off at 6:00 AM. For the first time in a very long time she did not press the snooze button five times. She quietly gathered her stuff and headed to bathroom for a shower, trying not to wake up Kevin. While in the shower she went back and forth in her own head about what to do with the strong pull she felt toward Luca. *I can't do this. I know if I do I will end up getting hurt or hurting him. Why is this happening I shouldn't feel this strongly towards a guy I don't even know? Then again I can't spend the rest of my life worrying about falling in love. LOVE! What the heck, you don't even know him and you're using the word love. Girl, are you out of your mind? Get it together Pres,*

seriously. After rinsing the soap from her long blonde hair she grabbed a towel from the counter in the bathroom and wrapped it around her head to dry her hair. She grabbed her pink robe off the hook next to the shower and went down stairs to start the coffee before going back to the bathroom to get dressed. When she got back to the bathroom the door was closed and when she tried to open it she realized it was locked. Figuring Kevin must have gotten up already and was taking a shower she went back to her room. Kevin had thought to put the clothes she had in the bathroom on her bed. ***He is so wonderful*** she thought pulling on a pair of Levi jeans and slid her black fitted v-neck over her head.

Presley was applying her make up when Kevin returned to her room fully dressed and ready to go. He was wearing an orange fleece pullover, loose fitting jeans and, as always, a pair of work boots. He was one of the only people Presley knew who looked good in orange.

"Does our deal still stand? Or did you talk yourself out of it already?" he asked while he sprayed himself with his Axe body spray.

"I just amended it again," she replied as she applied her lip stick, finishing her make up routine. "I decided I will be friends with him but I am not going to even consider anything romantic."

"Well, I guess that's a start. I mean it's not like you should go jump a guy you met yesterday!" He laughed while stuffing his clothes from yesterday in his overnight bag.

"Okay, you ready? Are you going to call Jimmy today?" she asked as she ran a brush through her hair one last time.

"First, we need to see how you do today then we will worry about me."

"Let's go," Presley told her friend.

The duo had just reached to bottom of the stairs when the front door opened.

Presley's mother, Brenda Kluttz, entered the room. She was a pretty and petite woman. Her beautiful tan complexion was envied by many who spent a lot of money and time trying to obtain the same skin tone she was blessed to have naturally. Her dark brown hair was cut just below her shoulders which she always wore in a French braid. Her deep brown eyes looked very tired. She was physically and mentally exhausted not only from working third shift as an ER nurse but also from the emotional roller coaster she had been on the past nine months. Nine months ago her daughter almost died. Physically Presley was fine but her mother knew that, like herself, mentally and emotionally she was not well at all. Brenda's husband had also left after the wreck when blood work done on Presley revealed there was no way John Kluttz was her father. That was also when the daughter she treasured quit speaking to her.

"Hi, guys. Kevin, I see you stayed the night again," Brenda said.

"Um..yeah I hope you don't mind Mrs. Klu.. Brenda." Kevin stopped himself from calling her Mrs. Kluttz. It was a hard habit to break but Brenda insisted on him calling her by her first name.

"No, it's fine. I like for someone to be here with Presley when I work third. Not to mention you have stayed here three to four nights a week the past seven months. It's a little late to ask permission now," she said smiling. Brenda would not normally let a boy spend the night at her house, especially in her daughter's bed. But not only was Kevin gay, he was also the only person Presley would talk to or listen to, and she knew that was what her daughter needed.

"You guys have a good day. I work third till Thursday. So Kevin you are more than welcome to stay."

"Thanks, Brenda."

"Alright, bye guys. I love you Presley."

Presley turned to her mother. She could see her eyes almost begging Presley to return the statement. Presley could also see the hurt in her pleading dark brown eyes.

"I love you too, Mom," she said and quickly headed out the door.

Brenda released the breath she hadn't realized she was even holding and a small flicker of joy lit up her very tired eyes.

Although Presley was still very hurt and angry by what her mother had done she did feel a small sense of happiness seeing the joy in her mother's eyes...even if only for a minute. ***Maybe, Kevin was right.*** Presley thought as she headed out of the door.

"Progress," Kevin said as the door closed behind them.

"Pick out your tux, Babe," she replied with a big grin.

The two friends laughed as they got into Kevin's Camry and headed to school.

Chapter Three

As Presley and Kevin walked toward school she was experiencing a feeling she hadn't had in a long time…excitement. She had this sense of happiness that, although she enjoyed it, also unnerved her. She couldn't wrap her head around the feelings just the thought of Luca gave her. "Kevin, do you think…" she stopped mid-sentence when she caught sight of Luca leaning against the school, one leg propped on the building and his arms folded across his chest. He wore a royal blue tee shirt with a pair of washed out, loose fitting jeans and black biker boots. *Oh God he is gorgeous* she thought. As if he heard her thoughts he locked his blue eyes with hers. She froze, and for a moment it seemed like nobody else existed in the whole world.

"Presley," Kevin said while snapping his fingers in front of her face.

"Huh what?" Presley gasped.

"Girl, really, you better watch yourself or that huge wall you built around yourself is going to fall on your head," he said while chuckling and pulling her toward the school.

"Hey, Luca," Kevin said as they approached Luca.

"Hey man," Luca answered.

"Hey, Luca" Presley said as she walked around Kevin giving Luca a little wave.

"Hello" Luca said as he grabbed her left hand, brought it to his lips and placed a small kiss on the back of it. "Glad, you didn't forget about me," he said as he lowered her hand.

"I wouldn't do something like that," ***How could I*** she thought as she spoke. Luca let out a little chuckle and raised one eyebrow. Presley could feel her cheeks turning bright red.

"Well, as much as I hate to break up this little gathering, I have to get to class. You two behave yourselves. I'll see you at lunch." He quickly gave Presley her normal goodbye kiss on the cheek and disappeared into the school.

"Shall we?" Luca asked as he placed his hand on the small of Presley's back.

"Sure, let go" she said with little smile and headed toward the door.

"Wait," Luca said as he grabbed Presley's shoulder. She spun to look at him, once again locking her eyes with his but she quickly dropped her stare.

"What?" she asked.

"Let me take this" he said as he pulled her backpack off her shoulder where it had been hanging by one strap.

"Oh, what a gentleman," she replied laughing just a little.

Then they headed into the school and their homeroom class. When they entered the class Luca saw Mrs. Farmer, a woman with red hair who sat behind a desk that was a cluttered mess. She was in her late 50's but looked much younger. She had almost no wrinkles on her face. Her stylish clothes hid the fact that she was slightly overweight. Getting up from her desk she walked toward Luca as he entered.

"You must be Luca Davenport," she said as she extended her hand to him.

"Yes, Ma'am," he said as he shook her hand.

"Well, I'm glad to meet you. Take a seat anywhere," she said motioning then the nearly full classroom.

Luca adjusted both backpacks he had been carrying and walked to the back of the classroom. That's where Presley was, already in her seat and giggling at him. He slid into the desk next to Presley.

"So, what exactly do we do in homeroom?" he asked as he handed her backpack.

"Nothing really. We're in here for about ten minutes and then off to first period," she said and then added, "It is really kind of pointless."

"I would have to agree it sounds pointless," Luca replied.

"Let me see your schedule," Presley said holding out her hand. Luca shuffled through the small pocket of his backpack and pulled out a green index sized card. The info on the card outlined his schedule for the next two and a half months. He handed it over to Presley. She looked over the schedule and then gave it back to Luca.

"Looks like you are stuck with me most of the day. We have all the same classes except sixth period. While you're working on your muscles in weightlifting I will be trying not to die of boredom replacing books to their rightful homes in the library."

"Good, I had a feeling today was going to be a great day," he replied with a wink.

She smiled "You're such a flirt and you know it. I bet you would be doing that little winky smiley thing to any girl sitting in this chair!"

Luca leaned closer placing his mouth right next to Presley's ear. "No, mio amore, I save all my winky smiley things for you." He slowly returned himself to a front facing position as Presley slowly released the deep breath she had been holding. A moment later Mrs. Farmer began to read the day's announcements and then she introduced the class to Luca. Presley couldn't take her eyes off of him as he stood in the front of class telling the students a little about himself. ***Oh Pres, you have got to get hold of yourself. You're acting like a love sick groupie.*** Once again that smug smile crossed Luca's face as if he had just heard everything Presley had thought. Those smiles were really starting to drive her crazy.

When Luca returned to his seat he again leaned close to Presley and whispered, "Mio amore, do you see something you like?" She whipped her head around quickly trying to come up with any smart-ass comment she could. However, for the first time that she could remember she drew a blank. So, doing the next best thing, she rolled her eyes and grabbed her backpack just as the bell dismissing class rang. Luca chuckled, then took her bag from her and threw it over his left shoulder. Rolling her eyes again Presley headed to the door and Luca followed.

The rest of the morning was full of math, political science and health classes, but it was also full of winks, flirty comments and a lot of eye rolling.

Kevin was sitting under the oak tree in the courtyard of the school where he and his friends always sat during lunch period. He was looking at his phone screen which displayed Jimmy's phone number. His finger hovered over the call button. He knew he needed to call Jimmy. They had only spoken three times since Jimmy had gone back to college after Christmas break. He wasn't mad at him. They hadn't fought but it was so difficult trying to make a long distance relationship work. Not to mention Jimmy had been very jealous of the time Kevin had spent with Presley while he was home for Christmas break. He just didn't understand how much Presley needed Kevin at that time. It was the first Christmas since her family had fallen apart and she was having a very difficult time dealing with all of that heartbreak. Jimmy thought Kevin was using Presley as a way to keep him at arms distance and this may have been partly true. Kevin pressed the cancel button when he saw Stephanie and Marcus heading towards him hand in hand. He slipped the phone back into his bag. Stephanie was wearing jeans and a tight v-neck sweater that was a little too low cut for her ample chest. Marcus didn't seem to mind at all. Marcus wore his usual tee shirt and jeans. Today's shirt was maroon and it looked good with his dark hair

"Hey guys. What's up?" he asked, trying to cover the sadness in his voice at not being able to call Jimmy.

"Well, our new little couple is causing quite the stir," Stephanie said totally oblivious to the sadness in Kevin's voice.

"Really, what kind of stir?" Kevin asked.

"Here we go." Marcus said as he sat on the grass next to Kevin pulling Stephanie down with him. It was pretty obvious he had already heard this story, probably numerous times.

"It seems that our class skank, Becca, has noticed the stunning new addition to the student body. She has apparently been trying to get his attention all day but he has been too busy ogling our sweet Presley to even notice her. She is fuming."

"Stunning, really, Steph," Marcus said with a little smile.

"Honey, you know you're the only one I love, but come on even you have to admit that is one good looking boy."

"Um...no I don't, and I won't!" he laughed.

"I will." Kevin popped in.

"You will what?" Presley asked as she approached her friends with Luca by her side.

"Oh, nothing," Kevin said clearing his throat.

"OOOkay," Presley said as she lowered herself to the ground looking curiously at Kevin.

"So, Luca, how's the first day been treating ya?" Marcus asked trying to change the subject.

"So far it's been great. Never enjoyed school so much," he said winking at Presley as he sat down next to her.

"Ugh, he has thoroughly enjoyed driving me crazy!" Presley said as she slapped his arm. He laughed and nodded.

Kevin couldn't help but smile at the two and how easy they interacted. It had been a long time since he had seen Presley truly enjoy herself and not just put on an act for everyone's sake. Maybe Stephanie was right, maybe Luca is exactly what Presley needs. Then the sadness hit him when he thought about Jimmy and their relationship. They had experienced that easy flirting thing but he may have blown it by pushing Jimmy away.

"Oh crap, here she comes," Stephanie muttered under her breath looking over Presley's shoulder. Presley turned her head and saw Becca heading in their direction. She and Becca had been best friends before the accident. Now Becca couldn't handle all the emotional stuff Presley had in her life. At first their conversations just got shorter, their time spent together was less frequent, and soon their friendship became a relationship filled with hate. Maybe hate was a strong word, extreme dislike was probably better. Neither girl knew how it got that way, it just happened.

Becca's dark hair was pulled back into a low pony tail. She wore a shear top with a bright pink tank top underneath, a pair of skinny jeans, and black slide on shoes.

"So, Luca, how do you like our little school?" Becca asked. She was practically drooling over the boy who sat in front of her while completely ignoring everyone else.

Luca turned to Presley as he answered. "Well, I love it and the view is spectacular," he said giving Presley another one of those winks that made her melt. Becca's face morphed into utter disgust when she saw Luca swooning over Presley.

"So, Pres, is this what it takes for you to get over Eric? One hot guy and you forget all about him," Becca asked in a pleasant tone that didn't disguise the venom in her words. She knew bringing up Eric would not only piss Presley off but she hoped it would cause Presley to distance herself from Luca out of guilt. Presley shot to her feet and was inches away from Becca's face in seconds.

"Don't you ever talk about him to me!"

"Did I hit a nerve? I'm simply saying it's the guy's first day and you haven't left his side. What do you imagine Eric would think?" she said in the same pleasant sarcastic tone.

All of the sudden Presley heard a loud smacking sound and the palm of her hand hurt. She realized she had just smacked Becca in the face. Becca stood there with her hand over her right cheek with a look of shock in her eyes. Although she and Presley argued a lot it had never gotten physical. Presley had the same look of shock on her face.

Presley spun around and headed straight to the women's restroom leaving her friends sitting where they were with dropped jaws. Kevin was the first to react standing up and walking towards Becca stopping mere inches from her face. Kevin noticed the fresh red hand print across her face and smiled for a quick second.

"You are such a bitch...you do know that right? I don't know what happened between the two of you to make y'all hate each other." Becca started to interrupt but Kevin wouldn't allow it. "And I don't care. What you just did was uncalled for and way over the line. You just deliberately hurt her in the worst way over some boy that not only do you not know but also a boy who clearly has no interest in you. I have known you for a long time Becca. You have always been shallow, immature, irresponsible and sometimes a little mean but you have never been cruel. What you just did was cruel." Kevin finished and headed after Presley before Becca could even respond.

Chapter Four

Kevin was waiting near the bathroom door for Presley when Luca approached him.

"What was all that about?" Luca asked, looking very puzzled.

"It's a long story. Pres will tell you if she wants you to know," Kevin answered.

"Okay, could you do me a favor?" Luca asked.

"What kind of favor?" Kevin asked not really in the mood to be passing out favors.

"You drove her to school, right?"

"Yeah, but what does that have to do with you?"

"Can you go home sick or suddenly have something to do after school?" Luca asked as he shoved his hands in his pockets. He looked embarrassed to be asking the question.

"Again why?" Kevin repeated with an impatient tone to his voice.

"I..I just want to spend some time alone with her away from school," Luca stuttered.

"I don't know if that's a good idea today. After that little altercation with the wicked witch of the south she is gonna need me. I don't want her to think I just ditched her," Kevin replied.

"Aren't you staying at her house again tonight?"

"Yeah, but man I don't know." Kevin said while rubbing his face with both hands. "What is the deal with you two? I mean I hate to point this out but you two just met and you're acting like…I don't know… but do you get my point?" Kevin said, feeling a little like a jealous boyfriend.

"I don't know what's going on, I just enjoy being around her and I have this uncontrollable urge to protect her. It's weird, right?"

"No, Presley has that effect on people. Trust me. Okay, give me your phone," Kevin said holding out his hand.

Luca pulled his phone out of his pocket and handed it to Kevin. "Why?" he asked.

"I am going to put my number in here. After you leave her house call me. I think we need to discuss a couple things," Kevin said as he typed his number into Luca's phone.

"Like what?" Luca asked as he watched Kevin messing with his phone.

"Let's just say I also have an uncontrollable urge to protect her," he said as he placed the phone back in Luca's hand. Luca just smiled. *This girl must be something to inspire such fierce loyalty* he thought. Marcus had said almost the exact same thing to him when he asked to meet her.

Just then Presley came out of the bathroom. Her blue eyes looked as if they were pools of deep blue water. Many tears were waiting to trickle down her cheeks. However, the swollen red skin around her eyes was proof that even though some tears remained plenty had already fallen. The sight of her like that sent a sharp pain through Luca's chest and filled him with anger which caught him by surprise. Now he was starting to worry about what was going on between them. First he had been unbelievably drawn to Presley when Marcus showed him her picture. Then from the moment he met her he just wanted to be near her. Next he was struck by an overwhelming need to protect her. Now just the sight of her in pain made him feel as if he had been run over by a Mac truck. **Oh** *yeah, something BIG is going on. I have never felt like this before. Love, could it be love after one day? I'm in BIG trouble*, he thought.

As Presley reached the two boys who were so worried about her she simply said, "I don't want to talk about it." She kept walking toward the tree where she had earlier left her backpack.

The second half of the day was not nearly as fun as the first half had been. Luca's once flirty comments and winks were now replaced with looks of concern and tenderness. Becca's cruel comments had achieved her vicious goal. Presley felt guilty not only about the feelings she had toward Luca but also about allowing herself to feel happiness. She was glad the sixth period had finally arrived. Not only because it meant the day was almost over but because being in the library alone gave her time to think. Many thoughts were racing through her mind, *I am a horrible person. The guy I loved so much and who loved me so dearly is dead and I am letting myself develop feelings for some guy I don't even know. Then I spend the day cutting up with him and flirting. Oh, my God! I am flirting while Eric lays in the ground. What kind of person does that? How could I let this happen? Eric must be so disappointed in me.*

Her unpleasant thoughts were interrupted by a hand coming to rest on her shoulder. She didn't need to turn around to see whose hand it was as soon as his scent hit her nose, accompanied by the warm feeling she was beginning to get in his presence, she knew exactly whose hand it was. When her eyes met Luca's she almost lost it again. *Presley, you will NOT cry twice in one day!* she scolded herself.

"Are you okay? You haven't really said anything since lunch," Luca asked with noticeable concern in his voice.

"I'm fine Luca" she said trying to sound cold and annoyed but she did not quite accomplish that goal. He could hear the underlying sadness in her voice.

"Don't do that. If you don't want to be around me that's your decision. Just don't make that decision because some jealous child made you feel bad. You have no reason to feel bad, you've done nothing wrong," he said almost in a whisper.

Presley turned her back to him. She couldn't look at him right now. She had to be strong and push him away but if she looked at him she knew she would fall apart. *Just do it! He's better off if he stays away from you. You're too damaged.*

Slowly she took a deep breath and let it out. "Look, Luca, you're a nice guy and I did have fun today. I'm just not interested. I have enough friends so I really don't think there is anything else to say," she finished still keeping her back to him unable to face him.

He placed a hand on each one of her shoulders. "Look at me," he said as he slowly turned her around. She let him turn her but kept her eyes focused on the ground. "Look at me," he said again as he placed two fingers under her chin and tilted her face up until their eyes met. "I know you don't mean that," he said still barely above a whisper.

"I do," she replied just as quietly.

"No you're scared and you feel guilty," he gently whispered to her.

"No, I'm not. You're wrong," Presley said softly.

"I'm not wrong, you know you can feel the pull between us. You are having feelings you think are too strong to have after such a short time. You don't want to have these feelings because you feel like you're betraying Eric," he said as he gently brushed the strands of hair that had fallen in front of her face behind her ear.

"How do you...," she began to ask.

"I know," he interrupted her, "because I feel them as well."

"This is too weird. I can't do this now!"

"Yes, you can," he said as he moved his face closer to her and kissed her forehead. When he pulled back she thought he might kiss her but the end of the day bell rang. At that point she didn't know if that bell was the best or worst sound she had ever heard.

"I gotta go find Kevin. He'll be waiting for me." She said pulling back to break the tension between them.

"No he won't," Luca quickly told her.

"What?" Presley spun around to face him.

"He had to go. He asked me to give you a ride home," he said with his usual cocky smirk.

"Why did he leave and why didn't he tell me?" she asked feeling slightly annoyed.

"He didn't say but he did say he tried to text you but you didn't respond so he asked me to find you."

"I didn't get any texts," she argued as she searched for her phone in her backpack. Pulling it out she looked at her screen: 1 NEW MESSAGE. She opened the message. It was from Kevin, "Sweetie, I had to go. Ride home with Luca."

"Okay, I guess you're right let's go," she said putting her phone in her bag and then throwing the bag over her shoulder.

"Did you think I was lying?" he asked removing her bag from her shoulder and putting it on his.

"No. You do realize I am capable of carrying my own backpack right? I mean I have been doing it for like twelve years."

"Yes, I am sure you are capable of doing anything you put your mind to but, I enjoy doing it, so I am," he winked.

"Man, whatever is your chiropractor bill?" she giggled as they headed out the door. She noticed she felt lighter somehow and, no, it wasn't because Luca had her backpack. Something had happened and she didn't feel so bad anymore.

She silently followed Luca to the parking lot where all the seniors parked. *He even has a cute butt. Is there anything this guy doesn't have?* Luca turned around and gave her another one of those cocky grins that caused Presley to blush. "What is up with you man? Are you a mind reader or something?" Presley wished she could take back that question as soon as it left her lips.

"No. Why, what were you thinking about?" he said with a raised eyebrow.

"Um nothing just which one is your car?" she asked knowing she was probably as red as an apple. Luca just chuckled and pointed to his blue mustang parked near the front of the lot.

"Haven't you already seen my car?" he asked knowing her earlier question was a diversion.

"Yea I guess forgot. I'm really not good with cars." **Stop talking NOW!** Her mind screamed at her. When they reached Luca's car he pressed the unlock button on his key chain. As Presley reached for the passenger side door handle Luca grabbed her hand. "What?" she asked as she looked up at him. He was just shaking his head as he pulled the door open for her.

"Oh. You really do like that whole gentleman thing don't you?"

"Yes, and I believe you like it as well," he said as he shut her door. Before she could even get her seat belt buckled Luca was already in the driver's seat buckling his seat belt.

"Dude, have you ever considered running track? You're really fast." she said in awe of his speed.

"Nah, not really a sports guy," he scoffed.

They pulled out of the parking lot and headed in the direction of Presley's house. As she gave him directions she couldn't help but feel she was right where she was supposed to be …with him.

Chapter Five

Luca pulled into Presley's driveway after a short ten minute drive. When he placed the car in park he looked over at Presley as she reached for the door handle.

"Really, haven't you learned yet?" he asked.

"I can open a door. I'm not helpless," Presley told him.

"Just let me, please," he said as he pulled her backpack out of the backseat and opened his door. She watched him walk around the car. She would never admit it but she liked that Luca was such an old school gentleman. It made her feel special like she should be handled with care. Not because she was an emotional wreck but because of who she was and she was worth special treatment. He opened the door and smiled at her.

"See, was that so hard?" he asked with that little smirk on his handsome face. She replied with the same eye roll she had been giving him all day when she couldn't think of a witty comeback.

When they reached the door she turned to look at him, "I am going to need my backpack. My keys are in it." Smiling he handed her backpack. She opened the door and walked in leaving the door open behind her. She realized Luca hadn't followed her into her home. She turned to him and asked, "Are you coming in?"

"Is that an invitation? "

"Yea, come on in. I thought leaving the door open was a pretty good signal I wanted you to come in," she laughed.

"It's not polite to enter someone's home without being invited," he said smugly.

"Oh well, excuse me. Please, kind sir...do come in," she said in an over the top southern accent as she curtseyed.

"Would be my pleasure my lady," he said and, going along with her teasing, he bent in a small bow.

They entered the house Presley threw her backpack on the floor next to the steps and headed to the kitchen. When Luca walked in he looked around the living room. It was not a big room but it had a very homey feel. The walls were painted in a light tan with white trim. The curtains were long and multiple shades of brown. There was an antique mahogany desk that sat in front of the big picture window on the front wall. The three mahogany bookcases lining the far left wall were full of books ranging from fiction to medical reference books. Sitting in the back corner was a small wood end table with a small reading lamp on it. A comfortable looking overstuffed dark brown recliner was beside the end table.

"Nice house," he said as he headed in the direction Presley had gone.

"Thanks. Would you like a snack?" she asked as he entered the kitchen.

"Sure" he said. He smiled to himself knowing nothing in that kitchen would satisfy his hunger...except maybe her.

She pulled a pitcher of sweet tea out of the refrigerator. "Tea okay?" she asked as she took glasses out of the cabinet.

"Perfect," he replied as he watched her move around the kitchen. He was relieved her mood had changed dramatically since they had spoken in the library.

"Sweet or salty?" she asked.

"What?" he asked, somewhat confused by the question.

"Sweet," she said holding a pack of cookies in her right hand, "or salty?" she asked holding a bag of potato chips in her left.

"Both," he said with a smile.

"Aw, a man after my own heart," she said placing her right hand, and the cookies, over her heart.

"That I am mio amore," he said with a wink.

She slapped his arm as she walked to the small round oak kitchen table with its four chairs. In the center of the table was a centerpiece with two small candles surrounded by blue and white roses. The kitchen didn't have the same brown theme the living room had. The decor was shades of blue with white accents.

"Well, we have spent almost the whole day together and I still don't know anything about you. Except there must always be something in your eye with all that winking you do!" she said sitting Indian style on her chair. She pulled her hair up into a sloppy bun on top of her head. She had always done that when she got home from school. It had been her habit since sixth grade.

Luca laughed and popped a chip in his mouth as Presley took a sip of her tea. After he finished chewing he asked, "What do you want to know?"

"Let's see, all I know is that you're eighteen and from Virginia." She said as she took a chocolate chip cookie out of the bag. "So, why did you move?" she continued.

"Just needed a change of scenery. There was no real reason for it," he replied popping another chip in his mouth.

"Your parents just decided they wanted to move for no reason?"

"I don't live with my parents. I haven't in a while. My mom died when I was a child and my dad lives in Italy."

"Oh, I am sorry. Do you have any brothers and sisters?" she asked. What she really wanted to know was what happened to his mother but she didn't want to ask. She knew from her own experience the death of somebody you loved was not something that you ever really wanted to be the topic of conversation.

"I have a younger sister, Nicky, well Nicolette, she lives with my dad. What about you?"

"I have an older brother, Brandon, he lives in Tennessee with his wife, Payton, and their son, Paxton, He's almost 2, and too cute. So that mio amore thing you keep saying is Italian I guess," she said taking a bite of the cookie she was holding.

"Yes it is. I usually just speak English but occasionally I will throw some Italian in for fun."

"Would you teach me?" Presley asked.

"Sure one day," he said.

"You and your friends seem real close. How long have you all been friends?" Luca asked her.

"We have known each other forever. Marcus and I have been good friends since like fifth grade. Stephanie and I became close when she and Marcus started dating about a year, year and a half ago. My sweet Kevin and I didn't get close till about nine months ago. Now he is my rock. I don't know what I would do without him," she replied thinking about how lucky she was to have such great friends. Before the accident she had a ton of friends and lots of people she would hang out with. After the accident she had narrowed her friends down to the people who truly loved her for herself, not her position on the school's popularity ladder. She was once on the top rung of that ladder but now she was glad to be off of it completely.

"How do you like it here so far?" she asked.

"I like it. The people seem nice and I have truly enjoyed your company," he said giving her the wink he knew she loved even if she said it drove her crazy. "Hey, are we just going to keep up with the small talk or are we going to talk about what we should be talking about?" he asked as he took a sip of his tea.

"What exactly is it we should be talking about?" She asked even though she knew he was talking about the conversation they had started in the library.

"Look. I know we are in a weird situation here and I really think we should talk about it. I am guessing we aren't going to have much time alone to talk so I think now might be the best time we have." He said, trying to gauge her reaction. He was beginning to think he should have waited to bring it up. *Smooth! Are you trying to get her to run screaming out the door? Man, your timing is impeccable!*

"First, before we get into some serious deep conversation, I need to know how you convinced Mr. Walsh to let you out of weightlifting early. He never does that," she said trying to stall. She knew they needed to talk about what was going on with them but she didn't know what to say. The whole thing had her so confused and unnerved she couldn't even think.

"Let's just say I can be very persuasive when there is something I want. It is seldom I am told no," he smirked while popping another chip in his mouth.

"I bet. Just know if you are going to be spending time with me I don't cave easily so you will hear no, I promise," she said with a firm tone.

"I have a feeling you, Miss Kluttz, are going to bring a challenge back into my life and I love a good challenge," he promised her.

"You have no idea, "she laughed and winked.

There was an awkward silence for a minute. Neither wanted to address the elephant in the room. Luca knew he jumped the gun trying to push Presley to talk about their feelings. Presley was feeling conflicted. She wanted to talk to Luca about what was happening between them but at the same time she wasn't sure she was ready to take that step.

Deciding to let her off the hook Luca rose from his chair and carried his glass over to the sink. "I better get going," he said as he placed the glass in the sink.

"Oh, okay well thanks for driving me home," she replied kind of disappointed as she stood.

"Anytime," he said as he put his arm around her shoulders and they both headed toward the front door. When they reached the door he turned her to face him and stepped closer to her. He pushed her hair behind her ear and looked into her eyes.

"What do you say we spend Saturday together and I'll teach you to speak a little Italian?" he asked, speaking in that very quiet tone that made telling him no even harder.

"I'd like that. I guess I'll see you tomorrow," she replied.

"You know it. Are we going to meet before school again? I could still use a tour guide," he said standing close enough for her to feel the warmth of his breath.

"You are such a liar. You didn't even need me to show you around today. Do you think I didn't notice I never once showed you how to get anywhere?" she smiled still looking into his beautiful eyes.

"Caught that did you? You're still going to meet me though, aren't you?" he asked with that cocky smile that looked so good on him.

"Sure, I guess I can make that sacrifice," she said very sarcastically.

"Alright, I'll see you tomorrow," he said as he leaned down and kissed her forehead before heading to the door.

"Bye" she said as she opened the door. She didn't want him to leave but she knew she wasn't ready to have the conversation they would have if he stayed.

She watched him head to his car giving another small wave as he pulled out of the driveway. She went back into the house and closed the door. **God I'm in trouble** she thought as she headed upstairs to her room grabbing her iPod on the way. She decided to clear her head. She put earphones in her ears and just listened to the music, trying not to think about Luca…it didn't work.

Chapter Six

Presley hadn't made it halfway through the first song on her Metallica CD when she felt light tapping on her arm. Opening her eyes she saw her mom, dressed in her work scrubs, standing next to her.

"Hey Mom, I didn't realize you were still here," Presley said as she pulled out her ear buds.

"I'm leaving in about thirty minutes. I was going to come downstairs and talk to you but you had company so I waited upstairs," Brenda replied as she sat on the end of Presley's bed.

"Oh, okay," Presley said as she looked at her mom. Brenda never told Presley when she was leaving anymore so doing it now caused Presley some concern. "What's up Mom?" she asked searching Brenda's face for any clue that might indicate what was on Brenda's mind.

"Nothing, just thought I'd touch base with you before I left. Um...who was that guy?" Brenda asked with a nervous tone to her voice and a look on her face that almost resembled fear.

"That was Luca. He is a new guy at school, just a friend," Presley answered, knowing it wasn't completely true.

"That looked like a little more than just friends," Brenda said with the same note of concern in her voice and trace of fear on her face.

"Mom, what's going on? Why do you look so scared?" Presley asked feeling a little put off by her mother's odd behavior.

"I'm just worried about you that's all. He is the first boy besides Kevin and Marcus I've seen you with and I just …I don't know why, but I'm worried. I wanted to make sure everything's okay," Brenda said as she softly rubbed Presley's leg. Presley didn't know how to respond. She and her mother had barely spoken in nine months and now her mother seemed to be acting like everything was back to normal. She couldn't hide the annoyance in her voice when she finally replied, "We are JUST friends. I don't want to talk about it!"

"Well then, I guess I'll just go to work. But, Presley, please be careful," Brenda said as she rose from the bed trying very hard not to let her daughter's obvious annoyance hurt her…but it did.

"See ya," Presley snapped as she replaced her earbuds and pressed play which effectively cut off her mother. The conversation had not gone the way Brenda had hoped but even though harsh words were spoken they had at least talked. Brenda left for work feeling sad about the turn the conversation with her daughter had taken but yet hopeful because they had spoken. Shortly after her mother left Presley drifted off to sleep.

∞

Presley sat on the bleachers of her high school football field. The sun was shining brightly and a cool breeze was blowing. When she looked across the football field her gaze fell upon a young man walking toward her. When the sun hit his golden hair causing it to glisten she realized who it was.

"Eric!" she yelled as she stood up, ran down the bleachers and on to the field. When she reached him she threw herself into his arms. "Oh my God, Eric!" she said as she wrapped her arms around his neck and kissed him. Eric let out a small chuckle as he pulled back slightly to look at her. "Hey, Babe, miss me?" he grinned as he lowered his mouth back to hers.

"I'm dreaming, aren't I? Please tell me I'm not. Eric, please tell me this is real," she said as a stream of tears rolled down her cheeks.

Eric pushed a strand of hair off the side of her face and gently guided it behind her ear. Then he softly ran his knuckles down the side of her face.

"Baby, this is like a dream. I'm still dead but I am sort of here. I need to talk to you but I don't have much time. Come on, let's sit down," Eric said as he intertwined his fingers with hers and led her back to bleachers.

Oh, God, Oh God Presley thought **He's mad. He knows about Luca and now he's pissed and hurt. Oh, God what have I done?**

When they reached the bleachers Eric sat down and pulled Presley onto his lap. "You are so beautiful," he said as he ran his fingers through her blond hair holding a strand of the red that was now part of her new look. "This is new. I like it," he grinned. "Is that what you needed to talk to me about?" She said cocking one eye brow.

"No, sorry, you know how easily I can be distracted. Anyway, it's about Luca."

"Oh, Eric, Listen it's noth..." she stopped when he started laughing. "What's so funny?"

"Listen to me, okay?" he pleaded.

"Okay go ahead," she replied preparing herself for a guilt trip like none she'd ever experienced.

"I need you to trust him. I need to know you're going to be okay and safe. Luca is the key to making that happen," he said watching her beautiful eyes widening.

"What are you talking about?" she asked very confused.

"I can't go into details and I am running out of time. I shouldn't even be here. I just need you to stop letting my death keep you from living. Soon Luca is going to need you to trust him. I need you to do that, too."

"I...I...don't understand. Eric, I ...love you. That is the only thing I know," she said placing a kiss on his lips.

"I love you, too, but I can't be here for you. You need somebody and it has to be Luca. Please, no matter what happens, or what he tells you, I need you to trust him to keep you safe. I can't rest in peace knowing you are hurting or in danger," he said as he placed his hand on the back of her neck.

"Eric, I am not sure what's going on here but I'll do whatever you need to be at peace," Presley told him even as her head was spinning and she was unable to put all the pieces together.

"Please, Pres, no matter what...live your life, open your heart and trust him. One day this will all make sense. I promise." He pulled her close and kissed her. "I love you. Be happy," he said as the wind picked up and he faded away.

Presley's eyes popped open as she sat straight up in her bed. When she heard the doorbell ring she was still spinning from the intense almost real dream she had just experienced. She couldn't think until she heard the bell again. Trying to clear her mind she got off her bed and headed to the door. As she started to feel more alert and "in the present" she twisted the door knob and opened the door. When she saw Kevin standing on the other side she lost any sense of calm she had gained. Tears burst out of her eyes as if a dam had broken, her knees went weak and she hit the floor.

"Oh, my God. Presley, what the heck happened? What's wrong Baby? Talk to me," he said as he wrapped her in his arms and pulled her from the floor.

"He..he..he," Presley tried to talk but she was crying so hard she couldn't speak.

"What did he do? I'll kill him!" Kevin shouted assuming Presley was talking about Luca and whatever he had done to hurt her.

"No, it wasn't Luca. It was...It was..." she couldn't get the words out. She knew it was a dream but it felt so real. She couldn't get her brain to put together a coherent sentence.

"Who was it Pres? You're scaring me. What is going on?" Kevin asked looking at Presley as if she had horns protruding from the top of her head.

"Eric," was all Presley managed to say.

"Eric? Presley, come here you need to calm down and tell me what the hell is going on," Kevin stated firmly as they went up the stairs to her room.

When they reached Presley's room Kevin guided her over to her bed and made her sit down.

"Okay, honey I need you to calm down and breathe," Kevin said as he placed one hand on each of her shoulders and leaned down to look in her eyes. Presley inhaled and released several deep breaths. Then, after taking a minute to gather her thoughts, calm her erratic breathing, and slow down her rapid heartbeat, she finally began to try to explain to Kevin about Eric.

"I fell asleep earlier and I had this dream. I mean...I guess it was a dream. Eric was here." She paused for a moment pushing tears back from her eyes. Then she continued "He was talking to me about Luca, telling me to trust him so I would be safe. I just don't know. I am so confused, Kevin. It was so real...I could feel him...smell him...touch him." As Kevin looked deep into Presley's eyes he was trying to figure out the best thing to say to comfort her. "Kevin, please say something," Presley pleaded as she pulled her knees to her chest and wrapped her arms tightly around them.

"Slow down for just a minute. Let me make sure I understand what you're telling me." When Presley nodded Kevin sat on the bed next to her and placed his arm gently around her shoulder.

"In a dream you had....Eric talked to you. In this dream he told you to trust Luca and also something about your safety. Is that what you are telling me?" Kevin asked in a tone of disbelief.

"He told me he wanted me to open up to Luca. He said I needed to trust Luca because he would keep me safe. Eric pleaded with me saying he couldn't rest in peace if I didn't agree to do it," she said with her arms still wrapped around her knees as she slowly rocked back and forth.

"Baby, it was a dream. Maybe it is your subconscious mind telling you to give Luca a chance...or something," Kevin said, still trying to process the information that had just been thrown at him.

"IT WASN'T JUST ANY DREAM!" she yelled. "It was real. I could feel him. I could smell him. He kissed me and it was just like old times...when he was here."

"Okay, I get it. Why don't you go take a warm shower? I'll make you a nice cup of tea and we will talk after you calm down a little," Kevin said trying to calm his best friend. He had said he understood but he didn't. He hadn't felt so useless since Eric had died. He had tried so hard to comfort her through that horrible time. Now he was grateful Presley agreed to take a shower because it gave him time to gather himself and find a way to get her through this.

Once he was sure Presley was in the shower he headed downstairs to make her tea. As he descended the stairs he pulled his phone out of his pocket and scrolled down his contact list till he landed on Luca's number. The phone rang three times before Luca answered. "Hello," he said, surprised to see Kevin's name on his caller ID.

"What happened here today?" Kevin demanded with hostility thick in his voice.

"What are you talking about man?" Luca replied feeling a little unsettled by the tone in Kevin's voice.

"Presley is here in tears freaking out about some dream about Eric," Kevin said. He quickly thought that Luca was probably the last person he should have called about this. However, something screamed at him that Luca was the only one who could help Presley.

"Is she okay? We didn't even talk about Eric! I'll be there in 15 minutes," Luca said, hanging up the phone before Kevin could reply.

Kevin looked at phone wishing he hadn't called Luca. Presley was not going to be happy and he knew it.

Chapter Seven

Fifteen minutes later Luca was pulling into Presley's driveway and running to the door. Kevin had been watching for him through the window and opened the door before Luca could even knock on it.

"Hey man, I should not have called you. She's really going to be pissed," Kevin said as he ran both hands through his hair.

"You called me because you know I can help," Luca replied. Kevin knew that was true. He had noticed the only two people Presley seemed to relax around were Luca and him. He also knew that he wouldn't be enough tonight. She was too upset. Before Kevin could respond he heard a small voice behind him.

"Luca, what are you doing here?" Presley asked standing behind Kevin in her pink bathrobe with her wet hair brushed back. Her eyes were still red and swollen from crying.

"Hey, I was on my way to get some dinner. I knew your mom was working so I thought I would stop by to see if you and Kevin wanted to join me," Luca responded not wanting Presley to know Kevin had called him. He hadn't known Presley long but he knew she wouldn't be happy with Kevin if she knew.

Feeling like she was missing something Presley looked back and forth between Kevin and Luca.

"I guess that would be okay. I haven't eaten yet," Presley responded. As she was speaking she was suddenly aware that she was wearing only a robe and not one bit of make-up.

"Great, Kevin, you cool with that? My treat," Luca said as he turned to Kevin.

"Sure" he replied with a sigh of relief. Glad Luca had so quickly thought of a way to keep Presley from knowing he had called him.

"Alright, give me fifteen minutes to get ready," Presley said heading back up the stairs.

"Thanks, man, I owe you one," Kevin said as he led Luca into the kitchen.

"You can repay me by telling me what's going on," Luca said.

"I would if only I could. She had a dream about Eric and it really upset her. I haven't seen her cry like that since he died. Man, it killed me seeing her like that again," Kevin said rubbing his face with both hands.

"What kind of dream? Did she say what happened?" Luca asked. He knew Eric was Presley's boyfriend for two years and he died last June. Marcus had told him all about everything when he had asked about her.

"She said she talked to him. She said she could feel him. She said it all felt real," Kevin told Luca. He still didn't totally get what had happened but he knew it had affected Presley profoundly.

"Did she say what Eric had said to her?" Luca was still trying to figure out as much as he could about what had Presley so upset. He needed to know as much as possible if he was going to help her.

"You...they talked about you. Something about her opening up to you and you keeping her safe."

"Me?"

"Yeah, look normally I would chalk this up to a very bad dream but her reaction to it was more than a bad dream. Don't think I'm crazy but, man, I swear I could smell his cologne on her," Kevin said. Before the boys could finish their conversation Presley entered kitchen. She had pulled her hair into a messy bun which she had placed on top of her head. She wore a pair of Levi jeans and an oversized NC State sweatshirt. She decided she was going for comfortable tonight.

"Wow, you look beautiful," Luca said as looked her up and down from head to toe.

"Boy, you need glasses," she replied as she grabbed her purse from the kitchen counter.

"Baby I promise there is nobody you know who has better eye sight then I do," Luca said as a sly grin spread across his handsome face.

"Oh crap, I left my phone upstairs. I'll meet you guys at the car," Presley said as she trotted back upstairs.

"Just keep doing that and she'll be okay…at least for a little while," Kevin said laughing and slapping Luca on the back.

"It'll be a hardship but I guess I can grin and bear it," Luca replied laughing.

The threesome arrived at the Waffle House and headed back to their usual booth.

"Do you guys eat anywhere else?" Luca laughed as he sat in the booth next to Presley.

"No, not really, I'm addicted to the coffee and Texas cheese steak sandwiches," Presley replied as she waved at Sarah who stood behind the counter.

"Hey guys, do you want your usual?" Sarah asked as she approached the booth.

"Yep," Kevin and Presley responded at the same time.

Luca laughed and told Sarah he would take a Pepsi and the Texas cheese steak sandwich he had heard so much about.

The group spent the next two hours laughing and joking. Kevin finally relaxed when he saw Presley was calmer. Now he was glad that he had decided to call Luca. His gut had been right. Luca was just what she needed to feel better, at least for a little while.

When they pulled back into Presley's driveway she was almost disappointed that the night was over. Although she still had the memories of the dream she had, in the back of her mind something about being with Kevin and Luca made her feel less alone, less sad. Luca opened the driver side door and walked over to open Presley's door. As she stood to leave the car their faces were only a breath apart.

"Are you gonna be okay?" Luca asked, letting on for the first time that night he knew something was wrong.

"He called you, didn't he?" Presley asked as she looked at Kevin who was entering the house.

"Yeah, don't be upset with him. He was just worried about you," Luca said as grabbed her hand and pulled her away from the car.

"I'm not. I'm not sure why he called you but I'm glad he did," Presley replied looking up into his eyes. Luca slid his hand to the back of Presley's neck as looked down into her eyes.

"I'm glad he did, too. I want you to know if you want to talk about it, I'm here. I know you have Kevin. I want you to know you have me, too." Luca said almost in a whisper.

"Does it scare you?" she asked, matching his quiet tone.

"Does what scare me?" he asked.

"This connection, this pull between us," she answered while taking a step backwards.

"No. It makes me look forward to something. I haven't done that in longer then I can remember," he replied pulling her back to him.

"Me too, but it scares me a little, too," Presley said still with a whisper tone in her voice.

Luca lowered his face to hers until their lips were almost touching. At that moment he whispered, "Don't be scared of me. Just trust me that everything will be okay." After speaking he gently pressed his lips to hers. Pulling back he took her hand and headed toward her front door.

"I'll see you in the morning." He winked and turned to head back to his car. Presley just stood in the doorway unable to speak as she watched him leave.

Once Luca's car left the driveway she turned to go look for Kevin. She found him leaving her bathroom shirtless and wearing sleep pants.

"You know, Luca has great timing. Don't you think?" she asked Kevin as she crossed her arms and raised one eyebrow.

"Figured it out, did you?" he asked with a smile as he walked past her into her bedroom.

"Why did you call him?" she asked as she plopped down on her bed.

"I don't really know. I just knew you were upset. Something told me he was the only one who would be able to make you feel better," Kevin said while sitting next to her on the bed.

"He did. He also just kissed me," she said as her cheeks warmed and turned pink.

"He kissed you, really?"

"No, I'm lying," she jokingly snapped.

"Well, what do you think about that?" he asked, turning to face her.

"I liked it but I…who am I kidding? I liked it. I like him. It scares the crap out of me!" she said exhaling loudly.

"Why does it scare you?"

"Because this is all too intense. After all, we have just met," she explained.

"You might be right, but just maybe you should quit trying to put a timetable on things and just go with it," Kevin said while rubbing Presley's back.

She pushed herself up from the bed and headed to her dresser to pull out her sleeping clothes. "Maybe, but Kevin, I don't want to get hurt and I don't want to hurt him."

"Hey, Pres...don't look at the worst case scenario. I get why you're a little worried. You're right, things heated up quickly but that doesn't mean it's bad. Just maybe it's too good to wait," Kevin said taking his place on his side of the bed.

"Always the optimist," Presley said going to the bathroom to change her clothes.

While in the bathroom Presley looked at her reflection. "You told Eric you would give this a chance and you will not break that promise. You are not a chicken. You will not let fear control you," she said out loud to the girl in the mirror. Once she was changed she headed back to her room and got in bed. Her earlier fears and tears had changed into a new determination. She would not cower from something that felt so right.

Chapter Eight

The rest of the week had gone by pretty much the same as it had started. The days were full of joking, laughing, flirting and a lot of winking. Soon after they met Luca had realized that not only did his winking drive Presley crazy but she also loved it. She just wouldn't admit it, so he did it constantly. Surprisingly by Friday after school Presley was feeling like things in her life were finally starting to go right. Stephanie and Marcus were their normal cute couple selves. Kevin had called Jimmy and they had decided to start talking more. Jimmy had agreed to come visit the following weekend which had improved Kevin's mood greatly. He actually didn't think he'd been in a bad mood but now he realized he had been in limbo...not up but not down...just caught in the middle. But now he had something to look forward to and that was a nice change for him. Presley and Luca were both very excited to be spending Saturday together...together and alone.

"So what are the big plans for this weekend?" Stephanie asked as the whole group gathered in the school parking lot near Marcus' black Chevy truck.

"I was thinking we should all get together Saturday night. You know hang out, watch movies, eat popcorn. My parents will be gone all weekend so y'all could come out to my house," Stephanie continued.

"Luca and I have plans during the day but I'm sure we could come to your house that night," Presley said as Luca stood behind her wrapping his big arms around her waist.

"I'm going to Skype with Jimmy around 6 but I can come over later," Kevin told them. He began to readjust the book bag that hung on his shoulder as he talked.

"That's good 'cause Marcus doesn't get off till 6 so why don't you guys come to my house around 7-730?" Stephanie said as she opened the passenger side door of Marcus' truck and began to climb into the cab.

"I'll get the movie, no chick flick!" Marcus' hollered as he closed his door.

Luca laughed as he put his arm around Presley. Then Kevin, Presley, and he headed towards Kevin's car. "I have ten bucks that says we end up watching a chick flick," Kevin chuckled as he watched the truck leave the parking lot.

"Alright guys I'll see you tomorrow night. Have fun," Kevin said as he placed a kiss on Presley's cheek and got into his car.

"Bye, Kevin call me later," Presley replied.

∞

Luca pulled into Presley's driveway a couple minutes later. "What time should I come get you tomorrow?" Luca asked as they stood on Presley's front porch.

"I'm not sure. What are we doing?" she asked.

"I thought you could come to my house. I could make us lunch then we could just hang out a bit. That is if that's okay," he said as he pulled her to his chest.

"Are you still going to teach me Italian? I'm really looking forward to that," Presley responded as she put her arms around his neck.

"Tutto quello che vuoi il mio amore, e' per vio. (Anything you want my love, it is yours)," Luca replied placing a gentle kiss on her forehead.

"I love when you talk like that. Does around eleven sound good?" Presley asked. She was somewhat disappointed that he had only kissed her forehead. He had kissed her once the other night but not at all since then. She really wasn't sure how she felt about him not kissing her more.

"I can't wait. I'll see you then," he said and turned to leave.

Presley watched him leave still wondering why he hadn't kissed her. Thinking maybe she would just ask him tomorrow she headed in the house.

"Mom, are you home?" Presley yelled as she threw her backpack next to the stairs and headed to the kitchen.

"Hey, how was your day?" her mother asked as Presley entered the kitchen.

"It was good. Same old...same old," she said while pulling her hair into her normal after school messy bun.

"What are your plans this weekend?" Brenda asked as she sat down at the kitchen table and took a sip of her coffee. It was her day off so she was relaxing in a light tank top and matching sleep pants.

"Just hanging out here tonight. Tomorrow I am going to be with Luca during the day then we are all going to Stephanie's tomorrow night," Presley replied as she searched the pantry for a snack.

"What's the deal with this Luca guy?" After the reaction she had gotten from her daughter when she asked about him last time she was almost afraid to mention his name. She just felt she needed to know more so she risked Presley being upset with her.

Presley headed toward the kitchen counter with a bag of pretzels in one hand and a pitcher of sweet tea in the other. She had convinced herself it was time to bite the bullet and have a real conversation with her mother.

"He's just a guy and we've been talking. He's not my boyfriend or anything like that. We are just getting to know each other," she told her mom. She left off the part about their undeniable connection and the fact she desperately wanted him to kiss her again.

"Okay, but what do you know about him?" Brenda asked. She was hoping she wasn't pushing her luck and that maybe her daughter would open up to her a little.

Presley was trying to remember that her mother was putting in an effort to repair their fractured relationship. Because of that, she pushed the annoyance her mom's questions had brought to the back of her mind before she answered.

"Well," she said while popping a pretzel in her mouth, "He's eighteen. His mother died when he was a child. He moved here from Virginia. He's really fun and really, really cute." She omitted the part about his dad living in Italy. She knew her mother was already worried about this guy. Since they were planning to spend the day at his place tomorrow she chose not to mention there would be no parental supervision.

"Well, I would like to meet him," Brenda stated taking another sip of her coffee.

"Okay, he's picking me up tomorrow at eleven. You're off, right?" Presley asked before taking a sip of her tea.

"They called me in because Iris is sick but I don't go in till two. So, yes, I'll be here."

"What's wrong with Iris, now?" Presley asked. Iris was a younger nurse who had started working with her mother about a year and half ago. She seemed to be sick, or have another reason to miss work, on a regular basis.

"Something about a migraine but I don't really know. I'm pretty sure she's on her last leg. Travis is getting very irritated by all her absences." Brenda said as she smiled. She hadn't smiled because her boss was most likely going to fire her co-worker but because she and her daughter were talking. No, it wasn't a deep conversation but there was no yelling. Also, she was getting more than one word answers to her questions, which was a nice change if pace.

"It's about time, if she gets sick that often the last place she should be working is a hospital." Presley chuckled as her phone chimed indicating she had a text message. She looked at her phone and saw she had a text message from Stephanie.

"Mom, Steph is texting me. Can I talk to you later?"

"Sure, I'll be here all night if you get bored. I'm sure Lifetime has a good movie on we can watch," her mom replied. Presley looked at her mom trying to decide the best way to respond. She knew her mom loved her and wanted things better between them. However, Presley was still hurt and angry with her.

"We'll see," Presley said as she headed out the kitchen and up to her room.

Stephanie: Hey girl I want details

Presley knew what Stephanie meant but she was going to pretend she didn't.

Presley: Details about what

Stephanie: Oh don't even try it. What's up with u and Luca.

Presley: Nothing we r just friends

Stephanie: Please shut up. U know as well as I do there is more now spill.

Presley chuckled she couldn't believe it took Stephanie this long to pry.

Presley: He's hot

Stephanie: Duh. Tell me sumtin I don't know

Presley: He kissed me the other day

Stephanie: SHUT UP

Presley: Fine I will

Stephanie: So r y'all like 2gether now

Presley: No he hasn't done it again since

Stephanie: What r y'all doing 2morrow

Presley: Going 2 his house. He's making me lunch & teaching me Italian

Stephanie: R u going 2 meet the parents

Presley: No he doesn't live with his parents

Stephanie: OMG! u know u r going 2 have to give me details

Presley: U r so nosy

Stephanie: It's not being nosey, it's a healthy thirst for knowledge. U r going to be alone with a hot guy who is totally in 2 u. damn straight I'm nosey

Presley: LOL. Don't get 2 excited unlike u I have self-control

Stephanie: have u seen Marcus really who wants self-control

Presley: u have issues

Stephanie: I know but u love my issues

Presley: I know

Stephanie: Marcus is here I'll talk 2 u latter

Presley: bye

Stephanie: DETAILS!!!!

Presley: Bye

Presley laughed and threw her phone on the bed. She grabbed her pajamas and headed to the bathroom to change her clothes. When she came back from the bathroom she decided to take a step by meeting her mother halfway to repairing their relationship. She would go watch a movie with her.

"What we watching mom?" Presley asked as she entered the living room.

"The Lacey Petterson Story," Brenda said. She was unable to hide the joy on her face because Presley was willing to spend time with her.

"Cool. I've wanted to see that." Presley said. She pulled the navy fleece blanket off the back of the coach and covered herself. She sat on the opposite end of the coach from her mother. Brenda smiled and placed a bowl of popcorn between the two of them. Brenda knew their relationship would not be fixed by one movie but she thanked God for small blessings. As much as she wanted things to get back to normal she knew they would never be the same. She also knew that sooner or later Presley was going to ask about her biological father. Truth be told, Brenda was hoping for later, much later.

Presley drifted off to sleep half way through the second movie in Lifetime's "Husbands That Kill Marathon." Brenda hated to wake her up but she knew there was no way she would be able to carry her.

"Presley," Brenda whispered as she gently shook Presley's arm.

"Huh?" Presley said half asleep.

"Honey, you need to go up to your bed."

"Okay," Presley said yawning. She slowly got up from the coach and headed toward her room. Turning back to her mother still half asleep she said "I love you, Mom. Things will get better just give me a little time."

"I love you, too, sweetheart. Take as much time as you need. I'll be ready when you are." Brenda smiled at her daughter and pulled her in for a quick hug. After their exchange Presley went to bed. Brenda stood in her living room amazed at the drastic change in her daughter in just one week. She had gone from not speaking one word to her mother for nine months to telling her she loved her and allowing Brenda to hug her. She seemed almost happy again. Brenda hadn't seen her daughter happy in way too long. Although Brenda was slightly concerned about this "Luca" boy she also couldn't help but feel he was part of the reason some of Presley's walls were cracking and tumbling down. If that was the case she would forever be in his debt.

Chapter Nine

Presley woke up at nine Saturday morning. She couldn't remember many Saturdays when she woke up before noon and even fewer when she had been happy to do so. She had decided to go ahead, take a shower and get ready for her day...until the scent of bacon hit her nose. Now that wonderful aroma was practically calling her to the kitchen...just forget everything else for now!

When Presley entered the kitchen she realized that her mother had not only made breakfast but also that she was already dressed in her work clothes.

"I thought you weren't going in until two," Presley said while pouring a cup of coffee.

"I was, but Travis called this morning and asked if I could come in early to talk to him. I'm leaving in about an hour. So your new friend has a reprieve." Brenda snickered as she made her daughter a plate of bacon, eggs, and French toast.

"Did he say what he wanted?" Presley asked as she eagerly took the plate of food from her mother and headed to the table.

"Nope, however he seemed to be in good spirits so I'm not too worried," Brenda replied as she joined her daughter at the table.

"I can't imagine they would have anything bad to talk about. I mean I don't think you have worked less than six days a week in like five years."

"If somebody wants to find something bad enough they will. I'm going to finish getting ready. I'll talk to you before I leave," Brenda said as she rose from the table and headed out of the kitchen.

Presley finished her breakfast and headed upstairs to shower. After her shower she needed to decide what to wear on this special day. After going through almost everything she owned she decided on her American Eagle skinny jeans with holes all down the legs. Her mother was not happy about paying so much money for holes! She just couldn't wrap her brain around paying that much for jeans that already had holes in them. Along with her jeans she wore a black tank top under a loose, off the shoulder white top. As she was applying her make-up her mother came in to let her know she was leaving. "What time will you be home from Stephanie's tonight?" Brenda asked.

"Not sure, but if it gets too late I may just stay. Is that okay?"

"That's fine, just check in with me around eleven."

"Okay, have a good day. Hope everything goes okay with Travis," Presley said as she continued to put on her eyeliner.

"Alright have fun but be careful. Okay?"

"Okay, bye Mom."

"Bye, I love you," Brenda told her daughter.

"Love you, too."

After hearing her daughter's wonderful good-bye Brenda was out the door. When Presley finished her makeup she realized it was already 10:45. She wouldn't have time to straighten her hair, which was a must if she was going to wear it down. So she decided to go with the messy bun she usually saved for down time at home. Luca seemed to like it that way last time. Plus they were just hanging out, might as well be comfortable. Just as she slipped on her black flats she heard the doorbell ring. Taking a deep breath, she headed to the front door. Even though she had been waiting for this day all week she still had butterflies in her stomach as she opened the door. Her breath caught for a moment when she saw him. He was in a blue button up shirt that matched his eyes with near perfection. His shirt was untucked and he had rolled the sleeves to his mid-forearm. He wore a pair of loose fitting jeans and black boots. Luca cleared his throat drawing her attention away from his gorgeous body. The smug smile on his face made it clear he had noticed her ogling him.

"Hey, come on in. I just gotta grab a couple things," she told him as she moved over allowing Luca to enter. He came into the house without saying a word. Something was different about him today but she couldn't quite put her finger on it.

"Be right back," she said and headed up the stairs. **Get a hold of yourself, girl. He didn't even say "hi!" Maybe he doesn't want to do this,** she wondered. When she turned around Luca was right behind her.

"Oh, where did you come from?" she said, startled by his sudden appearance.

"Just checking on you. I was lonely," he said, moving closer to her almost like a lion stalking his prey.

"I was only up here for a minute," she said laughing.

"A second away from you is too long," he said. He moved quickly as he completely closed the distance between them. As he moved his eyes never looked away from hers. Presley just stood there unable to move due to the intensity of his stare. He ran his knuckles down the side of her face. "You are so beautiful," he said. She opened her mouth to speak but was stopped short when his mouth crashed into hers. His left hand gripped the back of her neck holding her head where he wanted it. Her arms rose to wrap around his neck almost on their own because her brain seemed to have completely shut down. She just let herself surrender to the moment. He placed his right hand on her lower back and pulled her body close to his. She felt his tongue glide across her lower lip daring her to open her mouth...which she did. After a couple minutes of passionate kissing Luca finally pulled back. Presley opened her eyes and looked straight into his. They had changed. His pupils were so big his eyes almost looked black, except for a small ring of blue around them that seemed to be glowing.

"What's going on with your eyes?" she asked.

"Nothing. You ready?" That was all he said before quickly turning away from her.

"I'm sorry, did I upset you?" she asked placing her hand on his arm while attempting to turn him to face her. After a second he turned to her. His eyes looked normal. *Maybe I imagined it? Most likely that kiss had fried a few brain cells.*

"I'm sorry. I shouldn't have kissed you like I did. I just have wanted to really kiss you for so long. I just couldn't control myself," Luca confessed.

"Really? I am surprised to hear you say that. I didn't think you wanted to kiss me," she said almost in a whisper. Feeling a little embarrassed about what she had said, she tried to change the subject but Luca didn't give her the chance.

"Why would you say that?" he asked almost laughing.

"Well, you kissed me the other day but never even tried again. So I figured you regretted doing it the first time," she said still barely above a whisper and looking at the floor. She wasn't used to feeling so insecure with boys. She knew she was pretty. Since fifth grade boys had been telling her they liked the way she looked.

Luca laughed again, "The only thing I regret about the first time I kissed you was that it wasn't done properly. I didn't try again cause I was worried I was pushing you. I know you are not sure how to feel about what's going on between us." He placed his finger under her chin lifting her face to look at him.

"I guess I can understand that," Presley told him.

"You ready?"

Smiling again and feeling her confidence creep back in she smiled. "Yeah, let's go." She grabbed her purse and cell phone and they headed to Luca's car.

They drove in silence for about fifteen minutes. Presley took in the scenery as they drove through the back roads surrounded by only woods. Something about being in the woods always made Presley feel at peace. She never could explain it but she always felt most at home surround by wilderness. Luca could barely keep his eyes on road he was so distracted by the beauty sitting beside him. He found it very surprising she was so awed by the woods. He definitely would have pegged her as a city girl. Luca made a left on to a small dirt road. They had driven for less than a minute when his house came into view. It was a large two story house made of stone. His home, which had the most beautiful landscaping Presley had ever seen, sat on thirty acres of land. A large beautiful fountain, made of stone matching the house, was in the middle of the yard. On the left side of the yard was a gazebo surrounded with some type of flower that wasn't in bloom. The bushes surrounding the house were all perfectly pruned in square shapes. Presley could see many different flower beds that she had no doubt would soon be full of varieties of beautiful flowers.

"This is your house?" she asked still in awe.

"Yep, what were you expecting?" he asked with a little chuckle.

"Not this. I figured some messy apartment to be honest," she replied as he was opening his door and leaving the car. She waited patiently for him to walk around and open her door. She had given up fighting him about it. When he opened the door he laughed again as he saw the surprised look still on her face.

"It's been in the family for years."

"It's beautiful," she gushed.

Luca stood next to the car as Presley walked toward the house. He was enjoying watching her take in the scenery. Presley was so busy looking at everything around her she didn't notice the large rock right in front of her until it was too late, she tripped over it. She was sure she was going to land flat on her face, how embarrassing! She suddenly felt two strong arms wrap around her keeping her from face planting the ground. Presley looked at Luca then back to where he had been standing a second ago and then back to Luca.

"How did you?" was all she could get out before he stopped her.

"That rock gets everybody," he said trying hard to think of something to explain how he could have possibly caught her.

"You could have warned me," she said, not totally believing his explanation. She knew in her gut that something was going on and now she was determined to find out what.

Chapter Ten

After entering the house Luca led Presley to the living room. It was very elegantly decorated but still managed to have a homey feel. Even though the color scheme was black and gray it didn't feel dark. It felt warm with a touch of sophistication.

"Are you hungry?" he asked as they entered the living room.

"No, not right now, my mom made breakfast and there was bacon involved, so I'm stuffed."

"Bacon, I'll keep that in mind."

"So, we gonna start my lesson?"

"Is that really what you want to spend the day doing?"

"Sure, I really want to learn. That way when you try to be all secretive and flirty I'll know what you're saying," she smirked.

"Okay, let's take a walk and we'll work on it a little. But be forewarned I do not plan on spending my entire day with you teaching you Italian. I do have other plans."

"And what might they be?" she said with eyebrows raised.

"Tutto a tempo debito ma hai un gusto prime," (All in due time but you had a taste earlier) he said with a smug smile on his face.

"See that's what I'm talking about. What did you say?" she said as she crossed her arms and stomped her foot.

"Did you just stomp your foot?"

"Yes, now tell me what you said."

He laughed, grabbed her hand and headed toward the back door. "I said all in due time."

"Oh, no, there was more than that."

"How would you know?" he asked cocking one eyebrow at her.

"Ugh, this is not fair!"

They left his house and headed toward the wooded area behind it. He had realized on the way to his home that Presley seemed to like the woods. He thought she might like a walk among the trees. So he decided to take her for a walk on the trail that went through the woods behind his house.

"Wow, I love this," Presley said as she looked around the woods.

"I thought you might," he said grabbing her hand and interlocking their fingers.

"So what do you want to learn to say? Just so you know I will not be teaching you to curse."

"Party pooper," Presley said while as she made a pouty face.

"No, I just wouldn't want to hear such horrible things come out of your pretty mouth," he grinned.

"You're good," she laughed. "You want to hear something funny?" she asked.

"Sure."

"I really don't know what I want to learn how to say. I just want to know what you're saying when all of a sudden you start speaking Italian.

"I figured. How about I just start telling you what I say when I say it?"

"No, you lied to me earlier about what you said. How do I know you won't do it again?"

"'Cause I promise...no more lying," he said with a wink.

"Really, so I can ask you anything and you'll be honest with me?"

"Yea, why not?"

Ask him now you chicken. He said he would be honest. Just ask him.

"Ask me what?" Luca stopped in his tracks realizing the mistake he had just made. He had answered her thoughts before she had put them into words.

"That. I swear sometimes it's like you read my mind. You move way too quickly. Earlier your eyes, they were…..well different. What's up?"

"Okay, I will explain everything but first let's head back to the house. You're probably going to want to sit down."

The whole way back to the house they were both silent. Neither knew what to say or what was going to happen. Their conversation took a twist that Luca hoped would have happened later in their relationship. He knew it would happen sooner rather than later. He couldn't keep his guard up around her, but he had been hoping for a little bit longer. The whole walk back he went over in his head what he would say to her. He didn't want to lie but he didn't want to lose her. He didn't think he would be able to handle it if she feared him or turned her back on him. Presley had also been going over the possibilities in her head. The only constant thing in her head was Eric's voice telling her no matter what to trust Luca. She was beginning to believe that her dream wasn't a dream at all but Eric preparing her for this very moment.

When they reached the house he took Presley back to the living room and had her sit on the black leather couch. He sat next to her turning so he would be facing her. He started rubbing his face with his hands trying to find a way to start.

"Luca, it can't be that bad. Just tell me."

"Do you promise you will hear me out completely before you freak out?"

"I can promise to try but you're already freaking me out, so I make no guaranties," she said.

After listening to Presley Luca let out a small anxious laugh. "First, I need you to understand you will never need to fear me. I will never hurt you. I know what I am going to tell you is going to be hard to believe and might be a bit scary. Above all, I don't want to lose you," Luca said, his nervousness was very obvious.

"Luca, treat it like a Band-aid...just rip it off. We'll go from there. I'm a big girl. I can handle it," she said, placing her hand on his.

"IO.sono un vampiro." Luca said as he looked into her eyes trying to gauge her reaction.

"Okay, I don't know everything you just said but the last word sounded like vampire." As she spoke Presley jumped to her feet. Luca dropped his head. Presley ran her fingers through her hair as she tried to absorb this frightening information she had just heard. She couldn't think. All she could hear was Luca's voice saying he was a vampire...and Eric's voice telling her to trust Luca.

"Presley, mio amore, I won't hurt you. Please believe me. I would die before I let anything happen to you."

Suddenly something in her settled. She felt such a calm rush over her. She couldn't begin to explain. She walked back over to the couch and sat next to Luca. His head was still lowered. She placed her hands on each side of his face and gently lifted it to look at her.

"Let me see," she stated quietly.

"What?" he was totally dumbfounded by her response.

"Let me see what you look like when you're all in...your vampire mode or whatever!" Now her voice was a little bit louder when she spoke.

"Why?" he was glad she wasn't screaming, but he didn't expect her to be so calm.

"Because I want to know what I'm dealing with here." She stated frankly. But, truth be told, she was also surprised that she wasn't freaking out.

"Presley, I don't think you really want to do this right now. You can't tell me you don't have other questions we should address first."

"Do you kill people?" she asked bluntly.

"No, I take what I need and they never know what happened. I have learned to control myself so I don't hurt anyone. Worst case scenario they feel tired. They may have a sore neck the next day that they can't really explain. They usually just think they didn't sleep well."

"So they have no memory of what happened?"

"No."

"Have you ever bitten me?" she asked, almost ashamed to be asking.

"NO! I wouldn't do that to you!" He stood quickly, "I would never bite you!"

"Oh." Presley said. ***Why are you disappointed by that? Girl you have issues!*** She scolded herself. When she looked at Luca he had one eyebrow up and a smug grin on his face.

"Oh crap, you can read my mind can't you!" she yelled, jumped off the couch, and started pacing.

"Yeah." He said as he rubbed the back of his neck. He seemed almost embarrassed by his admission.

"Oh my god, Oh my god I can't believe this!" Presley exclaimed.

"Let me see if I have this straight. I just told you I'm a vampire. Yet the thing about this whole situation that bothers you the most is I can read your mind. Now you know that I know you're attracted to me."

"YES!" After a moment she added, "I guess that is kind of messed up, isn't it?"

"A little, I need to know how you feel about all this," he said as he walked over to her. He took it as a good sign that she didn't back away from him.

"Can't you just read my mind?"

"Yes, but I want you to tell me. Plus, I can read your thoughts but not your emotions."

Presley looked into his eyes searching for any sign of a monster. She couldn't find one. She knew she should be bothered by this, and that she should run. Something in her still cried out for him. She didn't think she could turn on him in any circumstance.

"First, I need to know if you can make me think or feel things I wouldn't normally experience."

"I can compel people to do things or forget things. However, I have no control over their emotions. But please remember because I can, doesn't mean I do. I would never mess with your mind. I promise."

"So here we are, all my cards on the table. I need to know if you are willing to put all your cards on the table, too."

"I just told you my darkest secret. There is nothing I have to hide."

"I know this should bother me or scare me but it doesn't. I feel I am safer with you then anyone else." She left the part out about feeling as if her soul called to him. She didn't want to deal with too many issues at one time.

"I would never hurt you, I swear," he said as he grabbed her hand.

"How often do you um....eat?"

"Every couple of days, because I don't drain them completely it doesn't last long. I take only what I need to get through a day or so to avoid any serious side effects to the human. Come back and sit down." He said as he pulled her to the couch.

"Anybody I know?" she asked sounding almost jealous.

Luca let out a little laugh, "No, I never um ....where I live. You do realize what a weird conversation this is right?"

"Yes, but I am trying. Give me a break."

"You're handling this great, Presley. I didn't want to tell you. I was worried you'd leave."

"I want to understand but you are going to have to bear with me when I ask stupid questions."

"You haven't asked any stupid questions."

"I guess this stays between us, right? I'm assuming you don't want me telling Kevin?" she asked.

"I would prefer you didn't yet," he said as he kissed her cheek. Again she didn't back away from him which comforted him.

"Yet, so I can at some point?"

"Yes, I'll let you know when."

"Good, just promise you won't eat any of my friends." She laughed and so did he as he said, "I promise."

"Okay, then we're okay. You don't kill people and you won't bite my friends. We're good."

"Wow, you are something else, Ms. Presley!"

"One more thing..."

"What's that?"

"When you do bite somebody, do they turn into a vampire?"

"No, there is a whole process to that. It requires more than a bite."

"So, if you bit me I wouldn't turn?"

"Don't."

"Don't what?"

"Don't talk about that right now."

"Why?"

"Because I already know that you're thinking about it. Talking about it is just going to make me want to do it more then I already do. You're not ready for all that right now. It's too much for one day," Luca said pinching the bridge of his nose while squeezing his eyes shut. He was trying to get the images of him sinking his teeth in the soft flesh of her neck out of his head.

"Will you show me now? What you look like."

"No, but I will soon. You already saw a little bit this morning. I lost some of my control when we were kissing."

"Oh," she said. A wicked smile crossed her face when she looked at his blue eyes and thought ***In that case...*** She wrapped her arms around his neck and pulled his face closer to hers. When he heard her thought he smiled just as wickedly, grabbed the back of her neck, and kissed her deeply. After a few minutes he pulled away from her and laughed when she whimpered. "You do like to push your luck don't you, Ms. Kluttz?" Then he lowered his lips back to hers.

"Yep," Ms. Kluttz answered with a big smile before pressing her lips to his.

Chapter Eleven

Luca and Presley headed towards Stephanie's house shortly before 7. "You, do realize I need her to invite me in right?" Luca asked Presley as he glanced over at her. He was quickly realizing having her in his car could be hazardous. He was finding keeping his eyes on the road was very difficult because his eyes only wanted to stare at Presley. "Got ya covered, Babe," she said as she pulled out her phone. He just laughed. He was still in awe about how she had handled his revelation. He had been sure she would run screaming but she didn't. Instead she had embraced both his secret and him. Presley scrolled down her contacts. When she found Steph's number she sent her a quick text message.

Presley: We r on the way.

Stephanie: U better have good details or I won't let u in.

Presley: LOL. Get Luca in the house and I will tell you as soon as we get there.

Stephanie: Will do.

"Okay, we're good. So you can't go in to people's house without be invited?"

"Nope, it's nature's way of keeping things fair. Each of us should have a safe place to go. However, public place likes school and stores are fair game."

"So what parts of the stories are true and what's not?"

"Well, obviously I can walk in the sun but we have to be charmed when we are turned to do so. Crosses and garlic don't bother me. A stake in my heart would hurt like hell but it won't kill me." He was once again realizing he was spending too much time looking at her and not enough time looking at the road. He couldn't believe how lucky he was to meet a girl he was so attracted to and surprisingly that didn't fear him.

"What would kill you?" She was very glad he was being so honest with her. Now that he had told her his secret she felt like he was an open book. God knew she loved a good book, and right now she was ready to read one about Luca.

"You planning something I should know about, mio amore?" Luca asked with a grin.

"Shut up! No, but I am assuming you are not the only vampire alive. Sometime in the future I may need to have that information," she said slapping his arm.

"The only way to kill a vampire is to decapitate it or to completely remove the heart from its body."

"Gross," Presley said scrunching her nose.

They pulled into Stephanie's driveway and saw her waiting on the front porch.

"Hey, guys," Stephanie said as they approached the house.

"Hey, Steph," Presley replied.

"Good evening, Stephanie," Luca said as he entwined his fingers with Presley's.

"Okay Luca get your sexy little butt in the house. I need to talk to my girl." Stephanie demanded playfully while throwing the front door open.

"Yes ma'am!" He laughed, then winked at Presley as he leaned down to kiss her cheek. After Luca entered the house Stephanie pulled the door closed and turned to Presley who had already joined her on the porch.

"Alright, spill," Stephanie said as she pulled Presley over to the wooden porch swing.

"Okay, well, you know how I told you that he kissed me the other day?"

"Yeah."

"Well that was not a kiss. At least not a Luca kiss. I was getting my phone from my room. When I turned around he was right behind me. He put his hand behind my neck, pulled me close and kissed me senseless. It was the most amazing, passionate, intense kiss ever. We are talking like movie quality."

"Really. Did he say why it took him so long after the first one?"

"Yeah he was worried that he was pushing me."

"So, what did y'all do the rest of the day?" Stephanie asked wiggling her eyebrows at her friend.

"We just spent the day getting to know each other," Presley said with a smile.

"Really...and just how well do you know him now?"

"Not like that. We had one other little make out session but nothing more than kissing...I swear," Presley told her friend.

"Um Huh...I bet!"

"Stephanie, I dated Eric two years and we never went all the way. How could you think Luca would get there in one week?" Presley said, smacking her friend's bare leg.

"I have a feeling that boy in there would make saying no very hard."

"No doubt, but it ain't gonna happen!"

Giggling the two girls rose from the swing and headed in the house. When they entered all three boys were laughing. Apparently, Marcus had lost the battle over what movie they would watch and the boys found it very amusing.

"What's so funny?" Presley asked as she shut the door.

"Sorry, Presley I tried but she just wouldn't budge," Marcus said as he turned to the girls. Stephanie just crossed her arms and smirked at him.

"Wouldn't budge on what?" Presley asked feeling very out of the loop.

Marcus exhaled a deep breath and explained, "She got ALL of the Twilight movies. I mean all of them!"

"Stephanie!" Presley whined.

"Oh hush, Pres. You know you like them. Just cause you're all Team Jacob doesn't mean you need to be a sore loser!" Presley's eyes were as big as saucers when she looked over to Luca. He was propped against the wall and his shoulders were shaking in silent laughter.

"Really, Team Jacob?" Luca asked cocking his eyebrow.

"Um..." was all Presley could manage.

"Yeah, she says vampires are sexy and all but they are wusses and werewolves are much manlier. I tried to tell her she was crazy but she just doesn't listen," Stephanie informed Luca.

"Really?" Luca winked at Presley who still stood speechless. Not sure what to say Presley just stood with her arms crossed and a pout on her face. ***This is not happening*** she kept repeating in her head. As Stephanie pulled blankets out of the closet toward the back of the living room she continued, "Personally, I think she just likes seeing Jacob with his shirt off. I mean I can't blame her, but come on vampires are so much hotter than werewolves."

"Stephanie, please just shut up!" Presley pleaded.

"Stephanie, you do realize that vampires and werewolves are not real right?" Marcus said looking at his girlfriend and very concerned for her sanity. Luca stood back watching, still silently laughing mainly at Presley's red cheeks and lost look.

"Yes, I do. I'm just saying if they were real I would be cuddled up to some sexy guy and Presley would just have a bad case of fleas." Stephanie said in a very matter of fact tone. At that point Luca's laughter was no longer silent as he let out a loud laugh. He tried to cover it with a cough when Presley turned to glare at him.

"Stephanie, how about you just worry about cuddling up with me," Marcus said as he pulled her down to his lap.

"I'll go get the popcorn," Kevin said as he rose from the couch shaking his head and laughing.

Just then Presley felt Luca's big strong arms wrap around her little waist. Then he placed his mouth right next to her ear and whispered, "Wusses, huh?" Then he kissed down her neck. When he reached the tender spot where her neck met her shoulder he gently pressed his teeth on her skin. Not a real bite just a little nip. Presley let out a small groan causing Stephanie to break her hold on Marcus. "Hey, what are y'all doing over there?" she asked laughing.

"Nothing!" Presley said as she elbowed Luca in the ribs. He chuckled and winked at Stephanie and Marcus.

"Oh, I love it. I knew that you two would click. I didn't realize it would happen so quickly, but God...I'm glad it did," Stephanie giggled looking at her friend. She had wanted for so long to see the carefree, fun-loving Presley again. Now Luca was bringing her back and that filled Stephanie with more happiness then she thought was possible. Stephanie always put up a good front of being cool, cocky and sometimes selfish. However, her friends knew she loved them and was fiercely loyal to them. That's why she and Marcus were such a good match. She didn't realize it until Eric died. When she saw Marcus with Presley after the accident she fell in love with him. When Presley's other friends ran from the emotional mess, too weak to help their friend, Marcus stayed. He supported her, and tried to ease her pain. Pain not only caused by Eric's death but also by the disappearance of her so-called friends.

The group settled down to watch the movie. Marcus and Stephanie cuddled on the big couch under a blanket. Kevin stretched out on the love seat covered in his own blanket. Luca laid on the floor with his head propped on a pillow and his left arm under it. Presley laid next to him with her head on Luca chest and his right arm wrapped around her. The blanket they were to share was only over Presley.

As they watched the movie they all laughed at Stephanie's lustful comments about the vampires and Marcus comical retorts. Every once in while Luca would lean down and kiss the top of Presley's head. He also gently rubbed her back. Every time she would start to dose off he would lean down and quietly howl in her ear, earning him several slaps on his tight six pack abs. Not long into the second movie Presley realized it was after eleven and she should have called her mother. She grabbed her phone and texted her mom.

Presley: Hey mom staying at Steph's

A couple minutes later her phone beeped to let her know her mother had responded to her text.

Brenda: K honey have a good night.

Placing her phone down Presley relaxed back into Luca's embrace. Before the second movie had ended everyone except Luca was fast asleep. Luca looked at the beautiful girl next to him and then around the room at the friends she held so dearly. Again he felt blessed, which was an odd feeling for the eternally damned. He had not only found a girl who could love him completely for everything he was. He also had made friends with a group of people who were truly incredible in every way. He wasn't sure what it was but he knew there was something very special about every person that lay in that room. Presley hadn't said that she loved him but he could feel it every time she looked into his eyes. He knew he loved her and would do anything for her.

Chapter Twelve

A beautiful woman with hair as black as midnight stormed into the Paris hotel suite she called home. She slammed the door behind herself. "That man is going to pay for this!" she shouted looking at the man sitting in a chair on the left side of the room.

"What happened?" he asked as he rose from the chair. To most people he would be very intimidating. He was 6'3 with a very muscular body. His shoulder length blonde hair was pulled back in a ponytail at the base of his neck which extenuated his chiseled face. However, his size was nothing compared to the rage coming out of the woman who had just entered the room.

"Basilio has my brother. They have arrested him for killing a human. Since it is his third offense Basilio is deciding between death and 100 years imprisonment," she replied with a voice filled with rage. She headed to the mini bar in the suite and poured a small glass of Scotch. As she downed her drink her companion walked over to her.

"Anthony killed another human?" he asked.

"Yes, Andrew, he did and the dumb butt got caught AGAIN!" she yelled.

"Ivy, you know Basilio will put him to death, right?" Andrew replied placing his hand on her back.

"Yes but I have month to figure out a way to save his butt. They are doing an investigation and I am sure this is going to get worst. You know they will find more human deaths attached to my brother."

"He does seem to have a problem controlling himself when it comes to human women doesn't he?"

"Yes, the combination of his hunger for blood and his lust for humans is becoming worst and causing all kinds of problems," she said pouring another Scotch. "I have to get him out of this and then rid our species of the self-righteous ass Basilio."

"You do realize that will not be an easy task. His people love him and he is well protected."

"Oh, I know, but I have a plan," she turned and smiled at Andrew as the evil danced in her eyes. Ivy was a smart, beautiful strong woman and her temper had often made grown men fear her wrath. Although at first sight most would more likely admire her beauty than fear her. She was a force to be respected. Her small frame was especially deceiving. She was extraordinarily strong, even for a vampire. Her ivory porcelain skin tone gave people the false impression she was fragile when that couldn't be further from the truth. She was turned into a vampire at the young age of twenty one so her face still held the look of innocent youth. However, if someone looked into her dark eyes they could see the evil she embraced so proudly. Her soul was as black as her hair. Her only desires in this world were to rule over the vampire species and to do it with Andrew by her side. She knew to accomplish this Basilio must die. The vampire world was broken up into several small clans spread throughout the world. Not only was Basilio the king of the Italian clan he was also one of the most powerful and respected vampires worldwide. He alone made the laws. Everyone obeyed his decisions, and if they didn't, they paid a price. Ivy was one of a few vampires who had a dislike for the way Basilio ran things. She passionately disliked the fact he protected humans, making it illegal to kill them. Of course their blood could still be used as nourishment. However, those humans were always to have sufficient blood remaining in their bodies to survive. Ivy thought of humans as cattle. She didn't like that they were protected by law. She also didn't like the fact vampires lived in the shadows. Vampires are some of the world's most powerful creatures. Despite their powerful attributes they live in hiding from a world they should be ruling. These things alone were enough to make her want Basilio dead. Now he had her brother and that just added to her already deep hatred of this man everyone else loved.

"What is your plan?" Andrew asked, pouring himself a drink.

"I'm going to get close to him and then I'm going to rip his damn heart out."

"I hope you have more than that. How do you plan to get close to him? Now that your brother is in custody Basilio will be even more suspicious of any actions you take to get closer to him."

"No, you know I am smarter than most people acknowledge. I had an angry outburst yesterday at the mansion. Yelling at Anthony about how stupid he was and how ashamed I am to have him as family...blah...blah...blah. Then I apologized to our great leader for my brother's behavior and swore to him I would to do anything to make amends for Anthony's actions. Now he believes I back him 100 percent," Ivy said as she searched through the clothes in her dresser.

"I haven't heard a plan yet, dear," Andrew said as he wrapped this woman he loved in his arms.

"That's all I thought about on the plane home. It's very simple, actually. I just want him to let his guard down. I need him distracted enough that he won't see me coming. Do you know the best way to do that?" she asked as an evil smile crossed her lips.

"How?" he asked, although he was fairly sure he knew the answer.

"I'm going to kill his precious prince. While he grieves I will go to him to offer comfort. When the time is perfect I will pull his heart from his chest."

"How do you plan to get that close to Luca? Do you even know where he is?"

"That will be the only tricky part. I need you to find Luca. I can't look for him now. It may look suspicious if I just disappeared considering my brother's current situation. So, you go find Luca. I'll head back to Italy and work on making amends with the king," Ivy answered, putting her arms around Andrew's neck.

"What do you want me to do when I find him? Do you want me to kill him?" he asked pulling her closer. There was no bigger turn on to this couple than an evil scheme.

"No. His death will come at my hands. I have wanted to rip that little twit's heart out for centuries. There is no way I will let this opportunity pass. Just find him, follow him, and find any weakness I can use."

"You are so sexy when you're bloodthirsty," Andrew said as he tossed her onto their king sized bed. He pressed her to the mattress as his body hovered over hers.

"Just wait and see, you haven't seen anything yet. You wait till Basilio and his brats are dead and we rule. I will bring this world to its knees. For every ounce of happiness it brings to me you will receive the same pleasure tenfold." She smiled and pulled his mouth to hers. Neither could deny the passion building any longer. Planning the down fall of a king had been more of a turn on then either one of them had ever experienced. Their wickedness consumed them as they ravished each other.

∞

Meanwhile back in Italy, Basilio paced his office replaying the events of yesterday in his head. Deciding that something wasn't right he grabbed his phone and quickly called his daughter's phone number.

After two rings she answered, "Ciao." (Hello)

"Nicky, cari per favore venite al mio ufficio," (Nicky, dear please come to my office) Basilio said to his daughter.

"Si, Padre," (Yes, Father) Nicolette replied. She quickly hung up her phone and headed to her father's office.

After ending the call with his daughter Basilio punched in another number on his phone. "Angelo," a deep voice answered.

"Ho bisogno de vederti," (I need to see you) was all that was said before Basilio hung up his phone.

A few minutes later both Nicolette and Angelo entered Basilio's office.

"Che cosa posso fare pe lei?" (What can I do for you sir) Angelo asked as he bowed his head to his king.

"First, from this point on let's speak English, you never know if someone is listening," Basilio answered his friend and guard. "Let me get Luca on the phone," he said while he pressing the speaker button on his phone and dialed Luca's number.

The phone rang a couple times before Luca answered with a whisper, "Ciao."

"Luca, son, we may have a problem," Basilio said when his son answered the phone.

"Hold on, let me walk outside." Luca gently slid away from Presley's sleeping body and exited the house through the front door.

"What's going on, Dad?" he asked after he closed the door behind him.

"First, know that I have Nicolette and Angelo here and you are on speaker phone."

"Okay. Why do I not like the sound of this?" Luca asked as he developed an uneasy feeling in the pit of his stomach.

"Hey, Luca." He heard Nicolette's tiny voice through the phone. Although Nicolette was centuries old she still had an innocence about her that their lives as vampires never destroyed. She was sixteen when she turned. She was still as sweet and innocent as she was that day.

"Hey, hun, " he replied.

"Okay, we need to get through this quickly. I don't know who else is in the mansion. I am pretty sure there is a leak somewhere so I want to get this done quickly," Basilio interrupted.

"Alright, go," Luca said

"I have Anthony DeCar in custody. He has killed another human. This makes three deaths we know about but I am sure we will find more. His sister, Ivy, was here yesterday. Although she says she supports us and believes her brother should be punished. I am not buying it. She is not as good an actress as she thinks she is."

"What do you think she's up to?" Angelo asked.

"If I had to guess...my death. Easiest way to get that is through my children. Luca, I need you to be extra cautious. If this gets bad you may need to come home."

"Dad, I can't leave."

"Don't argue with me now...we will cross that bridge when we get to it. Nicky, I want you to stay in the mansion with Angelo at all times. Angelo, I am going to move you in to the room adjoining Nicolette's. You are to stay with her at all times. Is this clear to each of you?" Basilio said in a tone thick with authority.

"Yes, sir." All three answered at the same time.

"Luca, let me know if anything happens. I will call you in a day or two with an update."

"Si, Padre," and with that Luca disconnected the call.

Basilio dismissed Nicolette but asked Angelo to stay. "Angelo, I'm placing my daughter's life in your hands. You must remember protecting her life is utmost...and anything that interferes with that has to be postponed at this time in your lives. Are we clear?" Basilio asked firmly. He knew Angelo and Nicolette were starting to develop feelings for each other and under normal circumstances he would be thrilled. He loved Angelo as if he were another son. However, he was well aware in situations such as the one they would be facing Angelo would need a clear head. He also knew that sometimes in stressful situations things could be done or said one may later regret...and that is when hearts are broken.

"Yes, sir," Angelo replied and left.

Chapter Thirteen

Luca pushed his phone back in his pocket as he paced Stephanie's front porch. Rubbing his hands through his hair he went over the conversation he had with his father. He knew that Ivy could be dangerous on a good day. He didn't want to think of the damage she could cause when she was enraged. She had once killed a woman in a bar because she smiled and winked at Andrew. She was cruel and heartless, a combination that made many fear her. Luca had never feared her. But now things had changed in his life, he had something to lose and that something, Presley, could also been seen as a weakness. *I hope I haven't brought danger to her. Maybe I should leave, they will never know of her if they don't find me with her.*

He was so lost in thought he didn't notice the front door open until Presley came up behind him and wrapped her arms around his waist. When he turned to look at her she squeezed him tighter. "Are you okay?" she asked her voice was quiet. She sounded as if she was still half asleep. Hearing her voice made the thought of leaving vanish from his mind. He knew there was no way he could ever leave her

"I'm fine baby, but you need to go back to sleep," he said while running his fingers through her long blonde and red hair.

Twisted Fate

"Are you coming with me?" she asked snuggling her face on his shoulder as she moved closer to kiss his neck.

"Yea, let's go," he said as he guided her toward the door. He knew he wouldn't sleep but he also knew if he didn't go back in neither would she. When they returned to the living room they took their places back on the floor. Luca laid on his back and Presley used his chest as a pillow. Because of his tightly toned muscles it wasn't the softest pillow...but it was quickly becoming her favorite.

Presley soon drifted back to sleep. Luca, however, couldn't clear his mind. He looked around the room at the sleeping teenagers who were rapidly becoming an important part of his life. He never allowed himself to become too emotionally involved with humans but there was something special about each sleeping body in that room. He couldn't quite put his finger on why but he knew he would die before he let harm come to any of them. He hoped that he wasn't putting them in danger by being with them. When he looked at Presley's face and he realized again that nothing could make him leave her side.

∞

The next morning Kevin was the first to wake. Luca realized then that Kevin spent a lot of time waiting for his friends. Whether it was them waking up or meeting somewhere, Kevin was always the first to arrive. Kevin looked around the room and saw that Luca was the only one awake. "Hey, man, you want some coffee?" Kevin asked as he pulled himself off the coach.

"Sounds great," Luca said as he slowly pulled himself away from Presley. Trying not to wake her he gently placed a pillow under her head.

"Don't worry about her. Once she's out an earthquake couldn't wake her," Kevin snickered as he headed toward the kitchen. After covering Presley up with their blanket Luca followed Kevin into the kitchen.

"So, we haven't really had a chance to talk," Kevin said as he put coffee and water in the coffee maker and started it.

"What do you want to talk about?" Luca asked leaning his back against the kitchen counter. He had known this was coming. Kevin was very protective of Presley. He had already told Luca they needed to talk but they hadn't had a chance yet.

"Well, for starters, what is your deal with Presley? I mean if this is just something you do to pass time you need to stop now. She already has feelings for you whether she will admit it or not. If you just decide to walk away you will hurt her. I do not want to ever see her again in that dark place she was when Eric died. I do not want her hurt, do you hear me?" Kevin said as he leaned against the counter across from Luca. Kevin believed Luca was a good guy but he didn't want Presley to get hurt. He believed it was time to figure out Luca's intentions.

"I really like her. I promise I won't do anything to hurt her. I don't think I could walk away if I wanted to."

"You need to know that she may put up a really good front but she is neither as tough nor as cold as she wants people to think she is." Kevin said as he pulled two coffee cups from the cabinet above the coffee maker. Then he continued, "Once she's in...she's all in. I'm pretty sure, as far as you're concerned, if she isn't all ready all in she will be soon."

"Would it make you feel better if I told you I think I'm already all in?" Luca asked.

"As long as you mean it. She isn't the kinda girl you can play games with," Kevin said as he poured two cups of coffee. "Plus, if you do, I don't care how ripped you are I will beat the crap out of you!"

Luca chuckled a little then responded, "I'm not playing games with her. She has become a very important part of my life. To be honest all of you have."

"Good. Do you want to cook some breakfast?" Kevin asked as he opened the refrigerator. Although it was not Kevin's house this group of friends spent so much time together they all felt right at home in each other's home.

"Sure. What do they have?" Luca asked as he joined Kevin at the opened refrigerator door.

"Eggs, bacon, sausage, and I'm sure they have bread and pancake mix. We are a breakfast group if you haven't noticed," Kevin said as he scanned the fridge.

"I make really good French toast," Luca offered.

"Perfect," Kevin replied.

"Alright, I'll do the French toast and you do the bacon. Presley is going to want her bacon," Luca said gathering what he would need to prepare breakfast.

"You're a quick study, grasshopper." Kevin laughed as he took the bacon from the fridge.

As the boys prepared breakfast Marcus and Stephanie entered the kitchen and each made a cup of coffee.

"So, I think it is time that we discuss prom," Stephanie said lifting herself onto a stool next to the counter. Even though she had just gotten up she looked like she was ready to go to the mall. Except for her tank top and pajama shorts, her hair looked like she had just brushed it and her face was flawless even without make-up.

"Stephanie, it is way too early in the morning to talk about prom," Marcus groaned as he sipped coffee. He, on the other hand, had obviously just woke up. He absolutely had major bed head. His sleepy eyes definitely showed he would be much happier if he were still in bed.

"Shut up. This is important stuff," Stephanie said as she glared at Marcus. "Luca, are you taking Pres?" she continued.

"Um…..to be honest we haven't discussed it. Does she want to go?"

"She is a seventeen year old girl and it is her senior prom, of course she wants to go!" Stephanie said with an "are you stupid" look on her face.

"Actually prom is on her eighteenth birthday," Kevin piped in while he flipped bacon.

"Hey, that's right," Stephanie said then looked back at Luca. "Hell yeah, she will want to go."

"Are you going, Kevin?" Luca asked trying to take some of the heat off himself.

"Don't know yet. Maybe, I have to talk to Jimmy."

"I'll talk to Presley about prom later," Luca said as he piled all the French toast on a plate.

"Okay, now go wake up sleeping beauty," Stephanie said as she popped a piece of bacon in her mouth and grabbed a plate.

"Yes ma'am," Luca said winking at Stephanie as he left the kitchen. He caught his breath as he entered the living room and his gaze fell upon Presley's sleeping face. He was still amazed by her beauty every time he looked at her. When he reached her he lowered himself so he could sit on the floor next to her. Leaning close to her he whispered in her ear, " Hey bella, ora di svegliarsi" (Hey beautiful, time to wake up).

Presley smiled as she opened her eyes and looked up at Luca's handsome face. "Good morning," she said, still smiling. He leaned down and kissed her. He tried to control himself but his control slipped away as soon as she opened eyes. Normally Presley would have been a little weary of kissing first thing in the morning, you know morning breath and all, but when Luca kissed her she reached up and locked her hands around his neck. When Luca pulled back Presley ran her tongue across her bottom lip and said "Be careful, I could get used to waking up like this."

"Tutto quello che vuoi, e' per voi" (anything you want, it is yours). Luca replied as he pulled Presley to her feet.

"Do I smell bacon?" Presley asked smiling.

"Yes ma'am, you do."

"Oh, yeah, I really could get used to waking up like this." Presley laughed as she headed toward the kitchen.

"Careful, Pres, Steph is already talking about prom," Marcus warned as Presley entered the kitchen.

"Took her long enough. I figured we would have been dealing with it last night." Presley was still laughing as she headed to the coffee pot.

"So you don't want to go?" Luca asked as he fixed Presley's plate.

"YES! She does!" Stephanie emphatically answered for her.

"Thank you Stephanie, but really, I haven't given it much thought," Presley said as she sat at the counter next to Stephanie. "I guess it could be fun."

"When is it?" Luca asked.

"April 19th." Everyone turned to look at Marcus surprised he was the one who answered. "What?" he asked as they all looked at him.

"Just surprised you knew, that's all," Kevin said.

"You do know who I'm dating, right" Marcus asked as he shoved his last bite of French toast in his mouth. "This is really good, man." he added with his mouth still full of food.

"Nice," Stephanie said rolling her eyes.

"You love me Baby," he said sticking his tongue out with chewed food still on it.

"You are so gross," Stephanie groaned while the rest of her friends just laughed. "Anyway, it's settled we are all going. Pres and I are going to look for dresses today."

"Today?" Presley asked choking on her coffee when went down the wrong way.

"Yes. Why not?" Stephanie asked.

"I don't know but I guess it's fine." Presley said as she looked at Luca who just shrugged. "Kevin can you take me home to get ready?" Presley asked as she turned to Kevin.

Before Kevin could answer Luca said, "I can take you." Sounding very confused by her asking Kevin instead of him.

"No you can't. My mom is going to be home and if you take me home she'll know you stayed the night."

"But it's okay that Kevin and Marcus stayed?" Luca asked, already knowing the answer but wanting to hear what Presley would say.

"Kind of different" Presley said. Her friends were trying to hold back laughter as they looked back and forth between the two. They also wanted to hear Presley's answer.

"How?" Luca asked.

"Um....Well... She doesn't see Kevin or Marcus as a threat to my virtue." Presley was not sure if she should have answered that way. **Probably should have said...just because...** She thought she saw a smug smile cross Luca's face. Then he said exactly what she was worried he would.

"Oh, so you're saying I am?"

At that point her friends couldn't hold their laughter any longer. They all three burst into laughter at the same time.

"Don't get too cocky there, buddy. She may think so but that doesn't mean you are." Presley said rolling her eyes as she got off of the kitchen stool. With that the group got up, cleaned their plates and prepared to leave.

Marcus and Luca went to their homes. Kevin took Presley home. Stephanie planned to pick her up around two. Presley wouldn't admit it but she was actually pretty excited about prom. She was also pleased to be having some girl time with Stephanie

Chapter Fourteen

Andrew sat on a private jet heading toward the United States. It had been easy for him to locate Luca although Ivy thought it was too easy. Andrew simply called one of Luca's poker buddies, Austin, under the rouse of trying to find a game to join. He knew Luca's absence would leave an opening in their game. So when Austin told him they had an opening due to Luca's trip Andrew simply asked where he had gone. Because Luca was away for a personal reason, not a safety one, Austin didn't think twice about telling him Luca was in North Carolina. Andrew didn't push for a specific town because he didn't want it to seem as if he was trying to find Luca. He knew the Davenports had homes all over the United States. He happened to be in Luca's home in North Carolina decades ago, when he was dating Luca's sister Nicolette and he still remembered exactly where it was located.

Just as Andrew was starting to doze off his phone buzzed indicating he had a text message. Opening the icon that held his text he saw that Ivy was texting him.

Ivy: Hey babe what is your E.T.A?

Andrew: Noon in the town by 1.

Ivy: Did some research. Think I may have found something. Sending u a pic.

Andrew waited for only a moment when his phone finally notified him the picture had arrived. It was a picture Ivy had taken with her phone of her computer screen. On the screen was a picture of a beautiful young girl with long blond hair with red streaks in it. Her face looked almost angelic. Andrew couldn't help but notice how pretty she was and that her blue eyes, even though a picture, were almost hypnotic.

Andrew: Who is this?

Ivy: Some teenager, Presley Kluttz.

Andrew: Where did you find this?

Ivy: Facebook.

Andrew: ?

Ivy: Luca is trying to fit in with a bunch of American teenagers, of course, he would have Facebook. He has 5 friends...1 guy named Kevin, 2 kids Stephanie and Marcus that are in a relationship with each other, and her. Surely you noticed how alluring she is. Luca is falling all over himself to be around this girl I promise.

Andrew: Anything else?

Ivy: The other girl, Stephanie, is going shopping 4 prom with her "Bestie" which I am assuming is Presley.

Andrew: How do u know that? What do u want me to do?

Ivy: Teenage girls put too much on Facebook. Follow the girl. Spook her a little that will send Luca into a tizzy and he won't be able to think straight. He won't want to leave her so he won't feed like he should and he'll be weak.

Andrew: Aw my little evil genius.

Ivy: U know it. Luv u

Andrew: u 2

With that Andrew replaced his phone in his pocket. Looking at his watch he realized it was about ten he had two hours, just enough time for a short nap.

Ivy paced her room. Everything was coming together but something in her gut was telling her it had been too easy.

She could almost feel there was something she was missing. Something big she wasn't taking into account. Deciding it was just her nerves getting the better of her she began to pack for her trip back to Italy. The whole time she was packing her attention kept being drawn back to her laptop screen which still displayed Presley's Facebook profile. Since she couldn't keep her mind on packing she decided to stop doing it and walked over to her laptop. "What am I missing?" she said to her screen. Now her focus was on Presley's eyes. "What is different about you? Pretty human girl but there is something else, what is it?" Ivy continued as the knot in her stomach grew. No matter how hard she tried she couldn't dismiss that feeling of doom. However, she knew it was something she would have to address later. Now she had bigger vampires to fry.

After Andrew's plane landed he procured a car from a small rental agency in the airport. Once in the car he turned on his smart phone and did a little research. After 10 minutes, and a visit to Facebook and the Yellow Pages, he had Stephanie MacLamore and Presley Kluttz's home addresses. "Got to love technology, makes my job so much easier!" he laughed to his empty car as he placed his phone in the car's console. Pulling out of the parking lot he headed toward the two addresses he had just found.

∞

Luca arrived home about noon. He decided to do a light workout. He knew he would have to go out that evening and eat but it was early. He had a lot of built up frustration that exercising would reduce. He removed his shirt, traded his jeans for a pair of black basketball shorts, and headed toward the back of the house where he had a small gym. With his mind bouncing in so many directions he hoped a light workout would help him put things in order. Starting with some 20lb curls his mind drifted toward his family and the danger that could be surrounding them. His curls became more rapid as he thought of his sister. Although Nicolette was a vampire she still had such an innocence about her which made her too trusting. She had placed that trust in the wrong man and had sustained serious injuries that even her vampire blood couldn't completely heal. Her vampire blood could only heal the physical injuries however the physiological wounds remained. Placing the dumbbells back on floor he moved toward his weight bench to do some presses. As he raised the bar up and lowered it again and again his thoughts went to Ivy, Andrew and their warped ideals. They believed that vampires should not live in the shadows of the world but should rule it. They also believed humans should be raised as if they were cattle. Just the thought of their arrogance and stupidity fueled Luca's anger. As his anger rose so did the energy he exerted as he raised and lowered the 200lb bar faster and faster. Resetting the bar on his bench he moved to his heavy bag. As he was throwing jabs his thoughts of Presley began to calm his temper. As he thought of her beautiful face and infectious smile he felt his anger subside. However, when his thoughts began to drift to thoughts of him sinking his fangs into her tender neck, his jabs began to quicken. Even as he tried to clear those thoughts from his head the idea of Ivy and Andrew causing harm to Presley crept into his head. With those thoughts now overtaking his mind his punches became quicker with much more power. When the heavy bag finally detached from the ceiling and flew across the room Luca decided it was time to stop. His "light workout" was causing too much damage to his gym. After grabbing a towel to wipe the sweat that covered his face he headed to the shower.

∞

At around two o'clock Presley heard Stephanie's car horn as she pulled into the driveway. "Mom, Steph's here I'm leaving. Do you work tonight?" Presley yelled as she put on her black Northface jacket.

"No but I am going out for dinner with Bonnie tonight. When are you planning to be home?" Brenda asked as she entered the front room.

"Not sure. I'll call you later," Presley said as she grabbed her purse and placed a light kiss on her mother's cheek. "Bye," she said as she left the house.

As Presley approached Stephanie's car she noticed a man in a black car across the street that seemed to be watching her. The same people had lived around there forever so she knew this man was out of place. She felt the hair on the back of her neck stand up as she climbed into Stephanie's red Jeep Cherokee. "Hey, did you notice the guy across the street?" Presley asked as she fastened her seat-belt.

"No," Stephanie answered turning to look out of her back window. "Where? I don't see anybody."

Presley turned to look out the back window as well, "I swear there was a guy out there."

"I can't believe after seeing Luca you even notice any other guy!" Stephanie laughed as she backed out of Presley's drive way. Presley just laughed with her.

Not feeling totally at ease Presley decided to try to enjoy herself but to remain vigilant. "Have you and Marcus made any prom plans?" Presley asked as she glanced into the side view mirror.

"No, not really. He's been working a lot trying to save money but I don't want him to spend it on prom. I mean I know he wants to move out as soon as he graduates to get away from his jerk of a father. I don't want him to waste any money he could use to make that happen," Stephanie said.

Presley looked at Stephanie with a look of total surprise at the words that had just come out of her friend's mouth. Stephanie has been talking about prom for like six months. As she turned to look at Presley Stephanie noticed the look of surprise on her face.

"What? I'm not that selfish. Yes, I have been excited about prom but what I want most is to see Marcus happy and he won't be as long as he lives there," Stephanie said as she returned her eyes to the road.

Presley knew Stephanie was right. Marcus's dad was a jerk. He was a big shot in banking until the economy crashed and he lost his job. He was a jerk before but after that he got worst. It was constant yelling and "put downs" to both Marcus and his mother. After he lost his job he began to drink a lot. That was when he became physically abusive to both Marcus and his mother. "You're right. I'm glad he has you Steph, I'm not sure how he'd get through without you." Stephanie just smiled at Presley's statement.

When the girls made a right into the mall parking lot Presley noticed the black car that had been parked across the street from her house turn in behind them. While Stephanie drove through aisles in the lot looking for an empty parking spot Presley lost sight of the car momentarily, but spotted it again when she got out of the Jeep. The car was parked two aisles over. A huge man, with long blond hair pulled into a low pony tail was exiting from the driver's side. Not wanting to alarm Stephanie nor look like she was insanely over- reacting she simply quickened her pace to the entrance of the mall.

"Why are you walking so fast?" Stephanie asked as she tried to keep pace with Presley.

"I have to pee," she said grabbing Stephanie's hand. She knew there was a possibility she was over-reacting but she could feel her heart beat quickening. After all she had just learned that vampires were real. Next there was some guy outside of her house who just happened to show up at the mall. Presley figured she was allowed to think the worst at this point. Her heart rate slowed slightly as they entered the mall. When the strange man entered an idea popped in her head.

"Hey, Steph, let's take a picture." She said as she pulled her iPhone out of her pocket.

"Oh that's a great idea! Let's start the prom memories early," Stephanie said, almost giddy. Presley raised her phone and both girls leaned their heads close to each other. As both girls made their normal duck faces Presley positioned the phone so that not only were both girls in the frame but the blond man was as well. After snapping the picture she sent it in a text to Luca.

Presley: hey, babe, do you know this guy? He was parked outside of my house and now he is at the mall. The big blonde guy behind us.

Chapter Fifteen

Luca had just laid on his bed and turned on the television when his phone beeped. He grabbed it and saw he had received a text message from Presley. The smile that had spread across his face faded quickly as he read the text and saw the picture. "Damn it!" he yelled jumping off his bed. Quickly he texted her back.

Luca: Where are you?

Presley: The mall. Do U know him?

Luca: Yes.

Presley: V?

Luca: Yes.

Presley: What should I do? Do U think he is following me?

Luca: Yes. Is there anyone at your house?

Presley: Maybe my mom. Y?

Luca: K. Walk around for like thirty minutes try 2 act normal. Like u don't notice him. Call ur mom see if she's there then text me back.

Presley: K.

Presley dialed her mom's number. After three rings her mother answered the phone, "Hello."

"Hey Mom, what time are you meeting Bonnie?"

"I'm leaving in an hour. We decided to catch a movie before we eat why?"

Searching her brain frantically for something to say Presley finally said, "We were thinking about having the guys come over and making dinner. I just wanted to know if it would be okay with you. We have a lot of prom plans to make."

"Sure, honey, that's fine."

"Okay, thanks Mom. Bye"

"Bye."

After ending the call Presley looked at Stephanie who was staring at her very confused by the conversation Presley had just had with her mother. "What was that?" Stephanie asked.

"Just keep walking. I'll tell you when we get to Macy's." Presley said as she began to text Luca.

Presley: She'll be gone in an hour.

Luca: Stay at the mall for an hour then meet me at your house.

Presley: K

Stephanie was still giving Presley a very odd look. Once they entered Macy's the girls headed toward the prom dresses in the junior section of the store.

"Okay, now can you tell me what's going on?" Stephanie asked as she placed her hands on her hips. Presley wasn't really sure how much to say so she decided to be as vague as she could be.

"The guy I saw parked outside my house followed us here," Presley whispered as she looked through dresses on a rack next to her. "Luca thinks he knows him and is meeting us at my house in like an hour," she continued.

"Why does Luca think he knows the guy? And what do you mean like an hour? Should we call the cops?" Stephanie whispered frantically.

"When I took our picture I made sure to get him in the background and sent it to Luca. We're going to hang out here for an hour then leave so Luca gets there first," Presley continued as she turned to another rack. She wanted to scan the store looking for the stranger following them. Sure enough she spotted him near the cosmetic counter.

"Why would you send it to Luca? What made you think he would know the guy? Presley, what is going on?" Stephanie said sounding scared and mad at the same time.

"Just a gut feeling. Stephanie, I need you to trust me right now that everything is going to be fine. Luca can handle this," Presley said as she pulled a red dress off the rack and held it up for her friend's inspection.

Stephanie laughed, "How do you expect me to trust you when you pick up a dress like that?" Presley joined in her laughter as she placed the dress back on the rack. "Which one is he?" Stephanie whispered as she pulled a sparkly black dress off the rack.

"Look's too clubby. The small blonde mountain standing by the cosmetic counter," Presley said taking the dress from her friend and placing it next to the other rejected dress.

When Stephanie moved to another rack she made sure to stand where she would have a clear view of the cosmetic counter in the process. "Holy crap, he's huge!" Stephanie gasped.

"I know, right," Presley said as she continued to sift through the rack of dresses. After about thirty more minutes of pretend shopping for dresses the girls walked to the shoe department of the store.

"How much longer?" Stephanie asked feeling very uncomfortable about the whole situation.

"Like fifteen minutes, then we will head out and stop by the pretzel place. That should give Luca enough time to get there," Presley said as she picked up a pair of red knee high boots.

"Since we have time let's stop by Hot Topic. I need a new belly ring." Stephanie said as she replaced a pair of sandals on the shoe display.

Presley stared at Stephanie with a surprised look. She was amazed that her friend actually wanted to continue shopping but, most importantly, how calmly she was handling this situation. "Okay, let's go." With that the two girls headed out into the main part of the mall.

"Is Luca into something bad?" Stephanie asked as she fidgeted with the strap of her purse.

"No, I don't think so," Presley said. She wasn't sure how to answer her question because she didn't really know why she automatically thought to get Luca involved. *Yes, you do. You called him because you knew there was a problem and you knew he would help you.* Presley thought as she watched her feet move through the mall.

Andrew continued to watch the two girls shop. He normally would have grown bored by now but something about both these girls was intriguing. He knew ahead of time Presley was different but Stephanie also had an aura about her. Something was up with these two girls. The more he watched them the less he thought about Luca. He began studying their movements trying to pinpoint what made these two girls different from regular teenage girls. When the two girls stopped by a pretzel place he used that opportunity grab a cold drink from the hot dog joint two shops down. He left the mall before the girls but made sure to keep an eye on their Jeep. While he waited he sent a text to Ivy.

Andrew: Found them. Check into these girls, something's up.

Before Ivy could text back Andrew saw the two girls leave the mall and get into their Jeep. "Alright I texted Luca, he is already there." Presley said after she shut the door.

"Are you sure we shouldn't call the cops? Should I call Marcus?" Stephanie asked with a tinge of fear in her voice.

"No and No. It's going to be fine. Luca can explain everything once we get there."

Stephanie was still not real comfortable about letting a teenage boy she had just met handle something like this. She did however, trust her friend. If Presley thought Luca could handle it, then Stephanie would go along with it for now. The two girls drove the twenty minute drive in almost complete silence, both of them not really sure what to say. They both were continuously checking the rear and side view mirrors.

∞

Luca ran out of his house as soon as he finished texting Presley. He drove well above the speed limit the entire way to Presley's house. He wasn't going to risk either the girls or Andrew getting there before him. He parked a couple houses down from Presley's waiting for Brenda to leave. As he sat in the car watching every car that drove by his anger quickly turned into rage. *How did he get here so quickly and how did he find her? How did I not know? How could I let this happen?* Those questions were dominating all of his thoughts. He was mentally beating himself up over something he could not control. He didn't see it that way... all he knew was he had brought danger to not only Presley, but to her friends as well. He knew he was going to have to discover Andrew's plan so he could protect Presley, her friends, and his family. He knew it had something to do with Ivy's brother, Anthony, and the fact his father, Basilio, had him in custody for killing humans. He just wasn't sure why he would be in the United States and what they could possibly want with Presley. He had been sitting there for about half an hour when Brenda finally left. Once her Volvo was out of sight he got out of his car and headed towards Presley's house. He decided to go around to the side where a large bush would block him from sight but still give him a clear view of the street. When he rounded the corner Mr. Harwood, Presley's neighbor, was taking his dog out to poop.

"Son, can I help you?" he asked obviously surprised to see Luca hanging out around the house.

Luca walked over to Mr. Harwood and looked straight into his eyes. He locked his eyes with Mr. Harwood's. He said in a very low deep voice, "You didn't see me. Go back in the house and make your wife a nice dinner. Don't come back out until after six." Hearing Luca's command, Mr. Harwood headed back into the house in a trance like state pulling his barking schnauzer behind him.

As soon as the back door shut behind the yapping dog Luca heard Stephanie's Jeep pull in the driveway. At almost the same time a black Honda Accord parked beside the curb in front of Presley's house. He waited for a moment for the Honda's engine to stop. When he saw Andrew leave the car and begin to move toward the girls, Luca walked around from the side of the house.

"Can I help you with something?" Luca asked. Andrew stopped dead in his tracks

Chapter Sixteen

"Ah, Prince Luca, How have you been?" Andrew asked with an over the top bow. Both of the girls jerked their heads toward Luca at the word Prince.

"What are you doing here?" Luca asked through gritted teeth.

Andrew let out a chuckle as a smug grin crossed his face. "You know how much I love home grown southern food," he said as his eyes slid over Presley and Stephanie. Each girl could feel her skin crawl as Andrew ran his tongue across his lips.

"You better stay the hell away from both of them. I promise you will be sorry if you even think about touching them." Luca said still clenching his jaw so tight there was a strong possibility he could crack a tooth at any second.

"You never were one for sharing your toys where you?" Andrew laughed as he took a couple more steps toward Presley and Stephanie.

"Um, a quick side note. I am not a toy," Presley snapped with her voice full of rage.

"Is that what you think? That's cute, really it is," Andrew said very much enjoying the affect he was having on everyone involved.

"I will rip your throat out." Luca stated very calmly as he positioned himself between Andrew and the girls. Stephanie was in utter confusion about what was going on around her.

"Temper, temper. I promise I won't break her. Well, I'll try not to," Andrew said, still acting like everything was one big joke. He had no intentions of messing with either girl…yet. However, he was really enjoying rattling Luca's cage.

"Girls, go in the house," Luca said without turning to face them. His eyes still glared at Andrew, almost as if they were locked together through their eyes. Presley grabbed Stephanie's hand, who just stood there staring at both men completely dumbfounded, and pulled her quickly into her house locking the door behind them.

"What's the plan Andrew? What have you let that psychotic woman talk you into doing now?" Luca asked as he took a couple steps toward Andrew making them less the two feet apart.

"I don't know what you're talking about. I just had a craving for some good old fashion southern cuisine," Andrew shrugged.

"Move on, this won't work out good for you or Ivy. If so much as one hair is touched on either of those girl's heads I will kill you."

"So which one is it, the blonde or the red head? Cause that blonde one looks tasty." Andrew said right before Luca grabbed him by the throat and flashed his fangs. "I guess that means the blonde one," Andrew gasped. Of course he already knew that but he decided to push a few more of Luca's buttons.

"If you think I'm joking try me. I will kill you. Then I'll be on the first flight to Paris and I will rip Ivy limb from limb. I know she sent you and, like the good little lap dog you are, you are following her orders." With that Luca released Andrew's throat from his tight grip.

"Alright, I'll leave for now," Andrew said as he turned to leave. When he got to his car he turned back to face Luca and asked, "Are Kevin and Marcus under your protection as well?" Before Luca could reply Andrew was in the car with the door shut.

Luca could almost feel steam rising from his head when he turned to the house where the girls were locked inside. He was weighing his options. He could either explain everything to Stephanie or he could just make her forget. Quickly he came the conclusion that if hers, Marcus' and Kevin's lives were all in danger it was probably better if they knew everything. Presley opened the door and threw herself into his arms before he could knock. "Are you okay?" she asked looking up at him.

"I'm fine, are you? What about Steph?" he asked as he ran his fingers through her hair.

"I'm fine, she, however, may be in shock. Are you going to tell her?" Presley asked, hoping he would. She hated keeping things from her friends. Plus, she knew if he told Stephanie he would let her tell Kevin. She desperately wanted to talk to Kevin about everything.

"Yeah, but I need you to call Kevin and Marcus and have them come here, now." Luca said as he grabbed her hand and they headed into the house.

When they entered the house Presley started making phone calls. Luca went over to Stephanie and sat next to her. "Are you okay?" he asked quietly as he placed his hand on her denim covered knee.

"I'm not real sure. That wasn't just some normal boy territory thing was it?" she asked. She looked at him looking almost child-like with her wide eyes desperately searching for a clue as to what was happening.

"No. Not really. Presley is calling Kevin and Marcus. When they get here I'll explain everything," he replied. He placed his arm around her shoulder trying to give her a little comfort. He truly believed her subconscious knew what was going on but wouldn't ask because she was worried Luca would think she was crazy.

"Was it just me or was that guy talking like he was going to try to eat us?" She asked as she leaned into Luca's shoulder.

"Steph, I promise I won't let anything happen to any of you."

Presley entered the room and felt a small twinge of jealousy shoot through her when she saw Luca holding Stephanie but dismissed the feeling as quickly as it emerged. "Hey, guys, boys should be here in ten," Presley said as she walked toward the couch where Luca and Stephanie were sitting.

"Thank you, love," Luca said as he pulled her to his lap. "Are you sure you're okay?" he asked sliding a loose strand of hair behind her ear.

"Yeah, are you? You have dark circles under your eyes."

"We'll talk about it later. Okay?" he said kissing her cheek.

The trio sat in silence waiting for the boys to arrive. Stephanie was trying to process the events that had happened earlier. Luca was concerned how his new friends would react to his revelation. He hoped they handled it as well as Presley did but he wasn't counting on it. Presley was worried about Luca. He seemed paler and tired. She could tell something was just not right. Then it hit her…he hasn't had any blood since he's been with her.

"Luca, can I talk to you in the kitchen for a minute?" she asked as she eased out of his lap and grabbed his hand. Saying nothing Luca rose from the couch and allowed Presley to lead him to the kitchen.

"What have you done this weekend?" Presley asked quietly as she turned to face him.

"What?"

"Run down your weekend since Friday after school."

"Friday night I cleaned the house so it wouldn't be a total pig pen when you came over. Saturday I was with you and today I went home worked out a little and then came here. Why?"

"When was the last time you ate?"

"Breakfast with you this morning," he smirked.

"Shut up you know what I mean," she said slapping his arm lightly.

"Wednesday night."

"Are you kidding me?"

"I thought I would have time Friday night but I didn't."

"You're weak aren't you? That's why you look so pale and have those dark circles under your eyes."

"Yeah, but it's not a big deal. I'll handle it. Please don't worry," he said pulling her into him. Looking down into her eyes he twisted his right hand into her hair and pulled her into a kiss. What he had intended on being a sweet gentle kiss quickly became intense when he felt her suck his bottom lip into her mouth. Before he knew what was happening he had her back up against the wall and his tongue deep in her mouth. When she let out a small moan causing his fangs to extend, he quickly pulled away from her turning his face so she couldn't see him. She placed her hand on his cheek and guided his face toward her.

"Open your eyes, Luca, look at me." Presley knew he wasn't looking at her because the vampire part of him was showing. She hated he was afraid to let her see him like that. She wanted him to know that she accepted it. That she wanted him for everything that he was, even the vampire. When he refused to look at her she decided to try a new approach. She knew he could read her thoughts so she thought **Luca, please look at me. Please trust me to love all of you.** His head snapped up and his eyes popped open looking straight into her eyes. His blue eyes were now black and encircled with a thin blue line, his canine teeth were now long white fangs. Presley ran her hand down the side of his face. As she leaned in to kiss him she was thinking **You are so beautiful.** When she wrapped her arms around his neck he grabbed her waist and lifted her up. Without breaking the kiss he backed her up against the wall and she wrapped her legs around his waist. Just as he moved his hand up to her hair they heard the doorbell ring. "Saved by the bell!" she said breathlessly. When she opened her eyes she saw that his teeth were back to normal and his eyes were their usual glowing shade of blue. Placing another quick kiss on her lips he lowered her to the floor and they headed toward the front door.

As Luca and Presley were walking into the living room Stephanie opened the front door and both boys were walking through it. Stephanie turned to look at Presley and Luca and she just grinned and raised her eyebrows. Luca laughed a little when he saw Presley's cheeks turn almost as red as the streaks in her hair.

"What's going on?" Marcus asked putting his arms around Stephanie's waist pulling her back to his chest. Kevin rolled his eyes, "You two just can't be in the same room without touching each other, can you?" he asked.

"Nope." Marcus replied as he tightened his squeeze on Stephanie's waist.

"Alright guys sit down and get comfortable we have some talking to do," Presley said as she motioned to the couch. Kevin and Marcus sat on the couch with Stephanie in between them. Presley stood next to Luca and intertwined her fingers with his. Looking up into his eyes ***You can do this baby. I'm right here and they will handle it...I promise.***

Chapter Seventeen

"Wait!" Stephanie said as she turned to look at Luca. "Did that crazy dude out there just call you Prince Luca?"

"Yeah," Luca said rubbing the back of his neck.

"So, you're a prince?" Marcus asked.

"Well, yes, you see.." Luca was saying when Stephanie interrupted.

"Are you like a Prince of a country?"

"Did you know about this?" Kevin asked Presley.

"No, I didn't know about the prince part but if you guys would calm down Luca will explain everything." At that point all three turned to look at Luca.

"Go ahead Luca, we're listening," Marcus said as he placed his right arm around Stephanie.

"Alright, I'm going to tell you guys something I don't normally tell people. Before I do I need you guys to know you have become very important to me. I would never do anything to hurt you or let anybody else hurt you." He said running his hands through his hair.

"Luca, just tell us it will be alright. You're our friend and no matter what it is that won't change," Kevin said as Presley grabbed Luca's hand.

"Yeah," Stephanie said giving Luca a reassuring smile.

Luca returned the smile then inhaled deeply. "Alright, I am a prince of sorts. Not of a country or anything. See I am...um... well, I'm a...um....I'm a vampire prince." When he finished he looked around at the shocked faces. When he felt Presley squeeze his hand he exhaled a breath he didn't realize he was holding.

Marcus was the first to break the silence "Is this a joke?" he knew it wasn't but he was having a hard time wrapping his head around what he had just heard.

"No," Presley answered hoping that her friends wouldn't freak out, that they would still accept Luca.

"So vampires are real?" Stephanie asked sounding almost excited by the idea. Marcus let out a big sigh. "Well, there goes my girlfriend," he laughed as Stephanie elbowed him in the gut. With that Presley knew everything was going to be okay. Then she looked at Kevin who had a very serious look on his face but hadn't said a word.

"Kevin are you okay?" Luca asked.

"I'm not real sure what to think about this to be honest with you," he said as he rose to his feet. "I mean I get you're a vampire and I get that you aren't going to hurt any of us and that you're the same person you were yesterday. What I don't get is you're from Italy right?"

"Yes."

"Why are you here? I mean why would a vampire prince come to a one stoplight town in North Carolina?" Kevin was beginning to get angry but not at Luca, just angry.

Presley crossed the room feeling the anger coming from Kevin. She grabbed his hand and kissed his cheek, "I'm sorry I didn't tell you, I couldn't, please don't be mad at me." When he looked at Presley he knew why he was angry. He was angry because she knew and didn't tell him. They always told each other everything and she knew something this big and said nothing.

"How could you not tell me this?" he asked. She could see the pain in his eyes.

"She wanted to but I asked her not to," Luca jumped in. He didn't want there to be a problem between them because of him. Kevin's attention was now drawn back to Luca.

"Look my feelings about you haven't changed, I still think you're a good guy but I want to know why you decided to come here?"

"Okay, fair enough," Luca said as he began to pace the room. "You see vampires don't go around turning random people into vampires. Generations of my family are vampires. We follow our blood line. We find and spend time with our descendants. When we meet one that we believe would make a good vampire, we give them the option to turn. The ones who decide they don't want to turn we make them forget being asked. Are you guys following what I'm saying?" Luca asked still pacing.

"What do you mean make a good vampire?" Stephanie asked as all her friends turned to look at her. "Oh come on, don't tell me the rest of you weren't thinking it," she said looking at each of them.

Then Marcus popped in, "Luca, stay away from her neck, okay."

"Sure thing." Luca laughed, then he turned back to Stephanie. "When a person becomes a vampire it doesn't change who they are. If they're good they stay good but if they are mean or greedy or anything like that they can become pure evil. The last thing you want is to have an evil person with vampire abilities. So we go meet our descendants and usually spend like 5 years with them before we make a decision. The offer is not normally extended till the person is at least 23 because by then their moral compass is pretty much set." Luca looked around the room to see if everybody was understanding what he was saying.

"So, if you don't believe they are decent people what do you do? Have you met any you refused to turn because of their personality?" Presley asked.

"Of course, I've met some that I didn't turn but they never knew what I was." Luca said.

"Wow! Okay, so I know this is none of my business but can you tell us about one? Ya know like why you didn't turn them," Marcus asked.

"Well, back in the eighties there was a guy who was a drug dealer and a pimp. So of course I didn't turn him."

"What happened to him?" Marcus continued. He found all of this very interesting.

"I discovered some of the girls he was pimping out were younger then thirteen. So I, well, I killed him." Luca said then quickly added, "I don't normally kill people even if I don't like the way they live, but then I saw what he was doing to those girls. I knew if he lived not only would those girls not be safe but he would make more young girls suffer. I couldn't let it continue so I killed him and did what I could to get the girls somewhere safe." At that point not only did Presley fall more in love with him but everybody else respected him even more than they already had. Not that any of them were in favor of killing people but to know that he did it to put an end to a bunch of young girls suffering made it a lot easier to accept.

"So if you spend at least five years with them and you offer them this gift at twenty three then you find them when they are about eighteen. Is that right?" Kevin asked beginning to pace the floor as he spoke. Presley could almost see the wheels in his head turning.

"Yeah, that's about right," Luca answered. He knew what Kevin's next question was going to be and he hoped his answer didn't change how well everyone was taking the news.

"Are you here because of one of us?" Kevin asked, crossing his arms in front of his chest. Every pair of eyes in the room were now fixed on Luca, all of them knowing that their life could change with his next word.

"Yes," he answered. Everyone took in a deep breath except Stephanie who was practically jumping out of her seat. "Who?" she asked sounding like a kid at Christmas. Luca scanned the room. He wasn't really ready to reveal that little tidbit but he had told himself he was going to be completely honest with them. After scanning the room again he fixed his gaze back on Kevin. "You," he said to Kevin not really sure what Kevin's reaction would be. Kevin just stood there quietly for a minute. Stephanie slumped back in her seat poking her bottom lip out and Marcus laughed at her.

Presley was right back by Kevin's side placing his hand in hers. He looked down at Presley "Did you know about this too?" he asked very calmly.

"No, Kevin, I swear I would have told you. No matter what I would have told you."

"Kevin, this isn't a big deal. You don't have to make a decision right now. I wouldn't normally reveal this this soon but I want to be completely honest with you guys," Luca said, still not real sure how Kevin was taking it.

"Okay, next question, what the hell happened here today?" Kevin asked changing the subject.

"That's it! You don't want to talk about this!" Stephanie yelled.

"Steph, calm down, he'll talk when he's ready," Presley said still holding Kevin's hand.

Luca cleared his throat and began to tell them about Andrew, Ivy and their views on vampire/ human relationships. He told them about Anthony and his habit of killing human females. Then he told them about the phone call he had with his father and his concerns that Ivy was planning his demise.

"So, this Andrew guy is here. Do you think he is going to try to use Presley to get to you? Then he would use you to get to your father. Do you believe that's his plan?" Marcus asked, not able to hide the irritation in his voice.

"I am thinking that is a possibility but I don't think that he is only planning to use Presley. He mentioned you and Kevin, too. Please, know if I had known any of this before I left Italy I would have never come here. I hate putting you all in danger," Luca said as walked over to Presley and pulled her to him.

"What can we do to help?" Marcus asked as he stood from the couch pulling Stephanie with him.

Luca was surprised and touched by Marcus's response. He couldn't believe how well these young people were taking everything he had just thrown at them.

"Really, there's nothing you can do. It's very important you don't invite anyone you don't know into your house. You must stay vigilant. I just found out he was here so I haven't had time to come up with a plan yet," he replied.

"Maybe we should work on that," Presley said. "But my mom will be here shortly so we can't do it here," she added.

"I need to talk to my dad before I do anything against Ivy and her clan, but first, and foremost, I need to make sure all of you are safe," Luca said. Looking around the room he noticed for the first time since he had met her Stephanie was very quiet. "Are you okay, Steph?" he asked.

"Yeah, I'm just trying to process all this. I do have an idea though," she said as her emerald eyes began to sparkle with mischief. She continued, "You can just turn all of us then we won't die." The entire group let out a loud sigh.

"I understand your thinking, but trust me this is not a decision you want to make in the spur of the moment," Luca said. He tried not to laugh when he saw disappointment spreading across her face. Presley couldn't stop laughing and said, "Steph, you do realize they don't really sparkle, right?" Everybody, including Stephanie, broke out in hysterical laughter.

Once the laughter stopped they all decided the best thing they could all do was that everyone, except Luca, would spend the night at Presley's. Brenda wasn't due home for another hour so while Stephanie, Kevin and Marcus went to get their stuff for the night and school the following day. Luca stayed with Presley.

Chapter Eighteen

Presley and Luca went to her room so she could straighten it up before the others came back. "So, do you have a plan?" Presley asked as she picked up dirty clothes off her floor. As she bent over to pick up a pair of jeans she felt Luca's hand on her hips. When she stood Luca whispered in her ear, "Right now, I just want to spend the little time we're going have alone together not talking about this mess." Presley turned to him and smiled, "What would you like to be doing?" She asked noticing again how pale he was. The dark circles under his eyes seemed to be getting darker by the minute. He leaned down and kissed her quickly but pulled away.

"Luca, what's wrong?" she asked.

"Nothing really, but earlier things got a little too intense. I'm in no condition right now to push myself, I may not be able to control myself," he said quietly.

"Because you need blood?" she asked as she sat on her unmade bed.

"Yeah. I've been careless letting myself go this long," he said as he sat next to her.

"Are you going to take care of that tonight?" She said as she tilted her head slightly to look in his eyes.

"I'm going to try but I have to call my father. Plus I plan on keeping an eye on your house to make sure Andrew doesn't get anywhere near you."

"We will be safe won't we? I mean as long as we don't invite him in he can't get to us, right?" she asked as she grabbed his hand.

"There are ways to get invited in and ways to get you out of the house. He has been around a long time; I promise he knows some tricks. Plus he has Ivy as a teacher. Trust me, you can't find anyone or anything more evil than that woman."

"You have to promise me you are going to take care of yourself. I don't know the guy but I would bet that if he sees you weak he will take advantage. Baby, I'm worried," Presley said trying to fight back tears. Suddenly the weight of the situation was hitting her. A single tear rolled down her cheek and Luca wiped it away with his thumb.

"Mio amore, don't cry. I won't let anything happen to you I promise."

"I know you won't. I'm worried about you. You've already weakened yourself because of me," Presley said as another tear rolled down her cheek.

"It's not because of you. It's because I was being selfish. I just wanted to sp..." he stopped when he heard Mr. Harwood's schnauzer barking and growling in the backyard. Luca quickly left the bed and walked over to the window. "What's going on?' Presley asked as she joined him at the window. "I'm not sure" he said as he opened the curtain slightly. When he caught sight of the mouthy schnauzer he followed the dog's line of sight to a dark figure behind the trees that lined the edge of the backyard. To the normal human eye the yard looked empty but with Luca's enhanced vampire vision he could see Andrew as clear as day standing beside a tree. He could see his bulky frame, his blonde hair and he even saw the wink Andrew sent him when he realized Luca saw him.

"Where is your mom?" He asked turning away from the window.

"I don't know" Presley said as she looked at the clock on her nightstand. Seeing that it was already 7:15 she said, "She said she would be home between 7:30 and 8."

"Call her. Find out where she is and, if she is close, find a way to keep her from coming home for at least thirty minutes. I'm going to text Kevin and tell him and the others to stay put until they hear from me," Luca said pulling out his cell phone.

"What's going on?" Presley asked as she headed toward the window.

"Andrew is in your backyard. Call your mom." Luca said while typing a text to Kevin.

After two rings Brenda's voice answered Presley's call. "Hey, honey," Brenda was laughing when she answered the phone.

"Mom, what's going on?" Presley asked. There was something different about her mother's voice, it didn't sound normal.

"Nothing," Brenda was still laughing almost uncontrollably.

"Where are you?"

"I'm still at Bonnie's. We decided to rent a movie and make dinner here."

"Mom are you drunk?" Presley asked, laughing herself.

"No, well, maybe a little." Brenda said. Presley was very surprised to hear that. She hadn't seen her mother drink in years and had never seen her drunk.

"Are you staying at Bonnie's?" Presley asked. She was sure her mother would say yes. As an ER nurse she knew what the damage drinking and driving could cause.

"Yeah, I'm sorry. We were just talking and laughing. We didn't even realize we had so much to drink."

Presley laughed a little, "It's fine. If anybody deserves a night to let go it's you. The guys are gonna spend the night, is that okay?"

"That's fine but not Luca. I'm not that drunk." Brenda said firmly but Presley could hear the snicker forming in the back of her throat.

"Okay, love you. Have fun."

"You too, sweetheart," Brenda said.

Presley hung up the phone. "Well, we're good. She won't be home until tomorrow." Presley smiled thinking of her mother and her lifelong friend drinking wine and, most likely, dancing around the house listening to music they had listened to when they were teenagers. Then she remembered why she had called her mother in the first place. "What now?" she asked.

"I'm going to go deal with him." Luca said as he headed towards Presley's bedroom door.

"No you are not!" Presley said loudly as she grabbed Luca's arm.

"I have to do something."

"You're right, you do. You need to bite me," Presley said looking up into his eyes.

"No!"

"Yes, look I get this whole noble I won't hurt you, I'm not going to use you as food crap but right now you have no choice. I'm the only one here and you need blood. You're weak and there is a big, mean vampire out there. My guess is he knew if he showed up here you wouldn't leave. Which would mean you wouldn't eat and you would be weak. Plus, you said it won't kill me right? Let me do this please," she was almost begging. She hated feeling helpless. She had felt helpless when Eric died and she wasn't going to go through that again. She knew she could help him if he would let her.

"Alright," he said as he grabbed her hand. He sat on the bed. "If it starts to hurt or you get dizzy you promise you will tell me?" he asked as he placed her in his lap.

"I promise," she said as she pulled all her hair to one side revealing the bare skin of her neck. Luca took in a deep breath as he looked at her neck. He felt he teeth lengthen. The urge to bite her became overwhelming. **Breath, you have to calm down. If you hurt her I will kill you** He said to himself as he tilted Presley's head to the side to get better access to her neck. When he moved his mouth to her neck he lightly kissed her neck. Then he heard her let out a quiet moan and that's all it took. He quickly but gently punctured her skin with his teeth. As he began to suck her blood into his mouth the first thing he noticed was how warm it was. All blood was warm but hers seemed to be warmer. When she placed her hand on the back his neck he noticed how sweet her blood was. As a vampire blood never tasted bad to him but it was never exactly something he craved but he could defiantly see himself craving her blood. When he pulled his teeth from her neck she turned to look at him and placed the other hand on the back of his head. She pulled him into a deep passionate kiss and they both forgot momentarily that Andrew waiting outside. "I need to deal with him," Luca said as he pulled away from her mouth stopping only a couple inches away. "But first let me heal your neck," he said as he glanced down to her neck. His eye shot back up to hers. "They're almost healed!" he said sounding very shocked.

"What do you mean?" Presley asked as she placed her hand to the spot he had just bitten.

"I mean there should be two pretty deep holes in your neck but there's barely a mark."

"Is that bad?" she asked feeling very self-conscious.

"I…..I don't know. I guess we'll talk about it when I'm back here with you. Stay put." He said as he lifted her to her feet.

"Be careful, please." She said as she wrapped her arms around his neck.

"I will," he said as he placed his mouth on Presley's. He moved his hand up tilting her head so he could deepen their kiss. "You better go or I may not let you," she said backing away slightly. Luca laughed, "I'll be back." With one of those famous winks she loved so much he left the room.

Presley plopped down on her bed **Oh my God, I'm in love with a vampire.** She thought as she covered her face with both hands. She rolled over and grabbed her phone to let Kevin know what was happening. Well, everything except the bite. She knew Kevin was already having a difficult time handling all this and she didn't want his head to explode. Not to mention Stephanie would probably fall over dead from jealously. After she finished texting Kevin she walked over to her window and peaked through the curtain. She was so worried about Luca she seriously thought she might throw up. How this boy had become so important to her in such a short time she didn't know but she did know that she couldn't imagine a life without him.

Chapter Nineteen

As Luca headed down the stairs of Presley's house he overheard her thoughts **Oh my God, I'm in love with a vampire.** Although he was walking into a potentially dangerous situation hearing her made him smile. His strength and energy had come back quickly. He actually noticed he felt stronger and had more energy than he ever remembered getting from human blood. He knew it probably just felt that way because he had let himself go so long without blood and had grown very weak. However, he had a nagging feeling there was more to it than that, but he didn't have time to dwell on it. He had yard work awaiting him.

He went out through the back door and was a few feet from Andrew in a second. The two just looked at each other for a moment. Luca was cracking his knuckles when he finally spoke, "What are you doing here Andrew?"

"Just couldn't seem to get those two girls out of my mind. Surely you understand," Andrew replied with a smirk.

"So what's the plan? You distract me while Ivy tries to kill my father or are you here to find me and kill me then Ivy kills my father while he mourns?" Luca asked cocking his head to one side.

"No plan, just needed a change of scenery. How about we split them? I mean you obviously want the blonde, so I'll take the redhead," Andrew said. Although Andrew continued to push Luca's buttons he was beginning to get an uneasy feeling. He could sense something different about Luca. Luca had always been a strong vampire and most wouldn't mess with him unless they had a death wish. Now Andrew could almost feel that power rolling off him.

"I'm warning you now, if you touch any of them I will tear you apart and enjoy every moment of it." As Luca was speaking Andrew noticed the small red stain on his white shirt. That's when it hit him. Luca was stronger because he had drunk Presley's blood. Judging by the power Andrew could see filling Luca he was right...there was something different about those girls.

"Come on Luca, looks like you've sampled, it's only fair to share."

"How do you think Ivy would feel knowing you're lusting after a human girl?" Luca asked with a raised eyebrow.

"I'm not lusting, I'm hungry. When I push my fangs into that little blonde's pretty neck I'll drain every drop while she cries for you. I'll be sure you find her bruised and battered body. Surely, you remember what I'm capable of, if not call your sister she'll remind you."

Andrew started to laugh until Luca grabbed him by the throat and lifted him two feet off the ground. Luca's fangs were out, his pupils were totally black and he let out a growl worthy of a powerful wolf. He was so enraged that he couldn't form a coherent sentence. Every fiber in him was screaming for him to kill Andrew and then he heard...***Oh my God***..

Presley's thoughts that he shouldn't have been able to hear out here. Pulling Andrew close to him he quietly said, "You need to get on your knees and thank God that she's looking out that window right now because if she wasn't you would be dead." When he went to put Andrew down he had intended on slightly tossing him to make him land on his back. However, not realizing his own strength, he ended up throwing him against a tree causing the tree to split almost in half.

Andrew stood up glaring at Luca with a new determination to unearth Presley and Stephanie's secret. He headed to his car. Once he returned to his cabin he would call Ivy.

As Luca walked back to the house he was running the recent events through his mind. He shouldn't have been able to hear Presley that far away and he was sure that he hadn't thrown Andrew hard enough to crack a tree. His phone began to ring pulling him away from his thoughts.

"Hello," he answered without checking to see who it was. He heard Marcus's voice on the other end.

"Is everything okay?" Marcus asked.

"Yeah, y'all can come back now," Luca said as he opened the back door.

"Got a problem with that, my dad, who normally doesn't care what I do, is giving me crap about leaving. Stephanie, and her infinite wisdom on all things fictional vampire, thinks you might be able to do some, and I quote, "vampire mojo" to help."

Luca chuckled. Shaking his head he said "I'll be there in a couple minutes."

Presley was standing in the kitchen when Luca entered the house. After he closed the door she threw herself into his arms. "Are you okay? What happened?" She asked as she nuzzled her face against his chest.

"I'm fine but we have to go to Marcus' and deal with his father." He said gliding his hand down the back of her head.

"What's that jerk doing now?" She asked pulling back slightly so she could look up at his face.

"I don't know. He won't let Marcus leave and Steph suggested that I could use some "vampire mojo" to change his mind." Luca said, doing air quotes when he said "vampire mojo."

Presley laughed and grabbed her hoodie off the back of a kitchen chair. "That girl," she said shaking her head. Then they headed to Luca's car.

Once in the car Presley turned to Luca, "So what happened out there?' she asked.

"Nothing he was just trying to piss me off and he succeeded. Um.. your mom might notice a broken tree in the yard, we're going to have to come up with a story for that," he said glancing at her from the corner of his eye.

"You broke a tree?"

"Well, technically Andrew's body broke it. I just assisted," Luca laughed.

"Okay. I guess I won't ask for details unless you think there are any I need to know," she said. Presley noticed when he had returned to the house after his "little altercation" with Andrew that his color was back. He looked healthy again. She had a sense of satisfaction knowing she had helped even if only in a small way.

"What's the deal with Marcus' dad?" Luca asked, trying to get her thoughts off Andrew.

"He's an ass. He was this successful business man with a major superiority complex. He was always nasty to Marcus and his mother, calling them names and flaunting affairs in his mom's face. When he lost his job, and started drinking, that's when he started hitting them. I do know Marcus doesn't like to talk about it," Presley said with a hint of sadness in her voice.

"Okay, we're here. Is there anything else I need to know before I go in there?" he asked as he turned off the ignition.

"Unfortunately, there's really no telling until we get in there." She said as he left the car. When Luca opened her door Presley stood up and kissed him gently on the cheek. They made their way to the house. The door opened before they reached it and Kevin came out. His face was blood red.

"Kevin what's going on?" Presley asked. She could tell by the look on his face whatever it was wasn't good.

"That man has lost his mind. He's totally wasted. He won't let Marcus leave because Steph and I are going to be there." Kevin said in a very irate tone.

"Why?" Luca asked. He thought all of them were good people and great friends to each other. He couldn't imagine anyone having a problem with any of them.

"Because according to him, Stephanie is trash and I'm a fagot." Kevin spit out the words like they were covered in venom.

"I'll handle this but someone has to get Marcus to let me in." Luca said patting Kevin on the back and stepping onto the front porch.

Presley poked her head in the door and yelled, "Marcus come here!"

Seconds later Marcus appeared at the door. "Can you invite me in?" Luca asked.

"Come on in, man. Maybe you can talk some sense into that idiot."

When they entered the house Mr. Morrison was coming down the steps. He had a small amount of blood on his bottom lip.

"What happened to him?" Presley whispered to Stephanie. Stephanie, who had obviously been crying, whispered, "Marcus decked him when he called me a slut." Presley just made a silent "O" with her mouth.

"Well, if it isn't the other piece of garbage my son insists on hanging out with." Mr. Morrison said looking at Presley. Luca could feel his blood boil as he clenched his fist and fought the urge to hit Mr. Morrison in the face.

"Dad, this is Luca Davenport." Marcus said pointing to Luca.

"Boy, you need to make new friends," was all Mr. Morrison said. A moment later a tall, skinny woman entered the room. Her blonde hair was pulled in a ponytail. She had a look of fear on her face and a black eye that had begun to heal. "Jeremiah, please just let him go," the woman pleaded. Jeremiah turned and looked at her as if she was an insect. "I don't think I was talking to you, bitch!" Jeremiah screamed at her. She simply hung her head. As memories of his sister with Andrew flashed through Luca's head he grabbed Jeremiah by both arms and looked him straight in the eye. Again fighting the urge to punch him in the face he quietly but firmly said, "Marcus is leaving with us and you're not going to stop him. You are also not going to physically harm your wife or your son again. You will treat everybody in this room with kindness and you will do all these things until I tell you otherwise. Are we clear?" Jeremiah simply nodded.

Marcus grabbed his bag from the steps and walked over to his mother. "I'll be back tomorrow. If anything happens call me," Marcus said as he hugged his mother. She looked at her husband who was standing in almost a trance state. Then she walked over to Luca. Looking into his face she squinted her eyes and said "I don't know what you did, but thank you." She said kissing his cheek. Next she turned her attention to Stephanie, Kevin and Presley, "I think you are all great kids. Please don't let him upset you," she said going up stairs.

As the group headed to their cars Marcus stopped everybody. "Guys, I'm sorry about all that," he said. Grabbing Stephanie's hand he said, "I love you. Don't ever listen to anything he says," then he leaned down and kissed her deeply. "I love you too," she said as their lips parted.

Moments later they were all at Presley's house. With everything that had happened during the day they all decided it was best to go to sleep. They could discuss everything and come up with a plan after they all had a good night's sleep.

Chapter Twenty

Andrew slammed the door of the small cabin he was renting, it was in a secluded place near a lake. Because it wasn't summer yet the area was basically empty making it easy for him to stay hidden. He jerked his phone from his pocket, quickly found Ivy's name and pressed the call button. After several rings, more than Andrew was comfortable with, Ivy's voice came across the line. "Hey, Babe" she said.

"What the hell took you so long?" Andrew asked. His foul mood came across clear as day.

"I was asleep; it's five in the morning. What is your problem?" Ivy asked obviously very irritated by the way Andrew had just spoken to her. He had forgotten about the six hour time difference.

"Sorry, just had a bad night. We are going to need to change your little plan." He said as he paced the small room.

"What happened?" she asked. Andrew was not easily rattled, and he was obviously rattled, she knew this couldn't be good.

"You were right about Luca not leaving that *girl* unattended once he saw me," he said saying the word "girl" as if it left a bad taste in his mouth. Then he continued, "However, you were wrong about him becoming weak because of a lack of feeding."

"You've been there one day, give it time," she said, trying to sound reassuring.

"It won't matter. He's drinking from her." He said with a huff, rolling his eyes even though nobody was there to see him

"Really..." she paused for a moment. She knew that Luca wasn't the type to keep little snacks around and then compel them to forget, which meant this girl knew what he was. He would only tell her what he was if he had fallen in love with her. "Oh, this is too perfect," she finally said.

"How can this be perfect?" Andrew asked. He had decided before he called her that he would tell her about Luca drinking Presley's blood. He was going to keep the part about her blood giving him new found strength to himself. At least until he knew what it meant.

"Simple, he obviously loves this girl or he wouldn't have told her what he was. We will just use her as bait. If I know Luca, and I do, if we take her he will come for her but he won't want to kill us in front of her," Ivy said. Andrew flashed back to earlier that night when Luca had told him to thank God that Presley had been watching from the window.

"Your insight into his mind is starting to bother me." Andrew said realizing that everything Ivy had said Luca would do...he did. **What happened between them? How could she know how his mind worked if they weren't close?** Almost as if she was reading his mind, which she wasn't. She couldn't vampires could only read human minds, they couldn't read the minds of other super natural beings.

She answered "I know how his mind works because my father was the same way. That's why he's dead now. His good heart and nobility got him killed and it will do the same to Luca Davenport." Ivy's father had been killed when he tried to protect a young boy from becoming dinner to a few hungry vampires. Standing between even one hungry vampire and his dinner would almost certainly end in your death but three vampires, is 100 percent chance of death.

"Okay, I guess I'll take that answer. Are you sure there is not more to you and Luca than you're telling me?" Andrew asked.

She simply laughed and responded with, "Aw, honey, you know those goodie two shoes don't do anything for me." She did however; leave out the part about how she had tried to seduce Luca simply because of his position but he had rejected her quickly.

"Alright, it's been a long night and my back hurts. I'm going to bed," he said and quickly wished he hadn't mentioned his back.

"What happened to your back?" she asked truly concerned.

"Oh nothing, Luca threw me against a tree, damn near broke the thing in half." He said quickly racking his brain for an excuse to how Luca had so easily over powered him.

"How did he do that? He's not that strong, is he?" she asked. She knew Luca was strong but Andrew was a six foot four over 200 pound vampire. He shouldn't have been so easily tossed.

"He caught me by surprise. Plus, I took a little bite out of the dad of one of his friends and the alcohol in his blood was unreal, I think it just had a bad effect on me." He knew she would buy that because it was sort of true. Anytime a vampire drank blood that contained drugs or alcohol it threw them off a little.

"Okay, well, go rest. Lay low I'll be there in two weeks. That's when prom is right?"

"Yeah. Well, not this Saturday but next."

"Okay, lure him into a false sense of security. I'll get there a couple days early and we'll make a plan. I love you."

"I love you too," he said then hung up the phone. He walked to the bedroom and sprawled out on the bed. Even though it was a queen size bed it almost seemed too small for him. As he laid there willing himself to sleep he searched his brain for any reason for Presley's blood to give Luca added strength. By the time he drifted off to sleep his search had revealed no answers.

Ivy paced her room going over and over the conversation she had with Andrew. He was holding something back and she knew it. **Maybe, he had fallen for one of those little humans.** She quickly dismissed the thought. Not because she trusted him, she loved him yes,...but trust him completely...that would be a big HELL NO! She knew human girls were never his thing because they were too weak.

She had convinced Nicolette and Angelo to have dinner with her that night. She needed to rest, putting on the 'nice girl' persona would be hard enough, but if she didn't get some rest it would be nearly impossible. Her plan was to start by trying to gain Nicolette's trust. After she accomplished that she would move on to the next prey on her way to destroy the Davenport vampire clan. Considering Nicolette's past with Andrew it wouldn't be hard. She would simply pretend to be done with him. She would give her some horror story about how he had treated her the same way he had treated Nicolette. Andrew's actions had not been limited to cheating and physical abuse. She positioned herself comfortably in bed and set her alarm to go off in three hours. Finally she laid down to try to get a couple more hours of sleep.

∞

Luca walked the streets in front of Presley's house. He kept thinking back to the altercation with Andrew and then the one with Marcus' dad. It had been a long time since he wanted to hurt two different people in the same day. He had controlled himself, but barely with both of them. If Presley hadn't been watching he would have killed Andrew and he knew it. He had wanted to since he saw his sister walk into their home with her body bruised and battered and any sign of life drained from her eyes. It took her a very long time to recover from the damage Andrew had caused her, both physically and emotionally. As he thought about how good it felt to throw Andrew into the tree he smiled to himself. Then he suddenly remembered what had stopped him from killing him. He had heard Presley's thoughts; he shouldn't have been able to hear them outside of the house. Vampires could read the minds of people but they had to be pretty close to them to do it. Not right next to them but at least within 20 feet. He had heard her as clear as if she had been standing right next to him. Then he thought about the power he had felt while he stood outside with Andrew. So many odd things had happened since he had arrived in this small town. He hadn't had time to examine any of them because there always seemed to be something else that demanded his immediate attention. He continued to walk the street around Presley's house keeping a close eye out for anything that seemed out of place. He would catch his mind bouncing between his need to be close to Presley and the strange things he had encountered since he first laid eyes on her.

It had been hours and he hadn't seen any sign of Andrew or any other vampire. Luca decided to head home so he could still get a couple hours of sleep before school. After doing one last walk by of Presley's house he headed home.

∞

Kevin sat in Presley's dark room. He was totally exhausted. He had just learned he came from a long line of vampires. One of them had found him and could possibly offer him a chance to become a vampire. All of that information bombarding his brain could surely make it difficult to sleep. In one day he discovered that one of his friends was a vampire; that if he wanted he could become a vampire; that another vampire had decided to cause trouble that could endanger him and all of his friends; and then to top the day off, he had to endure another friend's father being a hateful prick. He missed the days when his biggest concern was whether or not he should give his relationship with Jimmy a chance. Now his thoughts were on another problem, he hadn't yet thought about Jimmy being there Friday night. ***How am I going to handle that? I can't tell him but how do I hide something that in one day has become a major problem that all our lives are revolving around? CRAP!*** Looking at the clock next to Presley's bed he realized it was already 4 am. Deciding he would get no sleep tonight he got up and went to make coffee. If he was going to make it through a whole day of school he would need to spend the next four hours loading up on caffeine. After he started the coffee he headed back upstairs to shower.

Once he had showered and changed he went back downstairs, poured a cup of coffee and settled in front of the television. As he flipped through the channels he laughed when Bram Stoker's *Dracula* popped on the screen. "Yeah, not today." He laughed as he continued to flip the channels. "Not today what?" he heard Marcus' voice behind him. Marcus stood in front of the coffee pot wearing only plaid pajama bottoms, no shirt, and his hair was a mess. "Just trying to find something to watch on television. *Dracula* came on...really not in the mood for that right now," Kevin said as he took a sip of coffee. Marcus laughed, "I would guess not, could be worst though......it could have been *Twilight*," both boys laughed at the same time. "Wait, oh man, do you remember what happened at Stephanie's Saturday?" Marcus was trying to get the words out but he kept laughing, "When Stephanie was telling Luca how Presley thought vampires were wusses and she preferred werewolves?" Both boys were still laughing.

"I guess you couldn't sleep either?" Kevin asked when the laughter finally stopped.

"No, but I'm used to not sleeping much. Since my dad started drinking I never feel comfortable enough to get any good sleep," Marcus said sipping his coffee.

"I don't know how you manage to be normal dealing with all that crap," Kevin said. Kevin knew when it came to parents he had been dealt a better hand then his friends. Presley's mom had lied to her for her entire life and now she had no idea of her birth dad's identity. Stephanie's parents are never around, always on some extended vacation. They apparently feel that as long as Stephanie has an unlimited credit line she's good. Marcus had been dealt the worst hand, a dad who is an ass on a good day and a mom who is too scared to breathe. Kevin's parents were great, even when he told them he was gay. They were shocked at first but their love and support had never wavered.

"I don't know how much longer I can take it." Marcus said running his hand through the mess on top of his head.

"You're eighteen, move out I would." Kevin said standing from the couch to get another cup of coffee.

"Man, I got 800 dollars in the bank. Even if that was enough to get a place, prom is coming up. You know how much Steph is looking forward to going. I want to make it special for her and when it comes to prom unfortunately special means money," Marcus said rubbing the back of his neck

"You know she doesn't care about that. She would rather see you happy," Kevin said as he poured his second cup of coffee.

"I know but I care about it. Once I get out of school and can work full time at the shop I'll be able to get out of there," Marcus said as he sat on the couch. Marcus worked at a small garage in town, Right now he just changed oil and tires but Luca and some of the guys were training him on other repairs.

"Alright man but if I can help let me know." Kevin joined Marcus on the couch and they began watching *Jackass* the movie. As they laughed at the moronic things they saw on the screen Kevin thought...***This is what I needed, just a couple minutes to be a normal teenage guy and laugh at idiots who seem determined to kill themselves.***

Chapter Twenty One

The next couple days had gone by uneventfully. It was Thursday and there had been no sign of Andrew anywhere. Presley had wanted to believe it was a good sign but she knew better. There had been many times over the past couple of days when she could feel the hairs on the back of her neck stand at attention. She would have sworn somebody was watching her. She had decided not to tell Luca, he was already on edge and spent his nights patrolling around her house.

Presley was alone in the school library when she felt two very strong arms encircle her waist pulling her back into an inviting muscular chest. As the scent of Luca's cologne hit her nose she leaned back into him and let out a deep sigh. "Miss me?" he whispered in her ear. She let out a light laugh, "I just saw you last period," she said as she turned to face him. "Yes, but I haven't been alone with you since Sunday." He said pulling her by the waist to him. "It has felt like forever hasn't it?" She replied as she ran her hand down the side of his face. "Oh, yeah." he said as he caught hold of her hair and tilted her head back slightly.

Before she could think his mouth was on hers. As she wrapped her arms around his neck he slowly backed her up until her legs hit one of many small round tables scattered throughout the library. When they reached the table Luca moved his hands to her waist and picked her up sitting her on the table but never once taking his mouth from hers. With her now sitting on the small table he placed himself between her knees as his lips traveled across her jaw line and down her neck. When he reached the tender part of her neck where it met her shoulder he lightly nipped her. When he pulled back to look in her eyes she whispered "bite me." To say he was surprised to hear the words she had spoken would be an understatement. He ran his knuckles down the side of her face "not here; not now." He knew he should have just told her no, but truth be told, he wanted to bite her. Not because he needed to, even though he hadn't had any blood since Sunday he still felt good, he just wanted to taste her sweet blood again. He had been craving her all week.

"Okay, I guess the school library isn't really the place for such activities," she said as she lightly bit her bottom lip and a blush covered her cheeks. She wasn't normally so bold but since the first time he had bitten her she constantly replayed that moment over and over in her mind. At first when his teeth pierced her skin she felt pain but it was quickly washed away by a wave of pleasure.

He gently kissed her one more time on the lips. "I just wanted to spend some time with you." he said playing with one of the red streaks in her hair. "I'm glad you're here but Mr. Walsh is going to get pissed if you keep leaving class." She said as she fidgeted with the rolled up sleeve of his green button up shirt.

"He'll be alright," Luca said as he gently pulled Presley's hand to his mouth and lightly kissed it.

"What are you doing tonight?" She asked as he placed her hand in his.

"I have to work but it's my last night. I told Mr. Parker I would finish up the week before I quit." He said just as Presley's phone signaled her she had just received a text message. Presley jumped off the table and headed to her book bag.

Kevin: Do you have plans tonight? Can we hang out?

As she walked back over to Luca she said "Now, where were we?" and wrapped her arms around his waist.

"I think we were about here," Luca said as he leaned down to kiss her. Once again he grabbed her by the waist. When her feet were lifted off the ground she wrapped her legs around his waist. Luca placed one hand under her butt, while his other hand slid up her back and into her hair.

"You two really should find somewhere else to do that." Kevin laughed as he walked up behind his two friends who were in the middle of a pretty heavy make out session.

When Presley heard Kevin's voice behind her she pulled her face away from Luca. Licking her lips she whispered, "Maybe later." Luca laughed as he placed Presley back on her feet.

"I was just getting ready to text you," Presley said as she turned around to face her dear friend.

"Really, if you were even thinking about me during that little show you seriously need to reevaluate your priorities." Kevin laughed then kissed Presley's cheek. "What's up Luca...never mind don't tell me."

"Why did you text me if you were on your way here?" Presley asked trying to change the subject.

"I sent that text thirty minutes ago but I can see you were otherwise engaged." He laughed at the pink tone of Presley's normally ivory cheeks.

"Are you staying with me tonight?" Presley asked bouncing on her toes.

"I was thinking about it, unless, you were planning for an encore." Kevin said as he winked at Luca who just laughed.

"Shut up. You have to come over. My mom's going to be at work and I miss our little sleep overs."

"I've been at your house most of this week."

"Yeah, but I had to share you," Presley said as she hugged Kevin.

"Alright, I'll be there about seven with pizza."

"Extra cheese or I won't let you in."

"Girl, I don't know how you stay so skinny."

"It's a gift." She smirked.

The bell rang ending the school day and the trio left the library.

When they reached the parking lot they met up with Stephanie and Marcus.

"What's the plan for the weekend?" Stephanie asked as she approached the group. "Marcus and I are going to look at tuxes tomorrow but the rest of our weekend is open." She said as Marcus piped in, "I have to work Saturday. I asked Mr. Parker for some extra hours."

"I'll be with Jimmy most of the weekend," Kevin said as they approached his car and he unlocked the door.

"I was planning on spending tomorrow night with Presley, if that's okay with you," Luca said placing his arm around her shoulder. Before Presley could answer Kevin spoke, "Encore?" When Presley smacked his arm Stephanie's eyes widened, "Oh, I missed something and I want to know what it was!!" she said as she placed both hands on her hips.

"Just a little make out session in the library," Kevin said with a smug smile.

"IN THE LIBRARY!!!! You are my hero Pres, truly you are!" Stephanie exclaimed very enthusiastically.

Make it stop, make it stop Presley repeated in her mind as her temperature rose.

"Guys, I think that's enough," Luca said squeezing Presley's shoulders.

"Alright, fine, let's all meet at Waffle House Saturday night at seven. Kevin bring Jimmy." Stephanie shouted over her shoulder as Marcus pulled her to his truck.

"I'll see you in a little bit," Kevin told Presley as he got in his car.

∞

When Luca pulled into Presley's driveway he turned to her and said, "Do you think Kevin knows he can't tell Jimmy about any of this?"

"Um, I'm sure he does but I'll remind him." She gave him a reassuring smile.

He pinched the bridge of his nose and squeezed his eyes shut, "I know I am asking a lot of you guys. I'm sorry."

"This isn't your fault, Luca," she said as she grabbed his hand.

"You are all in danger because some blood thirsty vampires have a vendetta with my family. How is this not my fault?"

"First, you didn't know any of this would happen. Second, this is their fault. You didn't make them crazy. Their warped views on the world did." Presley said as she placed her hands on either side of his face.

Grabbing both her hands and removing them from his face he said in a very quiet deep voice, "You are amazing. You do know that, right?"

Before she could respond he opened his car door, got out and walked around the car to the passenger side. Presley just couldn't believe her luck ***How did I get so lucky?***

"I'm the lucky one, "he said as he opened the door. She smiled as she left the car. After closing the door behind her he pressed her against the car with his toned body.

"I know all of this is crazy but you guys are handling it better than I would have ever thought any teenager could." Luca said playing with his favorite red streak on the right side of her head.

"You know what I think is weird?" she asked looking up shyly from under her eye lashes.

"What?" he asked still twirling her red hair between his fingers.

"Math class," she said with a snicker.

"Math class?" he asked his fingers pausing momentarily in place in her hair.

"Yeah, I mean I find out my boyfriend is a vampire and there are two crazy vampires who want him dead. What am I doing? I'm sitting in math class worried about how I'm going pass tomorrow's test!" As she spoke she thought, **Oh crap, I just called him my boyfriend. He's never said anything about that. God, Pres you're an idiot!**

Presley felt Luca's hand gently lifting her chin. When their eyes locked he lowered his lips towards hers. They were a breath apart when he whispered, "I love you, Presley." Biting her lower lip she took in a deep breath. Softly she whispered, "I love you, too." Their lips gently pressed together. But hoping to avoid the inevitable total immersion to their intense passion they quickly ended their kiss.

"I'll call you when I get off," Luca said as he tucked a strand of her hair behind her ear. "Have fun with Kevin," he continued.

"Okay," Presley replied.

As she headed to the house she thought **Yeeeessssss! he said he loves me!**

"I heard that!" he shouted as he opened his car door and turned to look at her.

She stopped and turned to face him. "Stop that or I'll start thinking bad thoughts," she said as she crossed her arms over her chest.

"Really?" he said, almost daring her.

Cocking one eyebrow she thought *I just want to run my hands down his bare chest and....*

She was interrupted when he growled," Stop that, now!"

"I win," she laughed and headed to her house.

After entering her home Presley went to her room. She pulled out her math book and iPod. She put in her ear buds, turned on her Pearl Jam CD, her favorite study music, sat on her bed and began studying for her upcoming math test.

Chapter Twenty Two

Luca arrived at Mr. Parker's shop at 5:30. Marcus was already there sporting a brand new black eye.

"What happened to you? Did you make fun of *Twilight* while you were with Steph again?" Luca asked as he picked up the repair orders from his in-box located by the time clock.

"This?" Marcus pointed to his own eye. "This is just a gift from dear old dad." He said with a shrug, wiping grease off his hands with an already greasy towel.

"What? He should have...crap, he was drunk. He forgot everything I told him." Luca said shaking his head. "What are you going to do?" he asked, while pulling on his coveralls.

"I don't know but I have to find a way out of that hell hole. I talked to Mr. Parker, he said I can pick up more hours when school lets out. So hopefully, I can get out by August," he said releasing a deep breath.

"You could move in with me. I mean, I have plenty of room," Luca said sorting through the tools in his tool box. Luca was disappointed that his compulsion didn't stick with Mr. Morrison but he was going to do anything he could to help his friend.

"That's real nice of you but I couldn't intrude like that," Marcus said although he was thinking **When can I move in?** Of course, Luca heard those thoughts but Marcus didn't know about that ability yet.

"I'm not taking no for an answer. Pack your stuff tonight when you get home and you can either move in tonight or tomorrow after school." Luca said while popping the hood on the Dodge Charger that had been driven into his bay.

"Man, are you sure?" Marcus asked as he closed the hood of a Chevy Cavalier whose oil he had just changed. He was surprised Luca would make such an offer without a second thought. He knew vampires were supposed to be monsters but from where he stood they had more care and compassion then most humans he knew.

"Sure. I have plenty of room. You won't have to pay rent or anything but I should warn you, I'm not real good about keeping the kitchen stocked. I don't think about that stuff."

"Do you mind if I come tonight?" Marcus asked. He couldn't hide his excitement. Then he thought about Presley and asked, "Are you sure Presley won't mind?"

"First, yes you can come tonight. Second..., no, Presley won't mind, and if she did it really wouldn't matter it's my house," Luca said wiping the grease off his hands.

"Okay man, keep telling yourself that." Marcus laughed as he got in the Cavalier to drive it out of the bay. He was sure Presley wouldn't mind; however, he knew if she did Luca would probably reconsider his offer. As he backed the car out of the bay he could feel a wave of relief wash over him at the thought of no longer living under his father's roof.

∞

Kevin arrived at Presley's at seven with two large extra cheese pizzas. When Presley answered the door she placed one hand on her hip and the other on the open door she said, "I hope you got extra cheese." Kevin opened the lid on the top box of pizza, "Yes dear," he said in a whinny nasally voice. Presley took the top pizza, headed to the kitchen and placed it in the oven. Grabbing some paper plates and napkins she said, "I have already done all the studying I'm going to do so we have plenty of time to talk." Kevin took a deep breath and followed her up the stairs to her room. Once in her room Presley climbed on her bed and sitting on her knees she patted the spot on the bed next to her.

"Where do you want to start? The whole vampire descendant thing or the Jimmy coming this weekend thing?" Presley asked. She took a piece of pizza out of the box and placed it on the plate that sat on her lap.

"I don't even know where to start. All of it has my head spinning," Kevin said as he also took a piece of pizza. He wanted to stay with Presley tonight because he needed to talk to her. All his mind could do was bounce from one problem to the next. He still couldn't determine his own feelings on any of the situations. Taking a bite of his pizza he contemplated where to start when Presley beat him to the punch. "What are you and Jimmy doing this weekend?" she asked just before she took a bite of her pizza.

"Friday we're going to get dinner and catch a movie. I'm assuming he'll spend some time with his parents Saturday. He's leaving Sunday morning." He took a sip of his soda when he finished talking.

"Do you think he'll mind hanging out with us, or actually me on Saturday night?" She asked the question with her head lowered. She still carried an incredible amount of guilt over the void she felt she had caused between Jimmy and Kevin.

"Pres, don't do that. What happened between Jimmy and me was my fault."

"No, I was being selfish."

"You were hurting and you needed me. There is absolutely nothing selfish about that. I just need to learn better..." he paused for a minute trying to come up with the right word. Then he added "time management." Presley laughed as she took another bite of pizza, stretching the cheese between her mouth and the pizza.

"I really didn't want to do this but there is something I absolutely have to tell you," Presley said as she bit her lip.

"What now?" Kevin asked feeling like his head would explode if any more problems were crammed in to it.

"Well, Luca wanted me to make sure that you knew you couldn't talk to Jimmy about any of this vampire stuff," she said. With her head still lowered she was looking at him through her eyelashes. She waited silently for his reaction.

"Yes, I know." He sighed, then added, "I wouldn't have anyway. We have enough to work on without adding any of this paranormal drama."

"Have you thought anymore about being Luca's descendant or whatever?" she asked. She knew he wanted, and needed, to talk about the totally unexpected news he had been given. She was trying to open the conversation by taking some of the pressure off him.

"If you're asking if I have thought about becoming a vampire. I would be lying if I said no. But I can't make a decision like that right now. Pretty sure there's no changing your mind once it's done."

"Yep, I think it is pretty permanent. So, do you want to talk about it?"

"Yeah, but I don't really know what to say. I considered calling Jimmy and canceling but I just couldn't bring myself to do it. I don't know how I'm going keep this from him. I know I don't have to worry about Luca but what if that Andrew character comes around?" he said. Rising from the bed he began to pace back and forth. Presley was going to speak when Kevin continued "and as far as becoming one, I don't know. In theory it sounds great but there has to be a down side. The one major one I can think of is watching the people you care about die." Then he said something she hadn't thought of, "Do you think he'll want you to turn?"

"I...I don't know. I haven't even thought about that. I've been too worried about you."

"If he asked, would you?"

"I don't know. We'd have to be together a lot longer then we have been for me to make that decision. Kind of a big commitment you know?"

"Yeah, if I did it, would you?"

"I'm not answering that. This has to be a decision you make for yourself. For once you have to think about what you want, not what everybody else does."

"I know. So how are things going with you and Luca?"

"Nice change of subject. We're great. He told me he loved me today," Presley said with a smile that reached her eyes.

"Really, so I guess Steph was right," he said as he sat on the bed.

"Yeah, but don't tell her I said that," she laughed.

"I really wish you would've told me about the vampire stuff," Kevin said. Presley could hear the hurt in his voice.

"I'm sorry. If it makes you feel any better I only found out the day before you did," Presley said. She knew why she didn't tell him but she still felt guilty about it. Kevin had been there for her during the toughest part of her life and she kept a secret from him. She tried to make herself feel better by telling herself it was only for a day. However, she knew she would have kept it longer if the Andrew drama had not happened.

"I know why you did it. I know I shouldn't be upset about it but I was," he said shrugging his shoulders while taking another bite of pizza.

"Was? Does that mean you're not anymore?" Presley asked hopefully as she shifted her position on the bed and pulled her knees to her chest.

"I thought about it and I'm over it. I guess I'm just used to being the one you have secrets with, not from, but I'm glad you have Luca. He's been good for you."

"Kevin, he could never take your place. You're still my bff," She smiled rubbing his arm.

"I know, but I'm glad you have him. Now I can spend time with Jimmy and still know you're okay," he said while putting his arm around her.

"Was I that bad?" Presley asked leaning against his shoulder.

"I don't think you know how worried we were about you. Those first few months you were totally closed off, it was as if walls were instantly surrounding you. Then even when you started coming around you still had all those walls. I was truly worried you were going to grow up and live with like 100 cats. Before Luca I never thought I'd see you truly happy or relaxed," Kevin said holding her closer.

"He has made me happy but I never would have made it after Eric if it wasn't for you," Presley said as she wrapped her arms around his waist. "I love you, Kevin. Please don't think just because I have Luca I don't need you because I always will." A lone tear fell from her eyes as she spoke.

"I know, Babe, I love you too." Just as he kissed the top of her head she heard her phone beep announcing the arrival of a text message. She released her embrace, walked to her dresser, grabbed her phone and opened her text message.

Luca: I won't be at school tomorrow.

"Luca said he won't be at school tomorrow. Do you think something happened?" She asked Kevin.

"These days I'm afraid to guess." Kevin said standing to join her.

Presley: Y what's going on

Luca: Marcus is moving in with me. We r getting his stuff 2morrow

"Marcus is moving in with Luca." Presley told Kevin. Although she was shocked she felt a sense of joy knowing her dear friend was going to be away from his awful father.

"Really, I didn't think about that but it's a good idea." Kevin said as Presley responded to Luca's text.

Presley: That's great. Do you need any help?

Luca: No, it's just going to be the guys, but we r still on for 2morrow night.

As Presley was reading her text Kevin received one.

Marcus: Hey want 2 help me move 2morrow. We r doing it during the day.

Kevin: Sure pick me up in the AM. What time?

While Kevin was texting with Marcus Presley finished up with Luca.

Presley: You are wonderful you know that? What r we doing?

Luca: It's a surprise. Wear something warm.

Presley: Okay um kinda scared LOL

Luca: Don't be u will luv it ;)

Presley: k

Luca: I luv u baby

Presley smiled and felt her heart flutter just reading the text.

Presley: I luv u 2

After Presley finished she put her phone down. Between the fact that Marcus was finally going get away from his dad and the fact that Luca told her he loved her, she couldn't stop the huge smile that took over her face.

"They're picking me up at 7:30 in the morning," Kevin said as he pulled his shirt off and grabbed his pajama pants out of his bag.

"I am so happy for him. However, it's not fair that y'all get to hang out while Steph and I are at school," Presley said with a fake pout on her face.

"You'll survive!" He laughed as he left the room to go change.

While he was in the bathroom Presley changed into a pair of Spongebob pajama pants and a matching yellow tank top with Spongebob's face covering the entire front.

Once Kevin was back in the room they both climbed under the covers of her bed. She cuddled up next to him and said, "I love you Kevin, thank you for putting up with me," and kissed his cheek.

"Love you too, sweetie. I'm here for you always." Within minutes they were both sound asleep.

Chapter Twenty Three

Luca and Marcus each pulled into Presley's driveway at exactly 7:30 the next morning. As Luca left his Mustang Marcus hopped out of his truck. Before they could reach the porch of Presley's house she and Kevin came through the door.

"Good Morning, love." Luca said as pulled her into an embrace.

"Morning," Presley said kissing his lips.

"So what's the plan?" Kevin asked Marcus.

"I'm hoping we can get in and out of there before my dad wakes up." Marcus said shoving is hands into the front pocket of his jeans. He was hoping things would go smoothly. There was a strong possibility, that since it was so early in the morning, they could finish moving his stuff before his father woke from his alcohol induced coma.

"Does your mom know you're moving out?" Kevin asked. Kevin was glad his friend was finally getting out of his father house; however, he was worried about Marcus's mom.

"I'm going to offer to help her get out, too." Luca said as he and Presley walked toward them hand in hand.

"She won't leave," Marcus said as he exhaled a deep breath. "She says she loves him and she is convinced he'll get better."

"I'll offer her a way out but if she doesn't take it, there's not much I can do," Luca said. He had already tried to compel Mr. Morrison to stop the abuse but it didn't work, he wasn't sure what else he could do.

Stephanie pulled into Presley's drive while the others were still discussing Marcus's mother. She hopped out of her Jeep and ran into Marcus's open arms. She pressed a kiss to his lips while placing her hands on each side of his face. "Are you sure about this?" she asked. She was extremely happy about Marcus' decision but she didn't want her excitement to be the reason he made such a big decision.

"I am, Baby. As long as Luca's still okay with it," he said as he looked over Stephanie's shoulder to where Luca stood.

"I am," Luca responded with a reassuring nod.

"Alright, Presley and I will come by after school," she told Marcus. Although she and Presley had both wanted to help they knew that Marcus needed some guy time. They also realized that all the boys were worried about what might happen if Mr. Morrison was awake when they got there.

After the group parted ways Presley climbed into the passenger side of Stephanie's Jeep. "Thank you for picking me up." She said as Stephanie started the Jeep. "No problem," Stephanie answered as she steered the Jeep toward the school. Presley had a car but since the accident she didn't like to drive. Her friends didn't seem to mind driving her, or at least they never let on if they did. They seemed to understand.

As the boys pulled up to Marcus' house Marcus took in a deep breath, trying to prepare himself for a fight he hoped wouldn't happen. Kevin and Marcus climbed out of the truck and met Luca who had parked behind them. "You ready?" Luca asked when he saw the look of fear on Marcus's face.

"Yeah, this shouldn't take too long. I just need to get my laptop and clothes." Marcus was talking very quickly. "Breathe,"

Kevin said as he patted his friend's back. Marcus always gave the impression that he was fun loving and confident, which he was, unless his father was near.

"You and Kevin get your stuff. I'll talk to your mom and if your dad becomes a problem let me deal with him," Luca said.

"Alright," Marcus said as he was ringing his hands.

As the boys entered the house both Luca and Kevin could almost feel the muscles in Marcus's body tense up. When they heard Mr. Morrison's voice ask, "Boy, shouldn't you be at school?" they saw terror spread across his face. "Here we go," Marcus muttered.

"Just go get your stuff." Luca whispered. Marcus and Kevin ascended the steps while Luca stayed put on the landing at the base of the stairs. The boys had barely reached the top of the stairs when Luca heard the sound of a chair sliding roughly across the tile floor in the kitchen.

"What are you doing here?" Mr. Morrison asked as he entered the front room where Luca stood.

"Waiting on Marcus to get his stuff, he's moving in with me," Luca said calmly as he watched Mr. Morrison's face grow red with rage.

"You think so? KIMBERLY!" he screamed over his shoulder toward the kitchen he had just left. When Kimberly Morrison joined them in the front room Luca was glad to see she had no visible new bruises. However, he did know just because he couldn't see them didn't mean they weren't there.

"Did you know Marcus was planning on moving out with this…this kid?" Mr. Morrison asked with a voice filled with rage.

"No" she answered with her head hung low and her arms wrapped around her body.

"I hope you and Marcus realize I am not going to let that happen!" he said to Luca, trying very hard to be intimidating. Luca just laughed which only served to piss off Mr. Morrison.

"You listen, and you listen good. This is my family, my house and you will not come in here and tell me what is, and is not, going to happen. Do you understand me, boy!" Mr. Morrison yelled as he tightened his hands into fists. Luca simply laughed again. He figured as long as he could keep Mr. Morrison focused on him it would delay him fighting with Marcus. At least till Marcus was finished packing his essentials. While Luca laughed he saw Mr. Morrison pull his arm back and swing his tightly balled fist toward Luca's face. Luca caught his fist inches from his own face. With a tight grip on Jeremiah Morrison's fist he yanked on it, pulling him close to Luca's face. "I would be very careful right know if I were you," he whispered calmly. Then he released Mr. Morrison's fist with a slight push causing Mr. Morrison to land on his back side. Picking himself up Mr. Morrison headed back to the kitchen.

Luca then fixed his attention on Mrs. Morrison. "You can come, too." He said quietly as he walked toward her. She looked up at him, her bottom lip quivering. "Take care of my son." was all she said before turning away from Luca and headed back to the kitchen. Luca was disappointed she hadn't agreed to come with them but he didn't expect her to accept his invitation.

Luca continued to essentially guard the steps until the other two boys finished packing. Kevin and Marcus came down the steps about twenty minutes after Mr. and Mrs. Morrison had gone back to the kitchen. Each boy had two duffel bags on each arm. "I'm ready." Marcus said when he reached the landing of the steps. Right before they opened the front door they heard Mr. Morrison yell, "Leave your keys!" "Fine," Marcus answered back. Then as Mr. Morrison re-entered the front room he added, "All of them, the truck, too." With a look of smug satisfaction on his face Mr. Morrison crossed his arms over his chest and waited for his son's response. He truly believed Marcus would stay and continue to take his abuse if he threatened to take his truck. Luca looked over at Marcus, who was just staring at his father. ***Damn it! I can't not have a car, how will I get to work?*** Marcus thought. Luca could hear the mental debate going on in Marcus's head, so he decided this was a problem he could fix. "Give him the keys, Marcus," Luca said as he glared at Mr. Morrison.

"No, I make the payments on that truck. You can't have it," Marcus said gritting his teeth.

"That truck is in my name. If you no longer live here, you no longer have a truck. Make your decision," Mr. Morrison said, still displaying a smug look on his face. Luca, Marcus and Kevin wanted nothing more than to knock that look right off his face. Luca knew this because he heard their thoughts, and they were the same has his. All three involved flying fists and blood and teeth flying out of Mr. Morrison's mouth.

"Just give him the keys, Marcus; I'm not going to let you stay here over a truck," Kevin said placing his hand on Marcus' arm.

"Mind your own business, queer boy!" Mr. Morrison yelled. Marcus threw his keys, they hit hard on Mr. Morrison's chest. Then he said, "Take your damn truck, Jeremiah." He decided at that point he would no longer call him dad.

The three boys left the house and loaded Marcus' stuff into Luca's Mustang. "Kevin, I'm sorry about that," Marcus said as he fastened his seat-belt. As he spoke he looked over his shoulder at Kevin who was sitting in the back seat.

"It's not your fault. I'm curious about how normal and, well… nice you are after being raised by that?"

"Jeremiah didn't have much to do with my raising, that was all my mom," Marcus said. "I guess she said she wouldn't leave?" Marcus said as he turned his attention to Luca.

"We won't give up. We'll keep trying to find a way to keep her safe," Luca said trying to reassure his friend. Marcus inhaled a deep breath. Luca could see the concern on Marcus' face. He hated there was nothing he could do to change that, but he knew he would continue to try.

When they pulled up to Luca's house Kevin sat in awe at the sight of Luca's house. Marcus had the same experience the night before. Luca pulled around to a three car garage to the left of the house. Kevin slowly left the car while still looking around the large estate. Once out of the car they all pulled out the duffel bags containing Marcus' belongings. When they rounded the car Luca tossed his keys to Marcus who dropped his bags to catch them. "What's this for?" Marcus asked, still holding the keys in his cupped hands.

"There's a house key and car keys you will need to drive the Mustang," Luca replied as he continued toward the house.

"Wait, What? I can't take your car. What will you drive?" Marcus asked, still standing there motionless. Kevin was almost in shock as he stood next to Marcus. Luca turned to the boys and walked over to the garage. After he punched in numbers on the security key pad the garage door opened. Marcus' jaw dropped when the doors were completely open.

"Is that?" was all he could get out of his mouth. Luca chuckled at Marcus's reaction and said, "It's a 1955 Porsche Speedster." Marcus had such a love for cars and seeing that car was like a dream come true. "I can't believe you have this car...I have always had an interest in learning everything about the 1955 Porsche Speedster. Can I sit in it?" Marcus asked. Kevin thought for sure Marcus was about to start jumping up and down like a giddy school girl.

"Let's go get you settled. Then I'll give you a tour. After that I'll take you for a ride." Then after thinking for a second he added, "If we get finished before Presley gets here."

Luca hadn't had time to show Marcus' the entire house the night before so he took Marcus and Kevin on a tour to show them the kitchen, laundry room, gym and game room. Marcus really liked the gym and Kevin was thrilled to see the game room. The game room had a big couch with a 50 inch flat screen TV connected to an xBox One and a PlayStation 4. There was also a pool table, a card table and a small bar.

After showing Kevin and Marcus around the house Luca helped carry Marcus' bags to his room on the second floor. The room was awesome...Marcus could have never dreamed he would have a place like this to call "home." The room was furnished with a mahogany king size bed covered with a hunter green comforter, and matching mahogany dresser and armoire. On the wall opposite of the bed hung a large flat screen TV. "Um, this is...wow...it's great!" Kevin said. Luca smiled, then said "the girls will be here soon. Let's get this done."

Chapter Twenty Four

By the time the girls arrived at 4 the boys had already finished the unpacking. "Your house is amazing," Stephanie said as she Luca's home. "Thank you," Luca said while making his way to Presley. He wrapped his arms around her and lifted her off her feet. "Man, I missed you," he said as he kissed her more deeply then he normally would have in front of people. Presley giggled, "I missed you, too, Baby."

"Come on, man. How am I supposed to follow that?" Marcus laughed as he hugged Stephanie and kissed her. "How was your day?" he asked. "Fine, but it wasn't the same without you," she responded kissing him again.

"Okay, things are getting way to mushy in here...so, I'm gonna go. Jimmy should be here soon. Can somebody take me to my car?" Kevin asked.

"We'll take you," Marcus said and Stephanie nodded in agreement.

"Alright, bye Pres," Kevin said kissing her cheek. Then he faced Luca, "Bye man, thanks for this," he said referring to Luca having Marcus move in with him.

"My pleasure," Luca said then looked at Marcus and added, "I'm taking Presley out so y'all will have the house. Do whatever you want... just stay out of the bar," he laughed.

"Alright, see you guys later," Marcus said as they left the house.

Once the others had left the house Presley looked up at Luca and asked, "Where are we going?"

"E' una sorpresa il mio amore"(it's a surprise, my love), he said with a wink.

"Oh, here we go with all the foreign tongue and winks," she laughed rolling her eyes.

Luca leaned down, putting his lips right next to her ear and whispered, "You know you love my foreign tongue." Then he slowly pulled back just enough to move his mouth to hers so he could kiss her. As he pulled her close she opened her mouth allowing their tongues to meet. As the kiss deepened their tongues danced to music only they could hear. When the kiss finally ended she said breathlessly, "I guess you're right." Luca laughed a quiet but deep laugh. He grabbed Presley's hand and led her to the kitchen.

In the kitchen he grabbed a large duffel bag. "Let's go," he said as they headed out of the back door. They walked through the yard into the wooded area behind his house. "Where are we going?" she asked again when they reached the trail.

"Just a little spot I know," he said sending her another wink.

"I guess you're not going to tell me. I would have worn different shoes if I had known we were going hiking through the woods." she stated looking at her black boots which were soled with a 4 inch thin heel.

"No, I'm not going to tell you where we are going and I love those boots," he laughed.

"Tell me what happened today," she said as she grabbed his hand.

"Nothing really, we went to Marcus' house. His mom wouldn't leave with us. His dad...Jeremiah, we're not allowed to call him his dad anymore, was being a jerk and took Marcus' truck. Then we came here, unpacked and played some football on the PlayStation," Luca shrugged.

"He took his truck, but Marcus pays for that!" Presley yelled.

"It's in Jeremiah's name. It's fine though, I gave him the Mustang. We're here," he said. The first thing Presley saw was a large pond. Trees seemed to encircle the pond, leaving just a couple yards between the tree line and edge of the pond. On the far side of the pond were small waterfalls created by the creek, that ran through the woods, emptying into the tranquil pond.

"It's beautiful," she said as she spun in a circle taking in all the natural beauty surrounding her. When she turned back to Luca he had already spread out a large blanket and was pulling snacks out of the bag.

"Come here," Luca said motioning for her to join him at the blanket. She walked over to him slowly and lowered herself to the blanket. He smiled at her as he handed her a bottle of water. Then he joined her on the blanket, lying on his back. She laid down next to him, placing her head on his chest. "I thought we could just be alone and talk for a little while," Luca told her.

"That sounds perfect," Presley said as she moved so her chin rested on his chest and she could look at his face. "Tell me about your life," she said.

"That's a really long story. You want to be a little more specific?" he asked as she laid her head on his chest. He ran his fingers gently through her beautiful hair.

"The important stuff I guess. Like what happened to your mom, when did you become a vampire, and about your dad and sister," she said.

"Is that all?" Luca laughed still stroking her hair.

"Yep, that's it," she replied.

"Okay, let's see. My mom died when I was two during child birth with my sister. So I don't remember much about her. I just remember that she was kind and beautiful. My father was born a vampire," he stated. Presley moved her head from his chest to his shoulder and nuzzled her face to his neck. He kissed her on the forehead and continued, "When I was 18 and Nicky was 16 we both had the flu which turned into pneumonia. That was in the mid 1800's so it was deadly. I woke up one day a vampire. When my human body died from the illness my vampire gene took over and I was a vampire." He paused for a moment looking into Presley's beautiful eyes. "Anything else you want to know?" he asked placing a quick kiss on her lips.

After thinking for a moment she asked, "You were born a vampire? Do you like it?" He was quiet for a moment looking at the sky as the sun began to set.

"Yep, me and Nicky both were and I guess in general I do. It took some getting used to but once I learned how things worked and how to control myself it got better. Plus, it is somewhat comforting to know there is a good chance I will always be around to protect the people I love."

"So was your mom a vampire, too?"

"No."

"Why didn't your dad turn her?"

"I don't know. I figured she wanted to have children first. I guess there wasn't enough time to turn her."

"Tell me about Ivy and Andrew," Presley asked, not sure if he really would but she wanted to steer the conversation away from his mother's death.

"Ugh! Okay, they are monsters. Ivy is one of the strongest vampires I have ever met, women tend to be stronger."

"Really? Why?" she interrupted.

"I don't really know how to explain it but I'll try. It has to do with the blood they drink. If a vampire drinks blood from their own gender it amplifies their abilities. Women tend to not be bothered by biting other women where as men are a little more uncomfortable about biting other men."

"Hum, so that whole not being secure in their own sexuality extends to supernatural males too," she laughed. Luca laughed as well, "I don't know if that's exactly how I'd explain it but I guess you could say that."

"Okay, finish telling me about the gruesome twosome," Presley said as she used her finger to draw designs on his chest. Luca laughed and continued, "There's really not much to tell. There's nothing I know that would explain their behavior. Ivy is power hungry. Andrew is in love with her and does whatever she wants. Ivy has always been that way. Andrew was a friend of mine a long time ago; he even dated my sister for years until he met Ivy. After that he went crazy, first he cheated on Nicky with Ivy and then he started beating her up. I don't know why he wouldn't just leave Nicky, my guess is Ivy told him not to because of my father. She hates my father. I think causing him pain by causing his children pain is a thrill for her," Luca said still stroking Presley's hair. She sensed talking, or even thinking, about Ivy and Andrew was upsetting Luca so she changed the subject again.

"Do you think Kevin will make a good vampire?" she asked. Luca thought for a moment, thankful for the subject change, and then answered, "Yeah, I do. He's a good guy. He's calm, friendly and extremely patient." Luca said thinking back to the many times he had witnessed Kevin waiting on his friends. "Plus, he won't mind biting a dude," he added with a chuckle.

Presley began thinking about what Kevin had asked her the night before, not thinking about Luca's ability to read her mind. *I wonder if he'll want me to change?* She quickly remembered his ability when he asked her, "Is that something you would want?"

"Um…I don't know. I know I love you and I want to be with you but I haven't thought a lot about that." She said and then added, "Plus, I can't make that decision till after Kevin does because if I turn he will do it just to be there to protect me, or whatever, no matter what he wants for himself."

"Yeah you're probably right," he said as he noticed it was beginning to get dark. "Do you want to head back before it gets too dark?" He asked just as she slid to her back. He bent his arm and propped his head on his hand looking down at her.

"Why, are you scared of the dark?" she asked, poking his chest.

"Ha, Ha" he said pushing a strand of hair away from her face and behind her ear. "I thought maybe you wouldn't want to be out in the woods in the dark," Luca said in the deep low whisper that almost made her melt.

"I'm out here with a big, sexy vampire, why should I be afraid?" she asked while rolling her eyes. Running his fingers down the side of her face he said, "Maybe, it's the big sexy vampire that should scare you!" Then he claimed her mouth with his. He lightly bit her lower lip causing her mouth to open slightly. As her lips opened wider he slid his tongue into her mouth taking in every bit of sweetness she had to offer. His hand slid up from her waist to under the hem of her shirt stopping just below her bra. Presley ran her hand up his arm and into his hair pulling it lightly. He broke the kiss when he slid his mouth down her jaw line to her neck. As he lightly bit her neck followed by a swirl of his tongue on her hot skin she whispered, "Do it please, bite me." He wanted to tell her no because he knew telling her no was the right thing to do...but he just couldn't. He had a craving not only for her blood but for feeling his teeth puncture her soft skin. He moved his lips closer to his ear. "Are you sure?" He asked in that deep husky tone that made him impossible to refuse. "Yes, please," she said as she arched her neck to grant him better access. He kissed her neck again and again made a swirling motion with his tongue over a small bit of skin on her neck. When she let out a small moan of pleasure he used that as his clue and gently pierced her skin. He pushed his teeth into her neck causing her to let out another light moan and to wrap both her arms around his neck holding him close. He almost moaned, too, when her warm sweet blood coated his tongue. As he moved his teeth from her neck he licked the spot he had bitten and kissed it gently. Moving his mouth back to hers their tongues were once again intertwined. When he felt her hand slide between the cotton fabric of his shirt and his bare chest he pulled away. Knowing where both their thoughts were headed he decided they needed to stop. "We need to go back," Luca said, trying to convince himself as much as her.

"Why?" she asked pulling her lower lip between her teeth.

"Because, um…Marcus and Stephanie are probably wondering where we are," he said as his face hovered close to hers.

"Liar," she laughed, placing her hand on his chest.

"Okay, maybe that's not the only reason but that's the only one you're getting." He said as he rolled to a sitting position.

"I know the other one, so I won't argue," Presley said as she rose to her feet.

Together they put the uneaten snacks in the bag, folded the blanket, and placed it on top of the snacks in the bag. As they walked back to the house Luca began to feel guilty about biting her again.

"Presley, I um…you know that you don't have to let me bite you, right?" He was worried she had asked him to bite her because she wanted to make him happy, not because it was what she wanted. Presley stopped in her tracks and grabbed his hand to stop him. Looking at him, she said barely above a whisper, "I asked you, didn't I?"

"Yes, I know that, but I just need to make sure you didn't do it because you felt like you had to…because you don't."

"I asked you because I wanted you, too. I'm not the kind of girl who does things just to make other people happy." She was starting to get annoyed. She looked at it as a way for them to show they loved each other. It seemed he doubted her intentions.

"I just...I don't know. I love you and I don't want you to feel like I'm using you. What I do know is that I don't want to ruin what we have."

"You won't if you stop talking about it...now!" Presley said as she began to walk back to the house, pulling him with her. He laughed and followed her.

Chapter Twenty Five

Presley's phone rang at ten the next morning. Not removing the blanket from her head her right hand fumbled around her nightstand feeling for her phone. Pulling the phone under the blanket she looked at the caller id.

"Good morning, Steph" she said still half asleep.

"Get dressed I'll be there in one hour" Stephanie replied. Presley couldn't help but think **She's way to peppy in the morning**

"Why? Where are we going?" Presley said as she threw her blanket off her head and sat up in her bed.

"We have one week until prom and you don't have a dress."

"I doubt I'm going to be able to find one this close to prom. Maybe, I should not go" Presley said as she left the cozy warm embrace of her bed.

"Do you doubt my mad shopping skills?" Stephanie asked trying to sound hurt. Presley just laughed. "Alright, I'll be ready."

"Love ya," Stephanie said before disconnecting the phone call.

Presley headed down stairs. When she reached the kitchen she saw a note propped against the coffee pot. While pouring a cup of coffee she opened the folded piece of paper

Presley,

Had to run a few errands this morning. Stephanie called and said y'all were going shopping for prom. My credit card is on the counter. Don't go crazy with it. I work this afternoon so I probably won't see you until tomorrow. Have fun.

Love

Mom

Placing the note back on the counter she saw her mom's visa card lying flat on the counter. Presley knew she should be excited about getting to use her mom's credit card but it dawned on her that not only was her mom working almost every day lately but she was working nights. Presley couldn't remember a time her mother had been home at night. Blowing the thought off for now she headed upstairs to prepare for a fun filled day of shopping with Stephanie. When she reached her bedroom her phone was beeping with a new text message. A smile spread across Presley's face when she saw the message was from Luca.

Luca: Good morning, sweetheart. What r your plans for 2day

Presley: I'm going shopping w/Steph. What r u doing?

Luca: sounds fun. I have to call my dad then nothing really I'll pick u up at 6 for dinner

Presley: sounds great.

Luca: Luv U ;)

Presley: Luv U 2 <3

Placing her phone back on her nightstand Presley began getting herself ready.

Stephanie arrived at Presley's house around eleven. When they climbed in to Stephanie's Jeep Presley said "I don't even know where to begin looking."

"Lucky for you I have it all lined up." Stephanie smiled then continued "Nervous about tonight?" she asked.

"Yeah. It's going to be awkward at best and extremely hostile at worst." Presley answered releasing a long deep breath. All of her friends were going to dinner with Jimmy tonight and Presley felt very on edge about the whole thing. She knew Jimmy blamed her, at least partially, for the distance between him and Kevin. She did feel a bit responsible for some of their problems. If she hadn't been so emotionally needy when he last visited maybe Kevin would have spent more time with him.

"It will definitely be uncomfortable but if it gets heated we'll leave," Stephanie said as she maneuvered the Jeep through the little bit of local traffic on the roads.

"The problem is that if things get heated enough between me and Jimmy that I have to leave it will end things between Kevin and Jimmy. Kevin loves Jimmy I don't want to be the reason they aren't together," Presley said running her fingers through her hair.

"Do you really think he loves him? I mean I know he cares about him. But don't you think that if he loved Jimmy, Kevin would have spent more than like...five hours with him the two weeks he was here or Christmas? I mean if I hadn't seen Marcus in three months I would have spent as much time as possible with him." Stephanie asked occasionally glancing over at her friend sitting next to her.

"He didn't spend a lot of time with him because he was taking care of me."

"Marcus and I were there he could have made time for Jimmy if he wanted to. You have to stop blaming yourself for this. I think Kevin pulled away from Jimmy because that's what Kevin wanted." As Stephanie spoke Presley noticed that they had left their home town but they weren't heading in the direction of the mall, they were heading to the neighboring town that was as small as the one where they lived. "Where are we going?" she asked.

"My mom has a friend who owns a dress shop in Albermarle. She does all my mom's dresses for her galas and banquets and stuff."

"Oh, do you think she'll have anything for me?"

"Yep, I called her Tuesday she said my dress was ready and I told her about you and she is getting some stuff together for you to look at." Stephanie replied as she turned on to Main St. Presley grinned at her friend. Stephanie always seemed to surprise Presley with how much time she actually spent thinking about other people. People who didn't know her may think she was stuck up or a selfish little rich girl, when in all actuality that couldn't be farther from the truth. Although, her parents were very rich and held in high regard in the community, Stephanie was the most grounded and selfless person Presley had ever met.

When they walked into the small store named Brie's Bridal and Formal a small bell rang announcing their arrival. Presley stood in awe of the variety of dresses and colors that filled the small building.

"Stephanie, darling." the girls heard the loud voice Brie Overcash coming from the back of the store, they saw the short, silver haired woman making her way towards them.

"Hi, Mrs. Overcash" Stephanie said as Mrs. Overcash pulled her into a hug and kissed her cheek with her hot pink lips, which left a perfect impression of her lips on Stephanie's cheek.

"Who do we have here?" Brie asked as she grabbed both of Presley's hands in her wrinkled yet soft hands. Brie Overcash's appearance and personality was that of your typical and sweet grandma type. Mrs. Overcash had no children or grandchildren so Stephanie and Stephanie's mom, Olivia, filled the voids in her life.

"This is my best friend, Presley Kluttz, she's the one I was telling you about the other day," Stephanie responded with one hand on Presley's shoulder,

"Oh yes, come this way dear. I've got things all ready for you," Brie said as she pulled Presley toward the back of the store.

When they reached a small set of dressing room in the back of the building Mrs. Overcash handed a white garment bag that was hanging on wall to Stephanie.

"Go try that on, darling, make sure that all the alterations are right. As Stephanie headed into one of the dressing rooms Mrs. Overcash guided Presley to a small rack next to the dressing rooms that contained an array of red and black dresses.

"Stephanie told me you would probably like something in black or red, so I took the liberty of putting some of my favorites aside for you."

"Thank you, I really do appreciate it," Presley said as she lightly squeezed the small warm hand that was still in hers. Mrs. Overcash smiled up at Presley warmly. Presley could easily see why Stephanie and her mother were so fond of this women, she seemed to have the ability to make you feel special with a simple smile. Mrs. Overcash grabbed a black dress off the rack and handed it to Presley "Let's get started dear. Finding the perfect dress can take time." Presley smiled sweetly as she took the dress from Mrs. Overcash's extended hand and then headed into the dressing room next to Stephanie's.

Presley slipped into the simple floor length black gown. It was designed so that the left sleeve was long and the right shoulder and arm were exposed. She heard Stephanie squeal and figured she was probably jumping up and down as well. As Presley left the dressing room she saw Stephanie standing in an emerald green strapless dress. The top clung snugly to her ample chest, without revealing too much, there was a two inch wide band of diamond sequins separating the top from the full floor length skirt.

"Stephanie, you look so beautiful and elegant. I love it!" Presley said as she looked at her stunning friend. The emerald green color of the dress not only brought out Stephanie's stunning green eyes it also complemented her red hair perfectly.

"Thank you, I love it too." she replied as she spun in a circle. When she faced Presley again she scrunched her nose and said, "Um I'm not crazy about that one though, try another one," Stephanie said as she retrieved another dress for Presley to try on. Presley agreed, she wasn't really fond of the dress either, so she took the second dress from her friend and retreated back to her dressing room.

∞

After Luca had texted Presley he decided to go for a quick run through the trails behind his house. Marcus had left for work at 8:30 that morning so Luca had some time to kill. While he ran his thoughts where on Ivy and Andrew. He wanted to be able to relax and believe that Andrew's sudden disappearance meant he had left the area but he knew better. He wanted to believe that Presley and their friends were safe but he knew better than that, too. It took every ounce of self-control he had not to demand that he accompany the two girls on their shopping venture, especially after what had happened last time, but he knew that that would not have gone over well with either of the girls.

After he finished his hour run he arrived back at his house. Grabbing his cell phone, a bottle of water and a towel to remove the sweat from his face he headed to the back porch and took a seat at the patio table to call his father. After a couple rings his father's deep husky voice came across the line.

"Hello, son."

"Hey, dad, using English that's never a good sign," Luca said. He knew the only time his father spoke in English was when he was worried about who could be listening at the door. Some of the vampires in their clan knew how to speak English but most weren't fluent and would have difficulty understanding it while lurking in the shadows to eavesdrop.

"Just remaining guarded. How are things in the States any more problems with Andrew?" He asked while lowering himself into the large leather chair behind his desk.

"He's been suspiciously absent. I'd love to think he left but we know better than that. How are things with Ivy? Has she made any moves yet?"

"Well, she took your sister and Angelo to lunch the other day. Nicky says she's definitely up to something. She gave some sob story about splitting up with Andrew but Nicky thinks it's all a lie."

"I guess we should just be thankful we are each dealing with one at a time instead of them together. Dad can I ask you a question?"

"Sure, son, what is it?"

"Have you ever drunk blood that gave you an abnormal amount of power. You know made you stronger and able to hear things you normally wouldn't?"

His dad took in a deep breath and released it before answering, "I've heard of it but never experienced it myself. Rumor is if you drink the blood of another supernatural being it can cause that to happen, but the supernatural species are so separated and leery of each other it seldom happens. Why do you ask?"

"I had to drink from Presley the other night and afterward I was stronger than I think I've ever been. I heard her thoughts from a good twenty yards away and I was outside and she was in her house!"

"Hum, have you asked her about it? Are you sure she is human?"

"Yeah I'm sure.. I mean if she wasn't human I'm sure she would have told me when I told her what I was."

"Just keep a close eye on her. She may not even know. Most supernatural beings who are born and not turned don't come into their powers till they are at least eighteen."

"Alright, but I'm pretty sure she's human," Luca said, almost 100 percent confident in what he was saying.

"Keep me posted son. I have to go, I have a meeting with Angelo to discuss some security changes."

"I will, but real quick. How are things going with Angelo guarding Nicky?" Luca asked and laughed when he heard his father let out a deep sigh.

"All their smiling and flirting is giving me a tooth ache. I'm not sure this was my best idea."

"Aw, come on, Dad. Angelo's a good guy. You knew this was going to happen sooner or later. They've been dancing around it for almost a year. Plus, Angelo will protect her with his life. You couldn't ask for a better guard"

"I know but she's my daughter, who still looks the same as she did when she was sixteen, the idea of her with any man kicks in that fatherly protective instinct,"

"It'll be fine. I can't imagine a better man for her. He's honorable, honest, kind and scared to death of you. He won't do anything stupid," Luca said still laughing.

"We'll see, I guess. Call me in a week and let me know where things stand. I have to go."

"Bye, Dad."

"Bye, Son."

Luca ended the call still laughing. He knew that his father liked Angelo but also understood his need to protect Nicolette because he felt the same way towards his baby sister no matter how old she was.

Luca decided he needed to check on Presley. He couldn't shake the feeling that she wasn't safe, at least unless she was with him. Of course he knew that her safety was not the only reason he wanted her with him. He was finding it increasingly more difficult to be away from her and sometimes it almost felt painful. After dialing her number a knot formed in his gut when he was greeted with Presley's voice mail instead of her sweet voice. "Hey, sweetheart, call me when you get this. I love you." He reluctantly ended the call and decide to give her thirty minutes to call him back before he panicked. He would spent that thirty minutes showering and preparing to tear through every dress shop in a thirty mile radius to find her if need be.

∞

Kevin paced his bedroom nervously awaiting Jimmy's arrival. They had spent the evening before talking about everything but their relationship. Kevin knew that if things were going to work out between them they would have to address their issues. The problem was Kevin had so many other issues of his own, issues he couldn't tell Jimmy. How was he going to have a honest conversation when he had so many secrets he had to keep guarded. His natural instinct was to call Presley and get her advice, but he couldn't do that. He needed to deal with this on his own, this had to stay between him and Jimmy. He knew Jimmy would be beyond pissed if he knew Presley had any input in their relationship. But whatever happened between him and Jimmy he would have to live with it. If things didn't work out he knew Presley would think she was to blame and he didn't want that. He had been so lost in his own thoughts he didn't notice his father standing behind him until he heard his deep but soothing voice, "You okay, son?" Kevin turned to see his father leaning his shoulder against the door jam of Kevin's room.

"Hey, Dad, I'm fine... just thinking"

"You look like you're going to jump out of your skin. Are you nervous about Jimmy being back in town?" He asked as he entered the room and sat on Kevin's unmade bed.

"I guess, I just... I don't know. I don't know where we are." He said as he ran both hands through his hair and continued to pace the floor.

"Okay, first sit down you're giving me motion sickness." His dad chuckled and once his son sat next to him he placed a comforting hand on his son's back. "Now I'm going to be honest talking to my son about his boyfriend wasn't a conversation I had prepared myself to have but I'm going to give it a shot." Kevin laughed lightly again realizing how lucky he was to have such a supportive set of parents. He listened as his father continued to try to help him, "I know that you care about Jimmy and I believe he cares about you. Try not force things y'all are still young just let things take a natural course. If you two are meant to be together you will find a way to work through this. If you can't work through this it just means that there is someone else out there for you and Jimmy is just meant to be your friend. A friend who had helped you learn and mature so when you do find the person you are destined to be with you're ready. Do you understand what I'm saying?" his dad asked. He was trying desperately to help his son but wasn't confidant that he was accomplishing that goal.

"I get it dad. Thanks, I am just worried that to be with Jimmy I may have to sacrifice my friendship with Presley and I don't think I can do that," Kevin said as he released a deep breath.

"If Jimmy really cares about you he won't ask you to do that. Everyone who knows you knows how important she is to you"

"I know but he doesn't like her!"

"Did he tell you that?"

"No, not exactly"

"So you don't know. Until you do, don't worry about it. Enjoy your time with him this weekend without over thinking things. There's no reason to make any big decisions right now."

"Thanks Dad" Kevin said as his dad left his room. He actually did feel a lot better. His dad was right he didn't need to make any decisions right now. With a new determination to enjoy his weekend he felt like a weight lifted off his chest. He was going to push all of his concerns about everything to the back of his mind so he could deal with it all after Jimmy left.

∞

After discarding six dresses Presley was preparing to walk out of the small dressing room in dress number seven when she realized she had a missed call. Looking at her phone she saw that she had a voice mail from Luca. Deciding that she didn't want to keep Stephanie waiting she sent a quick text message.

Presley: Hey babe still trying on dresses

Luca: Call me I need to hear your voice

Presley got a strange feeling that something else must have happened with Andrew for Luca to demand that she call him. Not wanting him to worry and also wanting to know what was going on she shouted to Stephanie, "I'll be out in a minute." She quickly dialed Luca's number. "Are you okay?" Luca asked as he answered the phone before Presley even heard it ring.

"Yes, I'm fine. What's going on?"

"Nothing, I was…I don't know I just had a bad felling." Luca said frustrated with himself for letting Andrew put him so in edge.

"Babe, I'm fine but I won't be if I make Stephanie wait any longer to see this dress." Presley laughed trying to lighten the mood.

"Alright, call me when you get home. Okay?"

"Okay"

"Presley"

"Yeah"

"I love you."

"I love you too. Are you sure you're okay?" Presley couldn't help but worry because of the desperation she heard in Luca's voice.

"Yeah, I'm fine I just needed to hear your voice."

"Okay, if you're sure. I'll call you when I get home."

"Bye, sweetheart"

"Bye, Babe"

Presley paced her phone back in her bag and left the dressing room. As soon as the door opened she heard Stephanie squeal with delight "Oh, that's it. That is definitely the dress!" Presley walked a couple steps forward and did a little spin. She was wearing a red strapless dress that matched the red in her hair with near perfection. The skirt was short in the front but the back hit the floor. There was a delicate black satin ribbon separating the top from the skirt. "I think you're right!" Presley smiled at her friend unable to hide her excitement in finding the perfect dress.

"Oh, dear, you look beautiful!" Presley heard Brie's soft voice coming from beside her.

"Thank you." Presley said as she watched her reflection in the full length mirror that hung on the wall across from her.

"I have the perfect shoes wait right here." Presley was still grinning as she watched Brie head to the other side of the store. Stephanie, who had already changed back into her royal blue sweater dress and black leggings, came over and wrapped her arms around Presley "You look beautiful. Luca won't be able to take his eyes off of you." She smiled at her friend's reflection in the mirror. Brie returned with a pair of red heels that wrapped around the ankle. Presley fell in love with them instantly. After trying on the shoes and admiring herself in the mirror. Presley purchased her perfect prom dress and was now very excited that prom was only a week away. She didn't think she could wait much longer than that to wear her dress.

∞

Just as Brenda was heading into Mercy General Hospital for her shift her cell phone rang. After shuffling through her overstuffed purse she found and answered her phone without checking the caller ID. "Hello."

"Brenda, how are you?" She heard a familiar deep voice ask.

"I'm fine, father, how are you?"

"I'll be better when you tell me that you are bringing my granddaughter here for her birthday," he said not overly friendly.

"Dad, I don't want to go into this again. She'll be fine." Brenda replied not bothering to hide her annoyance.

"Don't be naive. Her eighteenth birthday is Saturday she needs to be here."

"There is no reason to believe anything is going to happen!" she shouted into the phone.

"Are you selfish or stupid? You know what will happen. You can hope it doesn't but it will. She's not prepared because you have been keeping what she is from her. It will be dangerous. Brenda, you have to bring her here…she needs to be with us. We can help her learn to deal with this and control it," Brenda's dad, Silas Rushing, said calmly but firmly.

"She has prom this weekend. She will go to prom and graduate high school like a normal teenage girl." Brenda said trying to control the rage boiling under the surface.

"You listen to me and you listen good. If anything happens to her because of your selfishness I will make sure you pay for it. I can promise you her father will feel the same way when he hears of this nonsense." Silas said still calm and firm.

"You don't even know who her father is, so don't threaten me with that!"

"I may not know who he is… yet. But I most definitely know what he is."

"I have to go to work. I don't have time for this," Brenda said disconnecting the phone call before her father had a chance to reply. Wiping the tears from her eyes and shoving her phone back in her purse she entered the hospital to start a long night of trying to focus on work and not the conversation she had just had with her father. She knew that what he said was true but Brenda still held onto the hope that since she had raised Presley away from the life she had grown up in that her worst fear wouldn't come to pass.

Chapter Twenty Six

After successfully following Presley and Stephanie while remaining undetected, Andrew had just returned to his cabin when he heard a light knock at the front door of his cabin. Not really wanting to deal with anybody he stomped across the room to the door and swung it open… his obvious annoyance for being disturbed was evident. The scowl on his face was quickly replaced by a big grin when he saw the raven haired beauty standing at his front door. As he pulled Ivy into his arms lifting her clear off the ground he said, "Wow, you're really early." Then he kissed her soundly on the lips before placing her back on her feet.

"I guess that means you're happy to see me?" She laughed as her feet finally hit the floor.

"I've missed you," he said still unable to release her from his embrace.

"Nobody knows I've left Italy yet. Basillio has two of his guard men following me. I managed to give them the slip so while I had the chance I figured I'd come here. Which means I'll need to go shopping. I didn't have time to pack," she said while nuzzling her face against his chest.

"I'm glad you did," he said sweeping her into his arms and carrying her to his bed. Just as he began to cover her body with his she placed her hand on his chest and said, "Down boy, first things first. I need to know what you know about Luca and his new little brats." Andrew let out a frustrated breath as he rolled his body off of hers. "Ugh…Where do you want me to start?"

"Just run down the list and let's see if we can find the weak link," she said as she sat up.

"Well the dark headed boy, Marcus Morrison, doesn't really help us at all. He's living with Luca now so getting to him will be hard. His parents, Jeremiah and Kimberly, are useless too. Neither leave the house often. When Jeremiah does leave he's usually so wasted that if you take a bite out of him your head will be spinning for a week, trust me I know. Plus, I think Marcus would let you kill his dad before risking his friends. Kevin, the light headed boy, is well guarded too. I think there is some kind of protection spell on his house I couldn't get within fifty feet of it."

"Spell? So his parents know a witch? That's interesting. Kevin is Luca's descendant right?" Ivy interrupted. Ivy began silently trying to make a connection to any witch she knew of but she couldn't think of any in that part of the country.

"I guess, it always amazes me how these small towns are so over run with the supernatural and no one ever seems to notice."

"Okay, file that info away for later move on," she said motioning for Andrew to continue.

"Stephanie Maclamore, her parents, Olivia and Brent, are never around. They boarded a flight to Cancun yesterday and she has been staying with Marcus and Luca. So getting to her will be pretty difficulty, too. Can't use her parents to lure her out cause they aren't here."

"Alright, let's get to the good stuff. Tell me about the little blonde who has stolen our prince's heart." Ivy said as a smile crossed her face and malice danced in her eyes.

"Presley Kluttz, Her mom is Brenda Kluttz, an ER nurse at Mercy General Hospital. Her dad, who just discovered about a year ago that he isn't Presley's birth father, is a surgeon at Mercy

General. Apparently, she was a daddy's girl until he found out he wasn't her biological father, now from what I've heard he hasn't spoken to her since. I have no idea who is her actual father. Somehow her mother has managed to keep that little tidbit a secret. Hard to do in a small town. You would be amazed how easy it was to get all this information. I didn't even have to try!" Andrew laughed and shook his head. The lack of loyalty among humans shocked him. A little smile and a wink and that teenage girl spilled everything she knew.

"We just found our weakness. I know how to get my hands on Luca's precious little human."

"How's that?" Andrew asked as guided Ivy's long black hair behind her ear.

"We use daddy." Ivy said sweetly as she pulled his body on to hers. Now she had all the information she needed to put her plan into motion. Deciding to put off their evil scheming for a short time they made up for the time they had spent apart.

∞

Luca arrived at Presley's house around 4:15, just as he was going to knock on the door it opened and Stephanie stood in the door way. "Hey, Steph." He said somewhat troubled by the weary look on her face.

"Hey, Luca. Presley's upstairs but I wanted to talk to you real quickly before you go up there."

"Okay. What is it?" Luca asked as he felt that familiar knot forming in his stomach.

"I think Andrew is still lurking around. I'm pretty sure he was following us today and I know he's been asking around about all of us, especially Pres," Stephanie said quietly.

"Why are you just telling me this now? Why didn't you call me as soon as you saw him following you?"

"Because one, I didn't seem him; I felt him. If I had seen him I would have called you. Two, Presley is going to prom and going to have some kind of normal life. She has been through so much I just want her to enjoy herself for a little bit," Stephanie said her voice remaining low but her irritation obvious. After taking in a deep breath she added, "I think he's up to something and we need to figure it out so we can stop him and protect Presley."

"You felt him, what does that mean?"

"The past couple of days I've felt like somebody is around. Which leads me to believe it's him and he knows that you'll know he's around." Luca ran his hands through his hair as Stephanie spoke.

"Damn it. I knew he wasn't gone. Who has been talking to him?" Luca asked as his temper rose.

"Becca. Jasmine Thatcher, a girl from school, told me when she was out with Becca the other night this, and I quote, "really big really hot blonde guy" asked Becca about us. She apparently got a bad case of diarrhea of the mouth and practically told him our whole life story. Including things that Presley doesn't need to know. Can you think of any other big blonde guy who would be asking about us?"

With every word Stephanie spoke Luca could feel the rage inside him growing. He opened and closed his fist numerous times, he was mad. He wasn't mad at Stephanie so he didn't want to scare her but he could feel his teeth lengthening and his eyes burning. The vampire part of himself that he usually kept hidden was responding to his anger and Stephanie could now see it. "Wow, you're hot when you're pissed!" she laughed. Luca just glared at her to which she responded, "I'm just saying. Calm down fang boy or she's going to know something's wrong." After a couple cleansing breaths he said, "That's definitely Andrew. I'll figure out what he's planning but we need to tell Presley. She deserves to know. She needs to know so she will be cautious."

"You're right she does but it can wait. She's going to have a hard night tonight with Jimmy and we don't need to add to it. She's finally excited about prom and it's been a long time since she's been excited about anything. We aren't going to ruin it. We can just make sure she's never alone between the four of us somebody can be with her."

"You don't think she'll notice that someone's always there?"

"Nope. One of us has been with her almost every day since Eric died; so things won't seem that different. Plus, we have you now and I know she will never complain about being alone with you," Stephanie winked as she walked past Luca and down the steps.

"Wait!" Luca turned to look at Stephanie. "What did Becca tell Andrew that you don't want Presley to know?" He asked with a furrowed brow. Stephanie moved closer to Luca so she wouldn't have to talk loud and risk Presley hearing. "Look, it happened a long time ago but if she finds out it will break her heart. I will tell you but you have to swear you won't say anything," Stephanie said as she looked around Luca to insure that Presley wasn't standing there.

"I swear."

"When Eric and Presley had been dating for like two months he kinda slept with Becca. Normally, I would tell a friend something like that but Eric is dead and it will serve no purpose but to hurt Presley."

"Okay, I get it." Luca understood why Stephanie wouldn't want to tell Presley. She was right it would open a wound that would never heal. With a small wave Stephanie climbed into her jeep and headed home. Luca entered the house and when he went upstairs he saw Presley laying on the bed reading a book.

"Hey," he said softly not wanting to startle her.

"Hey, I didn't know you were here," she said as she placed her book on her bed and sat up Indian style on her bed. When Luca reached her he cupped both sides of her face with his hands and pulled her into a kiss. Presley tilted her head to deepen the kiss. He leaned down slowly until she lay flat against her bed and he covered her body with his... never once moving his lips from hers. As she wrapped both arms around his neck he ran one hand down the back of her thigh till his hand came to rest on her bottom. When he finally pulled away from her he laughed when she let out a noise that sounded a lot like a whimper. "Well, that was a nice hello," Presley said as she tried to steady her breathing.

"I've missed you," he replied and rolled to his side, bending his elbow and resting his head on his hand. "Are you sure you want to go to dinner tonight?" he asked. He knew that she was nervous about going and was trying to give her an out although he was sure she wouldn't take him up on it.

"Yeah, I have to put in an effort for Kevin." She said as she also rested her head on her hand.

"Okay but if you start feeling like you want to leave you'll tell me... right?" Luca said as he began to play with his favorite red streak on the side of her hair.

"I will. How's it going with Marcus living with you?" Presley asked as she fidgeted with the rolled sleeve of his black button up shirt.

"It's good. I like having the company. I guess Stephanie is staying with us until her parents get back in town."

"Really." Presley said trying to hide the jealousy she felt but when Luca laughed she knew she had failed.

"Are you jealous?" he asked as he leaned in and started placing lite kisses down her neck.

"No," as she let out a small moan and added, "Maybe a little. I just wish I could spend that much time with you." In between kisses and light nips to her neck he said, "She's not spending time with me, she's spending time with Marcus. I spend most of the time she's there in the gym or my room."

"I don't care if you hang out with them I just wish I could be there, too, that's all," she said finding it increasingly hard to think or even to breath while he was kissing her neck.

When Luca found his face hovering over hers and his body covering her body he said, "I think maybe we should go down stairs or something."

"Why?" she asked softly as she ran her hand down his chiseled chest.

"Because the longer we stay up here like this the harder it is going to be for me to use the little bit of self-control I have when I'm around you."

Presley looked up at him debating on how much self-control she wanted him to use. When she rolled her lower lip between her teeth he pushed himself off her and moaned, "You have to quit doing that… please." She just laughed and pushed herself off the bed.

"Fine be that way," Presley said as she sat down at her vanity to touch up her make-up," we need to get ready anyway."

Luca just laughed and shook his head as he leaned against the wall next to her vanity. As she applied her make-up he found himself watching her every move. She was his favorite subject and more and more he found himself studying her. He was intrigued by the way she moved, the way her eyes lit up when she laughed, the way she chewed on the corner of her bottom lip when she was nervous and, most of all, the sexy noises she made when his lips were on hers.

"Why are you staring at me?" she asked, jolting him from his thoughts.

"You're so beautiful you know that?"

"Thanks, you're not so bad yourself." She giggled then rolled her lips to smooth her freshly applied lipstick. When she rose from her seat and headed to her closet to grab her black boots she asked, "Are we going to talk about Andrew or are you and

Stephanie going to keep pretending like nothing's going on because you're worried I'll have a nervous breakdown?"

Luca took a deep breath through his nose and released it slowly. "I don't know what's going on with Andrew yet so there's no need to worry about that tonight."

"Okay, but only because I have enough to worry about tonight but tomorrow we are going to talk about it okay."

"There's really not much to talk about yet."

"Okay I'm ready let's go," Presley said as she grabbed her purse and headed out her bedroom door.

Around 6:15 Presley and Luca arrived at Brooklyn's a small Italian restaurant in town. The original plan was to go to Waffle House, which Presley would have preferred, but Jimmy said he couldn't stomach it. Kevin and Jimmy were already there waiting, which Kevin always seemed to be doing. Presley took in a deep breath to try to steady her nerves when she spotted them across the restaurant... it didn't work. She did relax somewhat when Luca placed her hand in his. "Are you sure you want to do this?" Luca whispered. Looking up at him from under her long lashes she replied just as quietly, "No, but I owe it to Kevin."

"Hey guys," Presley said as she approached the table where the couple sat.

'Hey, Pres," Kevin said as he rose from his seat and placed a light kiss on her cheek. "What's up Luca?" Kevin asked.

"Not much man. How are you?"

"Alright. Luca, this Jimmy. Jimmy... Luca." Kevin said motioning between the two guys. "Nice to meet you," Luca said as he shook Jimmy's hand.

"Likewise, How are you Presley?" Jimmy asked, barely looking at her.

"I'm okay. How's school?" Presley asked as Luca pulled out her chair.

"Keeps me busy." Jimmy responded still not looking at her.

"Where do you go to school?" Luca asked placing a hand on Presley's thigh under the table. He found that touching her even in a small way seemed to calm her. Because he found it increasingly harder to keep his hands off her he didn't mind doing it as often as she needed.

"NC State."

"What are you studying?" Luca was trying to keep the conversation going so Presley didn't feel the pressure of making small talk.

"Large animal vet," Jimmy replied

"That's interesting. I have heard they have a pretty good veterinary program there."

"Presley, did you find a prom dress?" Kevin asked trying to pull Presley into the conversation.

"Um yeah. Steph, took me to Brie's."

"Well, what does it look like?" Kevin asked.

Presley smiled just thinking about the dress she had purchased today, "it's red and strapless It..." she was saying when Jimmy interrupted her.

"Kevin tells me you're from Italy. What's it like over there?" Jimmy asked Luca, ignoring Presley at the same time. Presley looked down at her hands trying not to make it so noticeable that her feelings were hurt when Jimmy had so rudely interrupted her.

"It's different. For instance over there people usually wait until one person has finished speaking before they begin," Luca said as he glared at Jimmy. Presley placed her hand over his hand on her thigh, and shook her head. ***Don't it's okay*** she thought knowing he would hear her. His temper began to recede when she touched his hand until he heard Jimmy's thoughts ***Stupid bitch always has somebody coming to her rescue.*** Luca didn't want to let that slide but he knew there was no way to call him out on it. Feeling the tension in the air Kevin spoke up," This was a bad idea, let's just call it a night."

"No, Jimmy may not like me, and that's fine, but we both care about you, Kevin. I'm sure we can have a nice dinner. Right Jimmy?" She asked looking at Jimmy with her eyes practically begging him to agree. Jimmy was silent for a second then with a forced smiled he said, "Yeah, I'm sorry Presley that was rude. How was your day with Stephanie?"

Kevin knew that Jimmy's feelings towards Presley wouldn't change right way but he was glad he was willing to try, or at least pretend.

"It was fun. I was worried that I wouldn't be able to find a dress this close to prom but Stephanie came through."

"That girl does have mad shopping skills." Jimmy laughed and the tension in the air stared to disintegrate.

"You know it!" They all turned to see Marcus and Stephanie approaching the table.

After Marcus and Stephanie arrived at the table the waitress came to take their orders. Once their orders were placed the group began talking and laughing like they always did and Jimmy was hanging right there with them. Throughout dinner the tension in the air began to fade, there were even moments where Presley and Jimmy found themselves not only agreeing on things but laughing and joking like old friends. When dinner came to an end Presley looked over at Kevin who had on arm over the back of Jimmy's chair and a huge grin on his face. She smiled at the sight and almost forgot why she had been so nervous go to dinner until Jimmy asked her if she would step outside with him alone for a minute. She agreed after reassuring Luca with her thoughts that everything would be fine.

Presley and Jimmy walked out the double doors of the restaurant leaving four very nervous friends behind them.

"I think we should clear the air a little bit." Jimmy said as he pushed his hands into the front pockets of his neatly pressed khaki pants. Presley noticed that the olive green polo he wore brought out his hazel eyes nicely. The warm evening air blew his shaggy sandy blonde hair as they walked.

"I think you're right." she said as she removed the black rubber band from around her wrist and placed her hair in a low ponytail to keep the wind from blowing her hair in her eyes.

The two sat on a bench close to the restaurant doors.

"Jimmy, I never meant to come between you and Kevin. I know now I was being selfish last time you were here but I didn't mean to and I didn't realize I was doing it at the time."

"I get it. I'm the one that was being selfish. I love Kevin but I'm not always sure how he feels about me so I guess I was just jealous of how openly he shows his love for you." Jimmy said grabbing Presley's hand.

"He loves you Jimmy he's just scared. He hasn't been in a serious relationship before… it's new to him."

"I know it would be easier if I didn't live so far away and I am glad he has you. I promise I'll try not to let my insecurities cause another problem between the two of us."

"Okay and I'll try to share better," she laughed and squeezed his hand.

"Deal!' Jimmy said and pulled her into a hug. Just then they heard Stephanie gasp behind them, "OMG...this is a total Mastercard moment.... Priceless!" Presley just smiled and kissed Jimmy's cheek.

"Now that everybody's all buddy buddy again, what are we going to do for the rest of the night?" Stephanie asked.

"We can all go to my house, play some pool or something," Luca said as he pulled Presley up off the bench she was sitting on and into his chest.

"I need to go home. I promised my parents I wouldn't be out late. I'm leaving tomorrow and they want us to spend some time with them," Jimmy said. Kevin sat down on the bench next to him and intertwined his fingers with his. Looking at Kevin he added "They would like you to come over for coffee and dessert."

"Um....Okay. We can do that." Kevin said.

"Are you coming back next weekend for prom?" Marcus asked Jimmy.

"No, I have finals the following week and I have to study."

"That sucks!" Stephanie stated a little louder then she had intended.

"Yeah it does. Are you still going, Kevin?" Marcus asked while wrapping his arms around Stephanie's waist and resting his chin on her shoulder.

"I doubt it." Kevin said right before Presley jumped in and said "You have to go!" as her black boot stomped the ground.

"Pres, you have to stop the foot stomping girl, really." Marcus said laughing at his friend's childish display. He knew she wasn't a spoiled brat who flung tantrums but occasionally they would slip out. All five of her friends laughing just increased when she crossed her arms in front of her chest and displayed on over the top pout on her lips.

When the laughter finally died down Kevin said, 'Maybe I'll go with y'all to dinner and meet up with you after but I have no desire to go to the actual prom." With a huff Presley responded, "I guess that's okay."

"I'll call you guys tomorrow," Kevin said as he and Jimmy headed towards Jimmy's silver Chevy Impala.

"Bye Jimmy!" they all shouted.

"Bye, guys I'll be back in a couple weeks." He waved as he climbed into his car.

When Jimmy's car was out of the parking lot Presley let out a deep breath and said, "Wow, that went better than I thought. I mean I knew we could be civil but I didn't expect him to actually try to be my friend."

"Sweetheart, be careful with him, please" Luca said as he squeezed Presley's body against his.

"Why?" She asked as she tilted her head up to look at him.

He pulled the black rubber band out of her hair releasing her red streaked hair so he could run his fingers through it.

"I could hear his thoughts, honey, he is being nice because of Kevin but his feelings for you haven't changed. They have softened slightly but he still thinks of you as an obstacle to what he wants." Presley's lips morphed into a frown as she leaned her head back against his chest. "I guess I should have known that." she said and felt the tears forming in her eyes.

"Baby, it's not a lost cause. He'll come around just be careful." He ran his fingers through her hair until he found his favorite red streak.

"Okay "she agreed barely over a whisper.

As Marcus sat quietly with his arms still wrapped tightly around Stephanie's waist he placed a gentle kiss on her neck. He watched Luca comfort Presley and felt a sense of satisfaction seeing the love between his two friends flow so easily. He had always considered himself a fill-in big brother to Presley. He did his best to protect her and keep her happy and between himself and their other two friends they did a semi-decent job; but they were no replacement for love. He had been worried since Eric died that he may never see his friend happy and in love again but as he witnessed Luca wrapping her in his big arms and soothing away her pain he knew he had worried for nothing. He would never say it out loud but he had never seen her so happy and loved not even with Eric.

"Let's go back to my house, okay." Luca said.

"Okay," she said softly and they got into his car. Stephanie and Marcus got into his newly acquired Mustang and they all headed to Luca's house

Chapter Twenty Seven

"WAKE UP!! Presley wake up, Baby!" Luca shouted as Stephanie and Marcus came rushing into his bedroom. Presley was thrashing and crying in her sleep. Her whole body was covered in sweat.

"What's going on?" Marcus's shouted while Stephanie stood beside him with her hand covering her open mouth.

"I don't know. She just started throwing herself around and I can't get her to wake up." Luca said sounding more afraid then anyone would imagine a vampire could. Just as they were all beginning to panic Presley's eyes popped open and she sat straight up. She looked at each concerned face in the room then around the room itself. When her eyes landed on the digital clock next to the bed the red numbers displayed 4:14 am. "Oh, my God, I have to go home!!!" she yelled and tried to get out of bed. Luca grabbed both of her shoulders to stop her. His eyes were black and his white fangs reflected the light from the full moon that shone through the window. "Are you okay?" he asked her. His hands were still trembling from the fear he experienced when he saw her body convulsing. He had felt so helpless when he was unable to wake her.

"I'm fine but I won't be when I get home at four o'clock in the morning." Presley said with a look of total confusion on her face. "How did I get up here?" she asked, realizing she was in

Luca's room. The last thing she remembered was lying on his couch listening to Stephanie complain about watching Fast and Furious.

"You fell asleep watching the movie. I texted your mom and told her you were staying with me. Luca brought you up here." Stephanie said the concern in her voice was very apparent. Presley looked down at her body and realized she was in one of Luca's t-shirts. When she looked up at Luca he pushed aside the hair that was clinging to the sweat on her face. "Are you okay?" he asked again.

"I don't know. I had a bad dream but I don't remember anything. I don't remember coming up here or changing or my dream." Looking at her body again and at Luca's bare chest she asked, "We didn't did we?" Both Marcus and Stephanie's heads snapped over to look at Luca. He laughed and cupped her face with both hands and said, "No, and not to sound cocky but if we had, I promise you'd remember!" Marcus and Stephanie both snickered a little. Presley let out a sigh of relief, although her cheeks were crimson red from her body heat...and embarrassment.

"You don't remember anything about your dream?" Luca asked. "You scared the crap out of me.

"I...I..don't...I just remember being scared and I don't remember anything else." She said as she leaned into Luca's chest and he wrapped his arms around her. Once he had her securely in his arms he felt his fangs retract and the vampire in him recede. She was safe in his arms and he needed her safe.

"Presley, what happened" Stephanie asked as she climbed onto Luca's bed and pulled at the shirt Presley was wearing. As she moved the shirt they all noticed five slash marks through the shirt and blood coming from Presley's skin under the shirt.

"Jeez, girl, were you dreaming about Freddy Kruger?" Marcus asked as he ran his hands over the bed sheets that had slashes identical to the ones on Presley's shirt. Presley's eyes were as big as saucers when she lifted her hands to see her fingertips stained with blood, her blood. She couldn't speak…she just stared at her fingertips. Her nails were barely past her fingertips, there was no way she could have done this to herself.

"Luca, what's going on?" Marcus asked, his eyes were wide with fear.

"I don't know!" Luca replied, feeling the fear he thought was gone crash over him like a violent wave.

"Can vampires, like get in your dreams? I mean could Andrew, or that Ivy chick, have something to do with this?" Stephanie asked as tears began to fall from her emerald eyes. All she wanted, all she's ever wanted, was to keep Presley and her friends safe but how could she save them from their dreams?

"No they can't. There's no way Andrew or Ivy could have done this," Luca said quietly racking his brain for anything to explain what had happened.

"God, I feel like I'm in a bad 80s horror movie!" Stephanie yelled as she hugged herself. Seeing fear take hold of the girl he loved, Marcus rushed to her and pulled her into a tight embrace.

"Luca, I'm scared," Presley said as her blue eyes began to almost glow with the moisture filling them. When the first tear fell Luca wiped it away with his thumb and pulled her on to his lap.

"I'll figure this out, Baby, I swear," he said hoping he could keep that promise.

"I'm so tired but I'm afraid to sleep. I don't even remember the dream but the thought of closing my eye terrifies me," she said as she wept.

"We aren't going to be able to figure anything out tonight. Marcus take Steph and go try to sleep. Presley lay down, I'll be right here. I'll stay awake and watch you. If it happens again I'll wake you up, okay?" He said trying to take charge of the situation and trying to make his love feel safe. Although they all knew sleep was out of the question they did as Luca requested.

Marcus closed the door behind him after he and Stephanie entered his room. Stephanie slumped down onto the bed and covered her face with her hands as her elbows rested on her knees. He sat down next to her and put his arm around her shoulders. "Are you going to be okay?" he asked softly lifting her face so she was looking directly into his eyes.

"I don't know. I'm scared for her. I mean when is she going to get a break? How can she possibly take anymore crap? Every time something good happens something bad follows," she said wiping the tears from her face. "She manages to survive the car accident when nobody thought she would. She doesn't even have any visible scars. Then Eric dies and so does the dumb ass who was more worried about texting his friend than paying attention to where he was going. She finds out her dad, who raised her and who she loves so much, is not her dad and he quits talking to her! Her mom is so wrapped up in her own pain that she only works nights so she doesn't have to face the lonely nights alone. However, she is leaving Presley alone to face the darkness and unanswered questions. She and Kevin become best friends but then she has to deal with the Jimmy drama. Presley closes herself off to everybody except Kevin, you and me. Along comes Luca and she finds happiness and love again. Now that is tainted by some crazy ass vampires hell bent on ruling the world. Are we surprised she can't sleep? I mean really, all this in one year! How can she possibly handle all this?" She finishes, barely taking a breath as the words tumble out of her mouth. Marcus was rubbing her back wishing he could take away her fear, yet at the same time falling more in love with her as he hears her speak of her love and concern for their friend. All he could say was, "We'll get her through this, no matter what it takes." Falling into a comfortable silence the two climbed under the overstuffed comforter on his bed and held each other...both lost in their own thoughts and worried about not only Presley, but each other, too.

Luca was lying in his bed with his arm around Presley as she slept with her head on his chest. He repeatedly ran his hand down the back of her hair. He was so angry, so mad because she was scared and there was nothing he could do to help her. She had laid in the bed for over an hour fighting sleep before it finally took over. He was going through every bit of information he had obtained over his long life trying to find any explanation for what Presley had experienced earlier that morning. He was drawing a blank. He would call his father in the morning and, maybe Wendy, a witch he had known for more years then he could count. He hadn't realized how long he had been lost in thought until he saw the sun coming up over the horizon. His breath caught in his throat when he saw how beautiful Presley was when the morning light hit her skin. His attention was drawn away from his favorite sight when he heard his bedroom door open. Marcus stuck his head through the small opening between the door and the wall. "How is she?" he asked.

"Finally asleep."

"Good. Do you need anything?"

"Can you sit in here for a couple minutes? I'm going to start some coffee and breakfast but I don't want her to be alone."

"Yeah, I can do that. Stephanie's already down stairs starting coffee but she'll need help with breakfast." Marcus said as he entered the room and walked over to a chair next to the bed. Luca slowly moved from under Presley's sleeping body.

"I'll be back up in 15 to 20 minutes," he whispered and left the room.

When Luca entered the kitchen Stephanie was standing at the counter leaning on it with her elbows and covering her face. Feeling him walk in the door she raised her head to look at him.

Her eyes where swollen due to lack of sleep and a whole lot of crying.

"No offense but you look like I feel," he said running both hands through his hair.

"Oh, I know. How is she?" she asked, sipping her steaming cup of coffee.

"She's still sleeping. She fought it for over an hour but finally fell asleep a couple of hours ago." After he poured his coffee he walked over to the fridge and searched for something to make his friends for breakfast.

"Did you sleep at all?" she asked as she hopped up on a bar stool next to the kitchen counter.

"Nope. What do you want for breakfast?"

"How are you even up much less thinking about cooking with no sleep?"

He laughed for a second and responded, "With everything you seem to know about vampires I'm surprised you asked that question."

"Oh yea, lack of sleep has my brain on strike."

"How about bacon and eggs?" he asked shaking his head.

"Sure. Do you have any idea what happened last night?" she asked, taking another big sip of her coffee.

"I have no idea. I've searched my brain all night and have come up with nothing."

"There's no way she could have done that to herself, is there? I mean her nails aren't long enough right?"

"You're right. I'm going to make some calls today and see what I can come up with but we've got to keep her from freaking out," he said as he cracked eggs into a large clear bowl.

"We'll just hang out here today. The hard part is going to be when it's time to go back to school or when she has to sleep at home by herself. I don't know how she'll handle those things."

"She won't have to. I'm not going to let that happen," he stated frankly as he scrambled the eggs.

"You let me know how Brenda handles that," she laughed and started separating slices of bacon.

"She won't know and even if she does, I don't care. I'm not leaving her alone at night ever again."

"Okay but I can help, too, you know. I mean my parents are gone for another two weeks so I can stay with her."

"Are your parents ever home?" he asked then thought about what he had said, "I'm sorry that was rude. I'm just a little on edge."

"Nope they're not, but I'm used to it," Stephanie said as she handed him a plate of separated raw bacon. "You have fun down here. I'm going to go take a shower and try to wake up."

"Alright it should be ready in ten minutes."

Luca had finished cooking breakfast and was placing the food on plates when Marcus came into the kitchen.

"Smells great man," Marcus said as he walked over to the coffee pot rubbing his hand over his bare washboard abs.

"Is she still asleep?" Luca asked handing Marcus a plate of food.

"No, she's awake but wanted to change her clothes. I thought maybe I should let her do that alone," Marcus said with a mouth full of bacon.

"Yeah that's probably a good choice."

Luca left the kitchen and headed upstairs with a plate of food in one hand and a cup of coffee loaded with cream and sugar, just the way Presley liked it, in his other hand. When he reached the door he lightly knocked on it with his knuckle.

"Come in." He heard Presley say from the other side of the door. Following her instructions he carefully opened the door successfully avoiding spilling any food or coffee. Presley was sitting on the corner of the bed she had just made still wearing his extra-large shirt but she had added her holey American Eagle skinny jeans. She was pulling her hair into a messy bun when Luca placed her food on the nightstand next to the bed.

"How are you feeling this morning?" he asked and went to sit next to her.

"Different. I mean I'm still a little freaked out about the dream but I feel good... really good. It's weird," she said fidgeting with one of the tears in her jeans.

"You scared me. Do you remember anything about the dream?" he asked pulling her into his lap.

"I...I do remember a little but I can't make sense of it," she said cuddling her face into the spot where his neck met his shoulder.

"What do you remember?" he asked stroking her hair.

"Well, I was standing in a black room and felt like something was trying to crawl out of my body. I guess that's why I scratched myself." She rubbed her hands over her belly where those claw marks now stretched across her skin. "I'm sure it's just stress or something," she said trying to reassure him, as well as herself, that everything was going to be okay.

"I was thinking I should call my dad or my friend Wendy about all of this," he said still stroking her hair.

"Wendy? Who's Wendy?" she asked surprising herself with the jealousy she heard in her own voice. Luca just laughed and lightly tugged her hair so that she was looking right into his eyes. "Wendy is just a friend I've had for almost 80 years. Trust me when I say you have nothing to worry about," then he kissed her firmly on the lips.

"You know I was never a jealous person before I met you. Now I can't stand the sound of another girl's name on your lips."

"I know the feeling," he said squeezing her tightly.

"So is Wendy a vampire?"

"No, she's a witch," he said waiting for her to freak out about yet another supernatural story coming to life, but she didn't. She simply looked at him and made an *"oh"* motion with her mouth.

"Look, I really don't think you need to call anybody. I know everybody's worried but I really think it was just a very bad dream, nothing more. If we are going to spend our time worrying about something it should be the real life vampires that are planning the demise of the human race as we know it." Presley figured if she kept telling people that her nightmare meant nothing, that it was just a dream maybe she, too, would start to believe it. She did, however, have an aching suspicion that wasn't the case.

"You hungry?" Luca asked as he pointed to the food that remained untouched sitting on the nightstand.

"Actually, I'm starving," she said getting out of his lap and walking toward the plate. After several bites of food and numerous sips of coffee Presley's phone began to beep signaling an incoming text message. When she looked at her phone and saw the message was from her mother she began to mentally brace herself for what she was sure would be a message demanding she come home. She knew there would be threats of punishment because Stephanie failed to mention they were sleeping at her boyfriend's house. She was surprised when she read it.

Brenda: Good morning sweetheart. Hope you and Stephanie had fun. I have some bday shopping to do b4 work so I'm leaving I probably won't see you till tomorrow. Luv u

Presley felt pangs of guilt hit her stomach like lightning strikes. Her mom had always trusted her. She had spent months punishing her mother for lying to her yet now she was lying to her mother. Her eyes began to burn with the urge to cry because not only was she feeling guilty but also because she realized she never saw her mother anymore. It was almost like she was doing the same thing her father was doing, avoiding the cause of their family's erosion.

"What's wrong, baby? Who is that?"

"My mom. She was just letting me know that she was gone for the day and I wouldn't see her till tomorrow." She forced the tears back and gently placed the phone on the bed. What she really wanted to do was throw it across the room or out of a window.

"Are you okay?"

"God, please quit asking me that!" she yelled as she shot to her feet. "I'm fine. I will be better when people quit treating me like some damn porcelain doll that's going to break any second!" she said in more of a growl then a yell.

Luca held his hands up in surrender. "I'm sorry. You just looked upset." he said as he slowly walked toward her.

Just then the bedroom door flew open and Marcus and Stephanie stood in the doorway. "Is everything okay?' Stephanie asked frantically.

"I have to get out of here!" Presley yelled as she rushed past her two friends and headed down the stairs. She didn't have her car there, as usual, so she stormed out of the back door and headed to the wooded trails behind Luca's house.

"What the hell happened?" Marcus said while looking completely lost by Presley's sudden outburst.

"A couple things actually." Luca said while walking toward the window in his room that looked out to the woods behind his house. As he watched Presley stomping into the woods he continued, "We are smothering her with all our concern. Making her feel like a child. Then her mom texted her to tell her that, once again, she would be gone all day. Presley thinks she is trying to avoid her." He turned to his friends who were now completely in his room. "She feels like she causes problems for everybody she loves. Blaming herself for us being up all night worried. Taking all the blame for her family falling apart and for the Kevin and Jimmy situation." When he finished speaking Stephanie was shaking her head. "Did she tell you all that?" she asked as an angry feeling washed over her at the thought of Presley feeling she was to blame for any of those things.

"No, but I could hear her thoughts," Luca answered her as he shuffled through the clothes in the dresser.

"You need to go find her before she gets her stubborn ass lost out there!" Stephanie yelled, not intending to take her anger out on Luca...but he was there, so she did. Luca simply looked at her with a smirk on his all too handsome face. He began to pull out a pair of jeans and a Pearl Jam concert t shirt. "Hurry up what the hell are you waiting on!" she yelled again. Marcus came up behind her wrapping his arms around her waist he whispered into her ear, "Calm down and what's with the language lately?" She simply glared at him for a moment then turned her scowl back to Luca.

"I'll get her. I know exactly where she's going but I'm giving her a minute to cool down. She needs to be alone for a minute." Stephanie stomped over to him and jammed her finger repeatedly into his chest while she said "If anything happens to her or she gets lost I will personally cook your fine butt. Got me?" Luca laughed although he knew she was serious he also knew that he was doing the right thing. If Presley needed a minute to breathe and think he would give it to her. "I need to change can you step outside and save the threats for later?" he asked with that cocky grin he was known for displayed proudly on his face. "Fine, but don't test me, Dracula, I'm dead serious," she said as she and Marcus headed out the bedroom door.

About ten minutes later after tying the laces on his black boots Luca headed out the back door and down the wooded trail he had earlier watched Presley take. As he walked down the dirt path he thought about what he would say to Presley when he found her. He was concerned about her, he loved her and just wanted to take care of her. He needed to remember that she was strong and independent. He couldn't take that away from her while trying to protect her. He stopped in his tracks when he heard the silence. He was in the middle of the woods and there was not a sound, not a bird chirping, no sounds of leaves rustling under the feet of a small animal and no crickets chirping. The only time he ever remembered hearing nothing but silence in the woods was when there was a large, hungry or angry predator around. With that thought he took off at vampire speed to the spot he hoped she'd be.

Chapter Twenty Eight

Presley sat near the bank of the small pond where she and Luca had sat at a couple of nights earlier. While listening to the soothing sounds of the small waterfalls she was mentally scolding herself for storming out of a house that was filled with people who loved her. She was beginning to feel like her life was once again spinning out of control. She was trying to remember the last time she felt at peace and, with exception of a few fleeting moments with Luca and her friends, it had been a long time.

"It's my fault." She heard Luca's soothing, sexy voice coming from behind her. He had heard her thoughts and they had sent a feeling of guilt throughout his body. As she stood and spun around to look at him she saw he was inches from her face. "I'm sorry, Baby, I wish I could say I would have stayed away from you if I had known Andrew had followed me. That would be the noble thing for me to do, but it would have been a lie. I don't believe I could have stayed away from you even if I tried. My soul is drawn to you. I literally ache when I'm not with you. I know I'm hovering and I'm sorry. I can't help it, you are precious to me and I will do anything to keep you safe. Even if it means I drive you crazy."

Presley looked at her feet feeling even worst about her tantrum. "Luca, I understand you're worried but I think everybody's overreacting. We haven't even seen Andrew in like a week. I'm sure he was just trying to rattle your cage and last night was just a bad dream." Presley said still staring at her feet. Luca closed the distance between them and lifted her face till their eyes met.

"Sweetness, I get why you might think he's gone or not going to do anything but I know him, and I know Ivy. They're up to something and I won't let them hurt you. Please just bear with me a little bit longer. After I have dealt with them I will try to calm down my protective streak, okay?" Luca said softly while running his fingertips down the side of her face and then down her neck. Gazing into his blue eyes and feeling his fingertips grazing her skin she inhaled deeply and said, "Okay, but can we pretend like everything is normal for a little while? Just be... together."

"Yeah, let's do that. Come here." He grabbed her hand while lowering himself to the ground and she sat between his legs, leaning her slender back against his chiseled chest. He wrapped his arms around her tightly feeling her relax almost instantly. He also noticed that the more she relaxed the more life returned to the woods around them.

They had been sitting in silence, simply enjoying being together, when Luca leaned down and pressed his moist lips against the tender skin on her neck. "I love you, you know that right?" Presley simply nodded and leaned back closer to him. "I love you too," she whispered. Placing more light kisses down her neck he said, "And I know you're strong, it's just one of the many things I love about you."

"I don't feel strong. I feel like I've been a burden to my friends the past year. I mean, it's our senior year of high school and instead of enjoying themselves they've been taking care of me," she sighed. Before Luca could argue his phone began to ring.

"Hello."

"Did you find her?" Marcus asked anxiously.

"Yea. We'll be back in a little bit."

"Alright man, Steph and I are going to get my tux and run some other errands. We'll probably eat dinner out so we'll just see you guys tonight."

"Okay, have fun," Luca said ending the call.

"Marcus and Stephanie are going out," he said as he resumed kissing Presley's neck. "By the way," he said as he lightly tugged her earlobe with his teeth, "you are nobody's burden, your friends don't feel like they are taking care of you. They are supporting you because they love you. There is a loyalty among you four that I've never seen amongst any humans." Presley shifted herself to her knees and turned to face him. Running her fingers through his short dark hair she leaned down and kissed him. Pulling back only slightly she said, "You always know what to say, don't you?"

"I speak only the truth my love," he replied. Then quickly, but gently, rolled them over so she was lying on her back in the grass and he was between her knees. Without another word he kissed her in a way that could only be described as claiming. She wrapped her arms around his neck grabbing the hair on the back of his head in her fist. Luca broke the kiss momentarily to look at her. "You are unbelievable in every way, you're beautiful, you're smart, you're strong, you're perfect and you're mine," he said moving a strand of hair from her face. Before she could respond he claimed her mouth again. He stunned himself when he murmured through their kiss…"Mine." When she responded with one word, "Always," he felt a sense of satisfaction he had never known. He was a 200 year old vampire he'd had other lovers but never had he considered them 'his' and never had he considered a commitment of forever. With Presley that's what he wanted and he would accept nothing less. Before he could stop it his fangs lengthened and grazed her skin. He closed his eyes and tried to fight his primal urge to take a part of her into his body. He lost that fight when he heard her moan out the words, "Please, do it. I want you, too." He kissed her neck one more time then ran his tongue over the delicate skin his teeth would soon enter. His razor sharp teeth pierced her skin as he gave into their mutual desires. After the initial pain of her skin breaking a sense of pleasure she only knew when they shared these moments, filled every cell of her body. Presley didn't have much experience with the opposite sex. She had never done anything with a boyfriend that required clothing to be removed. However, she couldn't imagine anything being more intimate then Luca taking her blood, not even sex. She was giving him what he needed to live, she was taking care of him instead of him taking care of her and it gave her a sense of empowerment, a sense of being...not only wanted...but needed.

He pulled his teeth from her neck and glided the tip of his tongue over the two puncture wounds they had left. Normally he would have moved off of her body but he couldn't bring himself to do it, he needed to taste her again, not her blood…but her mouth. He pressed his lips back to hers, she then boldly slid her tongue into his mouth wanting to taste him as badly as he wanted her. She was then overcome with an urge she had never experienced before. She wanted to bite him, to taste him the way he had tasted her. She heard her voice in her mind telling her to claim him, that he belonged to her and she to him and she needed to claim him. Without thinking she bit his bottom lip. "Hmm, feeling feisty today, are we?" he said as he pulled away from her. "Sorry," she said as she lightly bit her own lower lip.

"Don't be, I think it's sexy," his own desire for her had grown when he felt her small ivory teeth pinch his lip. "However, I think maybe we should go back up to the house."

"Why?" she asked and poked out her lower lip, pouting.

"Because, mio amore, I'm holding on by a strand here to be a gentleman and every time something like this happens that strand gets weaker." He said as he rose to his feet and held his hand out to offer her assistance in getting up. Looking at his hand she replied, "What if I want the strand to break?"

"You don't and when it does it won't be on the ground in the woods." Knowing he was right she placed her hand in his and allowed him to pull her to her feet.

"You just have to be so perfect, don't you?" she smirked at him over her shoulder as she began to walk away from him. He quickly grabbed her hips and pulled her back into his chest whispering in her ear, "This hurts me more than it does you…trust me." Presley responded with a giggle and the two headed back to his house.

∞

Luca was awakened by the sounds of tires getting closer to his house. He looked down at Presley's sleeping body spread out on his couch. He glanced over at the antique clock that hung on the wall across from the couch. The hands on the clock displayed 6:17. The two of them had apparently fallen asleep watching TV. He wasn't surprised considering what had happened the previous night. He did, however, wonder who was approaching his house. He figured it was too early for Marcus to be returning home. He moved from behind Presley and placed a blanket over her. Then he walked to the door opening it before whoever was there had a chance to wake up Presley. When he stepped on to his front porch he inhaled the fresh air and waited for his visitor to arrive. To his relief it was just Kevin. He didn't know why he was worried it would be anyone else ***It's not like Andrew is just going to drive up to your house idiot*** he thought shaking his head at his own paranoia.

"Hey Kevin."

"Hey Luca. Is everybody here?" he asked holding three pizzas in his hands.

"No. Just me and Presley but she's sleeping. We fell asleep watching some show that had a lot of screaming women and some dancing kids. I don't know what the hell it was supposed to be!" Luca said opening the door and Kevin walked in laughing. "She got you to watch Dance Moms, man, you've got it bad." Luca just laughed and nodded his head.

The two boys entered the living room where Presley still lay sleeping. Kevin placed the stack of pizzas on the coffee table and sat in the Lazy-Boy recliner next to couch. Luca lifted Presley's feet and sat underneath them, resting her sock clad feet on his lap. Listening to her heartbeat and breathing pattern he determined she was still asleep, so he directed his attention back to Kevin. "How were things with Jimmy when he left?"

Taking a deep breath with a smile, which could only be compared to a child's smile on Christmas morning, plastered on his face he answered, "Actually, really good. We hashed things out. Put all of our cards on the table and decided to put more of an effort into being together."

"Good, I'm happy for you. Do you think he'll ever accept Presley?"

"I hope so. He said he was going to try to be more understanding about our relationship. The only thing that really worries me is apparently it's not just my relationship with Presley that bothers him but my relationship with Marcus and Stephanie as well."

"Look, I don't know the guy all that well and I am most likely about to cross a line here but let me give you some advice," Luca said rubbing his forehead.

"Okay," Kevin said with nervousness apparent in his voice.

"You and your friends have a bond I've never seen before. I know you care about Jimmy but don't let him cost you your friends."

"I don't just care about him, I love him. I mean what would you do if you and Presley were in our situation?" Kevin asked.

"I love Presley and the only thing that is more important to me than her happiness is her safety. So I would never ask her to give up you guys and if Jimmy truly loves you he won't ask you to give up your friends."

"I know, I don't think he will. I think the problem is my inability to multitask. I can't seem to do what Presley does. I mean you know how deeply she loves you right?"

"Yes," Luca said as his gaze fell back upon Presley's sleeping face.

"See, I mean she has been able to remain a great friend to Marcus, Stephanie and me without sacrificing time with you. I couldn't do that with Jimmy. I really didn't try. I was so worried about her that I focused all my attention on her and none on my relationship with Jimmy," Kevin said slouching back in the recliner.

"Don't be so hard on yourself man. She needed you and you did what a good friends does. I mean it's not like she was just having a bad day or dealing with normal teenage drama. Her world was falling apart and Jimmy should have cut you some slack. Actually he should cut her some slack, too. If anybody has a right to be upset about this situation it's you."

"Me? How do you figure that?" Kevin asked leaning forward and resting his forearms in his knees.

"He put you in a position to feel like you had to choose between being there for the people whom you care about when they need you most and spending time with him, he should have never put you in that position." Luca finished and Kevin sat silently letting what Luca had said settle into his thoughts.

"I don't know. All I do know is that for things to work out between Jimmy and me it is going to take a lot of work from both of us. I really don't want to talk about it right now. I feel like it is all I've talked about, and thought about, all weekend," Kevin said reaching for a slice of pizza.

"I bet. Do you realize you and I haven't been alone since you found out what I am and what you could be, do you want to talk about that?" Luca asked spreading his arms across the back of the couch.

"To be honest I've been trying not to think about that this weekend. You know one problem at a time. But now that you mention it I guess I just want to know what it's like." Kevin had been avoiding the topic but after making progress with Jimmy and realizing things aren't usually as bad as you think they are, he figured he would spend a little time thinking about the vampire thing. He thought if he could dissect the problem and break down the pros and cons it may help him make his decision.

Luca took in a deep breath and searched his mind for a way to explain being a vampire to the teenage boy sitting before him. "That's a hard question to answer." He exhaled loudly, "I mean it is what you make it. You can remain the good person you are or you can let the abilities that come along with it turn you into a monster fit for nightmares. It opens some doors that before might never have been an option but it can close doors to the some of the things you want most. It can rid you of fears you thought you would never get past but it can give you new fears about things you never knew so you never feared. Do you get what I'm saying?"

"What doors does being immortal close? I would think it would open every door." Kevin said glad that he and Luca had the opportunity to talk alone, especially without Stephanie and her glamorized view on the whole vampire thing. He wanted the truth, the good, the bad and the ugly.

"Well, it does open a lot of doors, but mainly it closes the doors on the people you can have in your life and really the jobs you can do. You can only stay in one place for a short time after you turn. Which limits the relationships you can develop. You can't really start a career because your resume would show you with more experience than an 18 year old kid could have. I mean there are ways around some stuff; we all have social security numbers and stuff. You can only use that identification info for so long before you have to start over. I don't really know how to explain but you pretty much have to start a new life every five years or so unless you decide to live in a predominantly supernatural area."

"Okay, I get that. What about the fear thing? I mean what in world would you possibly fear?"

"A lot actually. I was scared to death to tell Presley what I was. I could have easily lost her because of it. So there is the fear of humans you care about being afraid of you. Then there are other supernatural beings out there that can throw that immortality thing out the window."

"There are more out there?" Kevin asked. Kevin knew it was stupid to believe that humans and vampires were the only things out there. If vampires existed he should have known there was a good possibility that other things he thought where only in works of fiction could exist as well.

"Yeah man, I hate to tell you but there are a lot more out there than you may think...werewolves, witches, warlock, wizards and fairies. None of them are what you see in movies. For instance, fairies are a lot bigger than Tinkerbell." Luca laughed as he thought about the misconceptions humans had about supernatural beings.

"Werewolves seriously? Dude I have had nightmares about those things for as long as I can remember. Please tell me they aren't like those big nasty things in Underworld."

"No they are actually very beautiful. They look a lot like natural wolves but bigger. They don't go out eating people but if you infringe on their territory or mess with their mates they can be ruthless. A werewolf could end my immortality in the blink of an eye." Luca said with a shiver.

"Have you met any?" Kevin was never into paranormal stuff, so he was surprised how fascinated he was by the information Luca was giving him.

"One, but it was before I turned. He was an Alpha my dad was working with to create a treaty between the supernatural species."

"If you had it to do again would you turn?"

"I was born a vampire I didn't have a choice but if I did yes, I would. I've had a great life and I've seen things most people never will. If I wasn't a vampire. I would have died at 18. Who wants to do that?" Luca said without hesitation. Just as he finished speaking Presley began to stir, slowly opening her eyes.

"Do I smell pizza?" she asked in a childlike voice.

"Yes," she heard Kevin say from the recliner behind her head.

"Kevin! Hey, how did it go?" She asked jumping from the couch and into his lap. She pressed a kiss on his cheek and he laughed at her excitement.

"It went good. Things aren't perfect but we're working on it," Kevin said as Presley reached for a slice of pizza but remained on his lap. She wanted to ask him if Jimmy had said anything about her. Since she knew this was about Kevin and Jimmy and Jimmy's opinion of her wasn't relevant so she didn't want to make it an issue.

"I heard you have been torturing poor Luca." Kevin laughed as he nodded his head in Luca's direction. Presley's first thought was that Luca had told him about their experience in the woods but she quickly remembered he wasn't the type to kiss and tell. With a look of confusion on her face she asked, "What are you talking about?"

"You made the poor guy watch Dance Moms. I bet that was the longest hour of his long life!" Presley lightly smacked Kevin's chest and glared at Luca when both boys started to laugh. A smile spread across Presley's face, this is what she wanted, her boyfriend and her best friend sitting in the living room laughing and joking. No talking about crazy vampires or nightmares.

∞

About two hours after Kevin's arrival he and Presley decided to head to her house where Kevin would again be spending the night. After entering Presley's house they headed straight up to her bedroom and got ready for bed. Once they were each comfortable on their side of the bed Presley laid her head on Kevin's chest. "I love you," she said sounding almost sad. "I love you too, Babe. Is something wrong?" he asked noticing that her voice was laced with sadness. "Nothing really, I just wanted you to know. Things have gotten a little nuts and I have a bad feeling it's about to get worst so I wanted you to know." Wrapping his arm around Presley he pulled her close, "It's just pre-prom jitters." He laughed and then added, "I mean you are going with a vampire." Presley joined in his laughter. Once the laughter stopped the two settled into the sleep they both desperately needed.

Chapter Twenty Nine

The week seemed to fly by and before Presley knew it was Friday night, the night before prom, was there. Her red dress was hanging on the back of her closet door. She looked at her dress and, instead of feeling the excitement most girls feel the night before their senior prom, she had an overwhelming sense of dread. She had tried to avoid everybody, especially Luca, all day she didn't want them to pick up on her feelings and she knew they would. Luca could, of course, read her thoughts and Stephanie seemed to be so in-tuned with Presley's feelings lately she almost wondered if she could also read her mind. She sat alone in her room for the first time in weeks, actually more like months. She had convinced her friends she had a lot of prom preparations to do and would just see them when they picked her up at 6pm the next day. They weren't very happy about it but finally relented when she pointed out that she wasn't a baby and was perfectly capable of being home alone. Luca insisted that no matter what she would only leave the house to go to her hair appointment and then straight home. He was overcome with the same sense of dread she was feeling. There had been a dark cloud over them since Andrew had made his presence known, the cloud just seemed to get bigger and darker the closer they got to prom. Wanting to get her mind off her own crazy reality she grabbed a book and settled in bed, reading had always been her way to decompress and relax. Getting lost in a fictional story of love, mystery or the paranormal always took her mind off her own problems. Since she had been dealing with entirely too much of her own paranormal drama she choose a trashy romance novel. Of course, it was a paranormal trashy romance but there were no crazy vampires in it so it would do.

∞

John Kluttz exited Mercy General Hospital through the staff exit around midnight. It was his weekend to pull second shift in the ER. He always hated when he worked in the ER because the chances that he would run into Brenda, his ex-wife, greatly increased. He tried to avoid her at all cost but this weekend it was essential that he not see her, he wasn't sure if he could control his temper if he did. This weekend Presley turned eighteen and he wasn't there. He knew he was being selfish by staying away from her but he couldn't get past his wife's deception. He loved Brenda, the family they had, and life they had built together but she threw it all away. Not only had she cheated, they could have gotten past that, but she lied to him for seventeen years. He was so hurt he drowned himself in work and avoided anything that reminded him of what he had lost, especially the daughter he loved so dearly. He was so consumed with his own thoughts he didn't realize he was being followed until he felt a hard blow to the back of his head. When his face came into contact with the pavement of the parking lot he lost all consciousness.

Within minutes of John being attacked his co-worker, Mark, was heading home and found him lying face down in the parking lot. The back of his head was red with blood from the impact, his face was in its own puddle of blood from the sudden stop on the pavement. Mark quickly grabbed his cell phone and called the front desk of the ER to send out EMTs and he followed that phone call with one to the police. Mark looked around the empty parking lot frantically while he spoke to the police, looking for any sign of who could have done this to his friend. When the EMTs joined him beside John's body, he watched in horror as they lifted John's still unconscious body from the pavement. The damage to John face was so extensive that when Mark saw it he had to turn away to vomit. Once his body was on the gurney John was rushed through the ER doors followed by his concerned colleague.

∞

Andrew lit a cigarette as he stood on the roof top of the hospital admiring the beautiful, yet deadly, woman who had stolen his heart. As he looked at her, Ivy watched with a smug grin as the human medical staff rushed her victim through the hospital doors. She knew he wouldn't die, she didn't want him to die, if he did it would ruin her plan. She had been watching all the people that surrounded Luca's new found love interest. She knew without a doubt that unless John Kluttz was to die nobody would tell Presley what had happened to him because they wouldn't want to ruin her prom. Their soft spot for the human girl that had become Luca's only weakness was going to work to her advantage. "It's all coming together," she said turning to face Andrew. With a look of disgust she added, "When are you going to quit that crap? It's disgusting." Andrew knew she was talking about his smoking, she made it very clear she despised the habit. Taking a long drag of his cigarette and exhaling it slowly he responded, "It's not like it's going to kill me."

"Yeah, well, the smell kills me." she said as she grabbed the cigarette he had put back in his mouth and extinguished it with the tip of her red high heeled boot.

"Why'd you do that?" he asked with a huff.

"I have to smell you and I don't want to smell cigarettes so you're quitting. Starting now," she said reaching for the pack he kept in the back pocket of his faded jeans. Before she could get the pack he grabbed her wrist and pulled her until she slammed into his rock hard chest. Tilting his face down till their noses were touching. He placed his hand on the back of her neck and kissed her fiercely. When he pulled back he said, "I'll cut down but I'm not quitting."

"We'll see," she smirked. "We need to get going, tomorrow's gonna be a big day." As she turned to leap off of the roof he grabbed her arm and spun her back to him. "Marry me," he said when he pulled her close. "What?" she asked honestly surprised by his statement.

"I love you. When this mess is done and the Davenports have been dealt with I want you to marry me," he said softly while lightly pulling on her black sleek ponytail. Ivy smiled sweetly and for a moment she felt the ice around her heart melt, not completely but enough to enjoy the moment. She loved Andrew. As mean and nasty as she was she still knew what love was and she loved him. He was her weakness which is why she knew Presley was Luca's. "Okay, but only if you quit smoking," she said and kissed him softly. "Deal!" he said with his mouth still on hers. They separated their lips but joined their hands and together jumped to the ground below.

∞

Brenda heard herself being paged to the ICU over the hospital intercom system. Figuring she was just needed to assist with a patient she headed quickly but calmly to the ICU wing of the hospital. She hurried through the numerous hallways all the while a sense of urgency began to fill her. The calmness she had felt was beginning to fade away although she was not sure why.

When she reached the ICU she saw Mark Russ standing next to one of the rooms. His pale face and expression sent Brenda into panic. "Mark, what's going on? What happened?" He grabbed her to keep her from entering the room.

"Brenda, it's John. He's been attacked," he said trying to remain calm.

"What? By who? Is he okay?" She knew asking if he was okay was a stupid question. If he was okay she wouldn't be standing in the middle of the ICU wing. Not waiting for his response she turned to enter the room but once again Mark stopped her. "You can't go in there. They are prepping him for surgery. They think he's going to be okay but they won't know until he regains consciousness after surgery. You need to call Brandon and Presley." Brenda thought for a moment as she leaned against the wall next to the room that held the man she once loved, the father of her son. "I can't call them yet," she said. Before Mark could argue she added, "I will after he's out of surgery. I don't know what to tell them till I know what's going on. Brandon lives eight hours away and if I call him he will come here now. It won't be safe for him to drive at night upset and thinking the worst. If I can tell him honestly that John will be okay he'll still come but he won't drive like a bat out of hell, with horrible thoughts running through his head, to get here."

"What about Presley?" Mark asked. He knew of their family problems but he also knew how close John and Presley once were and that they still loved each other very much. Brenda inhaled deeply and exhaled slowly before answering "I can't, not yet. I know you're going to think I'm being stupid and worried about trivial things but tomorrow is her prom. Her whole life has been a mess the past year. I want her to have that memory and if I call her she won't go, instead she will sit next to his hospital bed until he wakes up." Mark wanted to argue with her but having two teenage daughters himself he understood Brenda's thinking.

The two sat in silence until the door to John's room flew open and a group of hospital staff pushed the gurney that held John's body through the door and headed to the OR. Mark held Brenda when she began to sob at the sight of him so battered that he was almost unrecognizable.

∞

Ivy and Andrew arrived at the cabin they had been calling home since they arrived in the small North Carolina town shortly after leaving the hospital. Walking through the door Andrew asked, "Have you figured out how to get your hands on the blonde?"

"Yep," Ivy said and laid down on the bed on her stomach holding her chin in her hands.

"Care to share?" he asked as he joined her on the small bed.

Ivy adjusted herself so her body was snuggled close to his and her head rested on his chest. "I've been following her and found out her hair appointment is at 10. She's getting those hideous red streaks touched up and an up-do, so she should be finished between 12 and 1. I'm sure Luca will be watching her while she's out of the house. He's supposed to pick her up around 6. So he'll probably be there about 5:30. My window of opportunity is between 2 and 4:30. I'll trick her to get her out of the house and then snatch her," she said as if she was simply reading a grocery list.

"How are you going to get Luca here? He won't know you have her or where you are," he said while playing with her ponytail.

"I'll send you to tell him, before he leaves his house to go get her. You'll have him follow you and then we'll outnumber him," she said while drawing circles on his chest with her finger.

"I hope you know what you're doing."

Ivy's head popped up from his chest to meet his eyes. "You doubt my brilliant plan?" she said sounding almost hurt by his doubts in her.

"No, Babe, it's not that. I just feel like there is something big we're missing." He said and then decided to come clean with her about his suspicions about Presley. "There's something different about that girl. I can't put my finger on it but when Luca drank her blood his strength and power was beyond measure."

"Really, hum. Maybe she's his soul mate, isn't there some kind of lore about finding your soul mate giving you strength?"

"That's just a story. I don't believe it, I think it's something else and I would feel a lot better if we knew what it was."

"Don't you think Luca would know if she was supernatural or something?"

"I don't know. I mean if she is supernatural we would know right?" Andrew said still playing with her long ponytail. Both became distracted by their own thoughts. Ivy was piecing together her plan and trying to come up with any way it could go wrong. Andrew's thoughts were where they always were, on Ivy and what their life would be like once all this madness was over. He was content with just being with her but he knew the Davenports downfall would bring her happiness and he would do anything to give it to her.

∞

Two hours after the OR doors had closed they reopened. A tall blonde female doctor emerged from the operating room to talk with Brenda and Mark, who had both spent the past two hours pacing the short hallway.

"Kelly! How is he?" Brenda asked as she rushed toward the doctor with Mark at her heels.

"He's still unconscious. I think he'll be okay but we won't know the extent of the damage until he wakes up," Kelly replied pulling Brenda into a hug.

"When will he wake up?" Mark asked. He wasn't sure why he asked because being a doctor himself he knew what the answer would be. Sure enough Kelly responded to him with the same statement he had given hundreds of other families who had asked that question about their loved ones.

"Could be hours or days. I really don't know but we are keeping him in the ICU. We'll keep a close eye on him," Kelly smiled sadly at Brenda and headed down the hall followed by two nurses who were transporting John back to his room.

"Who would do this?" Brenda asked quietly in the now empty hall. Mark placed a reassuring hand her shoulder, "I don't know," he responded.

∞

Luca laid on his bed he wasn't trying to sleep because as a vampire he didn't require much rest. Instead he was trying to fight off the urge to camp out in Presley's front yard. He had reluctantly agreed to let her be by herself till it was time to go to the prom but he didn't like it. He knew something was bothering her, he knew she was afraid of something but neither of them knew exactly what it was. He was afraid, too, and that was not a feeling he had often so it was beginning to piss him off. He had talked to his father earlier that day and discovered that there had been no sign of Ivy there in days, which most likely meant she was with Andrew. Problem was Luca hadn't found where Andrew was hiding yet. He had been so convinced that he had to stay with Presley and their friends to keep them safe that he hadn't kept tabs on where Andrew was or what he was doing, now he was kicking himself for that.

Glancing at the clock he saw that it was 2 AM. He knew Presley would be leaving her house around 9:30 to get her hair done. He had already planned to follow her from a distance but he wasn't sure he could wait that long to see her. Again he felt a longing he had never felt before. He knew he loved her more than he had ever loved anybody but he never expected to crave her, not her blood but her. He craved the feeling he had just to be near her, holding her hand, twisting the adorable red streak in her hair around his fingers. His every thought and feeling had been consumed by only her since he saw a mere picture of her and now he felt he was on the verge of losing her. He knew if he didn't figure out Ivy's plan and stop it, it would cost him Presley. He refused to let that happen, he had been distracted for too long he had been selfish for too long. He should have put more effort into finding Andrew, he should have put a stop to it the night he found Andrew outside her house. He was so worried that if she saw him for what he truly was she would leave and because he gave in to that fear he may have cost her her life. Unable to fight his need to see her he left his home and headed toward her house. He opted to walk it would give him time to convince himself to stay out of sight, to just check on her and leave.

∞

Presley felt Luca's presence as soon as he stepped into her yard. She woke startled by the feeling and darted to her window. She scanned the back yard which her window faced and found him immediately. He was past the tree line and it was still dark she shouldn't have been able to see him but she could clear as day and when their eyes met he knew he had been caught. *You might as well come up* she thought shaking her head. She should have known he'd come to check on her. Truth be told she was glad he had. Ever since he had agreed to give her some time alone she had a persistent knot in her stomach and ache in her chest. Her dependency on him was starting to get on her nerves. She loved him, of that she had no doubt, but she had always been independent and her need for him made her feel like a silly love sick teenager. She really didn't like that feeling but she'd learn to deal with it. He was through her window only seconds after she had told him to come up. "Just couldn't do it could you?" she laughed placing both hands on her hips.

"Nope, I needed you," he said and she could hear the truth in his words. It was then, hearing the truth in his words and seeing it in his beautiful blue eyes, she realized that he felt the same need for her as she did for him. "How did you know I was out there? And why are you up? I figured you'd be sleeping?" he asked finding his favorite piece of red hair and twirling it between his fingers.

"Are you disappointed?" she asked jokingly. Presley was not really sure how to explain that even in her sleep she could feel him or how she could see him through trees in the dead of night.

"Of course not. Are you upset that I came when I promised I wouldn't?"

"No, I'm glad you did," she said leaning into him, pressing her body flush against him as she wrapped her slender arms around his waist.

"How did you know I was out there, Presley?" he asked again his tone making it pretty obvious that he wasn't going to be distracted.

"I don't know. I was sleeping and I...I...I felt you. It woke me up so I went to the window and there you were," she said so quietly that had it not been for his vampire hearing he would have missed it.

"You felt me here when you were sleeping and you saw me without any trouble. Do you feel okay?"

"Actually, I feel great, Better and more complete then I ever have now that you're here. Will you stay with me?"

"Anything you want, mio amore, it's yours," he said squeezing her tightly. "Is your mom here?" he asked. He had never really put much thought into meeting Presley's mother but suddenly it felt very important. After thinking for a minute Presley said, "I don't know, she should be. Wait here I'll go check." Presley quietly left her bedroom and headed down the dark hall to her mother's room. Before opening the door she knew the room would be empty and after opening it her suspicions were confirmed. She felt her heart sink to her stomach. The absence of her mother was starting to weigh on her, she did find the feeling odd since it wasn't long ago that she would avoid her mother at all costs. As her eyes began to fill with tears she heard Luca's voice, "I'm sure there's a good reason she's not here. I'm sure she'll be here to see you before we go tomorrow." She turned and pressed herself back into his embrace. Being in his arms had become the only place she felt safe or wanted anymore. "Come on, let's go to bed...to sleep," he said as she giggled when he added the last part.

While she climbed under her overstuffed comforter Luca grabbed the book she had been reading. She blushed a deep shade of red as he read the title *Dark Wolf Rising*. "Do I want to know what this is about?" he asked with a questioning eyebrow lifted. "Probably not," she laughed and bit her bottom lip. "Let me see if I can guess," he said joining her in the bed. Positioning himself so he could put an arm around her, she cuddled against his side laying her head on his chest. He said, "Some trashy romance novel about werewolves?" When her cheeks became redder than the blanket that covered her body he laughed, "Thought so."

"Shut up!" she said slapping his chest lightly. Still laughing he rubbed the spot she had just hit as if it actually hurt.

" Alright, but you do know they write these things about vampires, too, right?"

"That probably wouldn't be a good thing for me to read right now." she stated. Quickly catching her meaning he agreed. They sat quietly, him stroking her hair and her rubbing her small hand over his chiseled chest until she drifted to sleep.

Once she was in a deep sleep Luca got out of her bed with his vampire grace never once disturbing her sleep. He walked to the window and looked out to the trees where he had once been standing. *She shouldn't have been able to see me. What am I missing?* He thought. He was now certain that she was more than just a beautiful teenage human girl. He could figure out what exactly she was later, but he knew she wasn't human. He swiftly jumped from the window and headed home deciding that after prom he and Brenda would be having a little heart to heart.

Chapter Thirty

Presley woke up with a feeling of emptiness. She had become used to having that feeling whenever Luca wasn't with her but this time it felt worst, deeper. She forced herself to get out of her bed, trying to ignore the way her body ached. When her feet hit the floor the dread she had felt the past couple of days was in its place in the pit of her stomach. Rolling her eyes at herself she headed to the shower. She had an hour and a half before she had to be at Simply Stylin' Hair Salon. She sat on the side of her bath tub adjusting the temperature of the water. As the temperature of the water rose so did her anger. It was the day of her senior prom and her eighteenth birthday but she didn't feel the excitement most girls felt, all she could feel was the fear that something bad was going to happen and it pissed her off.

After reluctantly getting out of the warm shower she wrapped herself in her fluffy pink robe and headed downstairs for breakfast. She was starving, the hungriest she had ever been. When she walked through the entryway of the kitchen she saw her mother sitting at the table with her head bowed. When Brenda lifted her head Presley knew immediately something was wrong. Not only was it clear that Brenda had not slept a wink all night but also that she had spent her sleepless night crying. "Happy Birthday, Sweetheart. How are you feeling today?" Brenda asking lifting her steaming cup of coffee to her lips with one hand and pushing a plate of food toward the empty chair across from her with the other.

"Thanks, I feel fine, I guess. Are you okay?" She asked walking to the coffee pot.

Brenda took in a deep sigh of relief after everything she had endured last night. The fact that Presley felt no different on the morning of her eighteenth birthday gave her a bit of hope that her plan had worked. She had kept Presley from the life she had been raised in and because of that Presley wouldn't have to deal with the nightmare she had before she left. "A um....coworker of mine was hurt last night so it's just been a long night. I have to head back to the hospital to… cover his shift. I know I should be here today and I want to but..."

Presley could sense that her mother was hiding something but didn't want to deal with it right at that moment. She figured whoever it was had to be more than just a co-worker and maybe the reason she was spending so much time away from home. "It's fine, Mom, really not a big deal." Presley interrupted figuring if her mother could lie so could she. Joining her mother at the table she said, "I have to leave in about thirty minutes anyway to go see Amy."

Brenda smiled but because of the sadness she felt that smile never spread across her face to reach her eyes. "Here," Brenda handed Presley a red envelope. Presley took the envelope but was slightly disappointed when she opened it. Inside was $200 in cash which was great but she was hoping to find a sweet, heartfelt card, a thoughtful present or at least a small note but all that was in the envelope was the money. "Thanks, Mom," she said with a smile. She finished her breakfast, excused herself from the table, and headed back to her room to get ready to go to Amy's.

∞

Luca parked his car about a mile from Simply Stylin' Hair Salon, he knew Presley would be arriving soon. Strolling down the main street of the small town he watched families enjoying the peace they felt living in the small tight-knit community. He laughed wondering how at peace they would feel if they knew that walking amongst them was a vampire or that somewhere in their small town were two vampires that wanted to treat them like cattle. The sight he saw was proof that sometimes ignorance was bliss. He spotted Presley as she walked through the doors of the salon. He settled on to a bench down the street keeping a close eye not only on the door but the people around it. Pulling his phone from his pocket he sent Presley a quick text message wanting to give her the impression that he was still at home.

Luca: Good morning birthday girl.

Presley: Good Morning

Luca: What's the plan today? When do you want me to pick you up?

Presley: Looks like you already know the plan. Is that bench comfy ;) BUSTED!

Luca: I tried.

Presley: I know

Luca: Just pretend like I'm not here

Presley: I intend to Luv u

Luca: U2

Luca laughed as he shoved his phone back into his pocket, he should have known that she'd know he would follow her. He was becoming pretty predictable when it came to her. He spent the next two hours simply observing the people of the small town until Presley finally emerged from the salon, still pretending that he wasn't watching her. His breath caught at the sight of her, something was different. It wasn't just her hair, she was revealing a confidence and strength he had never seen in her, but he liked it. She looked more woman then girl and he found that incredibly sexy. Since Luca had known Presley she had always exhibited a strength and confidence that was remarkable for someone her age. Yet at times he felt she used that demeanor as a façade to protect herself. But now she totally radiated a true sense of confidence and inner strength.

∞

Presley returned home shortly after noon and was surprised that her mother was still home. "Mom!" she called out as she entered the house. "Up here!" Brenda yelled from her upstairs bedroom. Presley trotted up the stairs and went into her mother's bedroom. "Hey, I figured you'd have left by now," she said plopping down on her mother's bed. "I told them I'd be a little late. I know it's early but I was wondering if you could go ahead and get ready so I can see you before you leave?"

Presley thought about it for a minute, it was way too early but she did want her mom to see her in her dress. "Okay, just give me a couple minutes to get it on and do my make up." Presley jumped from her mom's bed and hurried into her room. She sat on the small bench in front of her make up table. Brenda remained in her room getting ready to head back to the hospital. She did feel guilty about not telling Presley about John's condition but seeing the excitement on her face when she asked her to put on her dress she knew she had made the right decision.

After applying her make-up a little darker and more dramatic than usual she slipped into her dress. The light fabric hugged her upper body like a second skin and the skirt, short in the front and long in the back, accentuated her long slender legs. High heeled shoes put the toned muscles of her legs on display. Admiring her reflection in her full length mirror she finally felt excited about the upcoming night. She pulled herself away from the mirror and went to find her mom who was still in her room getting ready for a night at the hospital. "Oh, my, you look stunning," Brenda said breathlessly. Presley simply smiled at her mother's praise and turned in a slow circle. Brenda walked toward Presley grabbing both of her hands in hers. "I have never seen anybody look more beautiful than you do right now," she said honestly.

"Thanks, Mom."

"I really need to go but I want to get a couple pictures so I can show you off at work today," Brenda said going to retrieve her iPhone from its charger on her nightstand.

Fifteen minutes and a ton of pictures later Brenda was gone and Presley stood alone in the living room. She thought about changing out of her dress, feeling a little silly just hanging around the house in it by herself, but she couldn't bring herself to do it. Carefully sitting down on the couch she found a Law and Order SVU marathon on TV and settled in for couple hours of relaxing watching one of her favorite shows. It was about 4:00 and the start of the second episode of her show when she heard her phone began to chime with the arrival of a text message. Walking to the counter to get her phone she rolled her eyes sure that the message was from one of her friends checking on her. Her heart skipped a beat when she saw who the message was from.

Dad: Hey, Sweetheart, happy birthday. I would really like to see you we have a lot to talk about. Will you see me?

Barely thinking she responded to the message but found it hard to type with the tears welling in her eyes and her hands trembling.

Presley: of course come on over.

Dad: I can't come in there it's too painful meet me at the corner.

Presley: Ok when?

Dad: now

Presley: Ok

Not taking the time to think she rushed to her front door. Feeling something inside her stir telling her not to open the door she froze with her hand on the knob. She stood still for a moment having an internal debate with herself. ***You shouldn't leave the house you promised Luca you wouldn't but it's your dad you've been waiting for this almost a year. How can you possibly pass this up?*** Thinking for a moment she answered herself out loud "you can't" with that she swung open the door and headed down the street.

∞

Luca looked at his clock it was 4:00 and time to get ready. Marcus had already dressed and was rushing Luca to get ready they had to go get the girls and bring them back for the romantic dinner both boys had spent most of the day preparing. While Marcus took some photos of himself to send to his mother Luca headed to his room to take a quick shower and get ready hoping it would calm Marcus's nerves. Luca couldn't figure out what had Marcus so rattled. He was acting like it was his first date with Stephanie even though they had been dating over a year. Then it struck him, it may not have been their first date but Luca was willing to bet that Marcus was planning on tonight being a different first. Marcus had once told Luca that all though he and Stephanie were very affectionate and she often joked about sex it was a step neither one of them had ever taken. After getting out of the shower he quickly dressed and headed downstairs so Marcus would know that he was ready....way too early in his opinion.

∞

The closer Presley got to the corner the more she began to doubt her decision to leave the house. The corner came into to view but her dad was nowhere to be seen. The only person there was a young dark headed girl talking on her cell phone. When Presley reached the corner the girl smiled sweetly and stepped to the side letting Presley pass. Looking down both sides of the street she saw no sign of her father. "You look very pretty, Presley," said the girl standing on corner. Spinning around to look at the girl she was going to say thank you until she realized the girl, she didn't know, called her by her name. When their eyes met she knew exactly what and who she was looking at, not only was this girl a vampire but this was…"Ivy?" Presley said, not able to hide the fear in her voice. "So you've heard of me. Good, I hate wasting time with introductions," she smiled at the fear she saw in Presley's eyes. "What do you want?" Presley asked trying to push down her fear and her urge to rip off the girl's head. Ivy was a vampire and Presley knew she wouldn't stand a chance in a physical altercation but she had never wanted to do anything so badly. Ivy laughed for a moment and the sound sent chills down Presley's spine. "All I want is to talk, but privately get in the car," Ivy stated.

Presley turned to her left when she heard a car door open and almost broke into tears as she saw Andrew emerge from the car. She held back her tears, she wouldn't give them the satisfaction of seeing her cry. "Yeah, um that's not going to happen," Presley stated, impressing herself with the firmness in her voice despite the fear she felt inside.

"You can get in the car under your own power or I can drain you to near death and put you in myself. The choice is yours, I suggest you choose wisely," Ivy said her voice remaining calm and low. Which Presley had decided was more threatening than if she had been yelling. Ivy was in complete control of this situation and they both knew it. Presley looked at Andrew who had a cocky grin that Presley wanted to rip off but he was beaming with pride watching this woman terrify her. "Fine," Presley walked slowly toward the car. She felt her skin crawl when Ivy wrapped her ice cold fingers around her upper arm. When the two girls reached Andrew Presley said, "Whether I live or die I hope Luca rips you both apart and I hope it hurts." Andrew and Ivy both laughed as they pushed Presley into the back seat of the car. **Luca where are you I need you. HELP!** Her mind was screaming even though everything in her told her he wouldn't hear it.

∞

Luca had just stood after tying the second of his shiny black dress shoes when he dropped to his knees. Presley's voice came tearing through his head **Luca where are you I need you. HELP!**

"Luca, man, what's wrong?" Marcus asked as soon as he saw Luca hit the floor.

"I don't know but we have to go now!" Luca yelled heading to the door and without any more questions Marcus followed.

"You take the car, meet me at Presley's quickly," Luca instructed. Not giving Marcus time to respond he took off at inhuman speed heading toward Presley.

He reached her house in a matter of minutes. Swinging the door open he searched the house frantically but found no trace of her. Just as he was leaving the house the blue Mustang that once belonged to him was coming to a screeching halt in the driveway.

"What the hell is going on?" Marcus asked jumping from the car.

"They have her," Luca said looking up and down the street. "Damn it! How did I let this happen?"

"Andrew?" Marcus asked, already knowing the answer but hoping he was wrong.

"Both of them, Ivy is here. I know it."

"Okay, calm down, we'll get her back. Let me call Stephanie and Kevin, get them over here and we'll come up with a plan."

Luca nodded, not really sure they could help but right now he didn't have a better idea. He was once again haunted by the fact that he never took the time to find Andrew's hideout.

∞

As Presley sat silently in the back seat of the car she had been forced into she was trying to come up with some kind of a plan. She had briefly considered jumping from the car but knew she couldn't outrun them. She also had entertained the notion of causing the car to wreck but knew that she was the only one that could be truly hurt in that situation.

"Where are you taking me?" she asked trying to sound bored by the whole scenario.

She knew they were headed out in to the rural part of town but landmarks were hard to find in those parts. Nothing but trees and dirt roads surrounded them.

"Like I would tell you that," Ivy answered looking back at Presley. Presley couldn't help but notice Ivy looking around, as if she was searching for something.

"Why? You have my phone. It's not like I can tell anybody where I am." Ivy thought for a minute pondering Presley's words. She was right Luca didn't even know she was gone. If he did, he wouldn't be able to read her thoughts until Andrew brought him back to the cabin. Looking over at Andrew who just shrugged, she said, "A small cabin."

"What are you going to do with me?" Presley asked, still trying hard to hide her fear and so far she was doing a pretty good job, which surprised even her. The cruel smile that spread across Ivy's lips as she turned to face her caused the already present knot in her stomach to grow tighter.

"I haven't decided yet. First I was going to have your little boyfriend watch as I broke your neck. However, now I'm thinking maybe I'll let you watch him die before I drain you dry, or maybe I'll turn you. Wouldn't our little prince love that?"

"You're a twisted bitch," Presley spat out before she could stop herself.

"Shut your mouth or I'll rip your tongue out," Andrew shouted. Ivy just winked at her. Presley turned her head to look out the window and as soon as she did she saw them drive past Piney St. She knew exactly where they were taking her. When she was dating Eric they used to go to parties at cabins in Eudy Park. She couldn't explain her feeling but something about knowing where they were taking her made her feel as if things weren't totally hopeless.

∞

Minutes after being called Stephanie and Kevin's cars almost collided pulling into Presley's driveway at the same time.

"Where is she?!" Kevin shouted jumping from the car racing over to Luca. When Luca answered him with, "I don't know." Kevin punched him square in the jaw. "How could you let this happen!" he shouted. Marcus and Stephanie, who were both dressed in their prom attire, pulled him away from Luca. Luca simply hung his head. Normally anybody who dared to hit him would have hell to pay for their bad decision, but he understood Kevin's anger toward him because he felt the same anger, if not more, toward himself.

"Calm down!" Stephanie shouted and all three boys turned to stare at her. "We don't have time for this crap. We have to find her and we aren't going to be able to do that if we're too busy blaming each other to look for her. We are all to blame for this, we all knew something was going to happen today and we ignored it. Now let's figure out where they would take her.

Luca, they aren't going to do anything to her until they have their hands on you."

"You're right," Luca said feeling a bit of hope breaking through the despair he was feeling, "but we need to find them first. We have a better chance of taking them if they don't know we're coming." He was beginning to pace the yard trying to develop a plan.

"Stephanie, you look beautiful," Marcus said. He hadn't been able to take his eyes off her since she arrived. "But if we're going to go hunt down vampires maybe you should go to Presley's room and change." Looking down at her dress that already had a small tear from pulling Kevin away from Luca. "You're probably right," she said and hastily made her way to Presley's room to change.

After throwing on a pair of jeans and black v-neck tee she sat on the edge of the bed pulling a pillow to her chest and looked around the room. Her tears began to fall freely as she tried to focus on items that reminded her so much of her best friend.

"Stephanie, are you okay?" Marcus asked as he entered the room.

"How did we let this happen?" Stephanie asked through her tears.

"We'll find her," he said pulling her into a tight embrace.

"Okay, let's go," she said pulling away from him and wiping the tears from her eyes. "We don't have time for me to fall apart"

When they joined Kevin and Luca in the front yard Marcus asked, "Have y'all thought of anything yet?" Kevin and Luca both shook their heads.

"If Andrew or Ivy have a house around here I don't know about it." Luca was still inwardly blaming himself for putting Presley in danger. Now she was in the hands of two vampires who would kill her and not think twice about it. ***Oh, Presley, where are you?*** He thought, raking his hands through his hair.

∞

Presley had to hold back a gasp when she heard Luca's voice in her head *Oh, Presley, where are you?* She knew it shouldn't be possible but at this point she would take what she could get. *Luca! I hope I'm not imagining your voice in my head. If you can hear me they are taking me to a cabin at Eudy Park.*

Luca stopped dead in his track and almost fell to his knees again when he heard Presley tell him where she was. Not having time to dwell on the fact this should be impossible he turned to Kevin, "Do you know how to get to Eudy Park?"

"Yeah, why?"

"Because that's where they're taking her."

"How do you know that?" Stephanie asked.

"She told me through her thoughts."

"That's not possible," Kevin stated shaking his head.

"Kevin, you're right it shouldn't be but you're standing here talking to a vampire. Do we really need to have the anything is possible conversation?"

"You're right, let's go."

All four loaded into Stephanie's Jeep and headed full speed to the place they hoped they would find Presley.

A small smile slid across Presley's lips when she heard Luca's deep voice in her head saying **Don't worry baby I'm on my way. I love you.**

Chapter Thirty One

The car was silent until they arrived at the small cabin that had become Andrew and Ivy's hideout. The car came to a stop, Ivy reached for the door handle but stopped short when she felt Andrew's large hand wrap around her upper arm.

"Get her in the house and then meet me on the porch," he said sternly. With a look of confusion on her face Ivy nodded and got out of the car. She pulled the back door of the car open with so much force that it almost came off the frame, "oops" she laughed as she grabbed Presley's arm and jerked her from the car.

"Hey, you don't have to be so rough. It's not like I'm going anywhere!" Presley yelled and glared at Ivy.

"Oops, " Ivy repeated with an evil grin. Jerking her by the arm Ivy led Presley through the small door of the cabin and tossed her on the couch that was against the opposite wall.

"Geez, what the hell is your problem? I mean I know you're going to kill me but can you stop with the jerking and throwing?" Presley said while rubbing her arm.

"Sit there and shut up! If you move from that spot I'll break both your legs."

Presley didn't know how to respond to Ivy's threat so she simply rolled her eyes.

When she had Presley settled in the cabin Ivy joined Andrew on the front porch. "What's wrong, Babe?" she asked as she nuzzled herself into his muscular chest.

Wrapping his arms around her tiny body he asked, "Can you read her mind?"

"I..I... no. I haven't heard a single thought," Ivy responded stunned by the sudden realization.

"Ivy, I think you should really reconsider this. Something's off. She's terrified, her mind should be practically screaming."

"No, this ends tonight. I'm sure Luca just taught her to block it or something," Ivy said removing herself from his embrace.

"Ivy, I don't like this. I don't want to leave you alone with her," he said pulling her back to him.

"Don't you think if she was anything more than human she would have escaped by now, or at least tried?"

Andrew thought for a minute and, against his better judgment, he agreed she was probably right. "Just be careful," he sighed.

"Go get our little prince and get back here quickly," she said following her words with a deep passionate kiss.

"Alright but at least tie her up, or something, please."

"Okay, Okay. You're no fun you know that, right?" she smiled.

"I know. I love you."

"I love you, too." After another kiss Andrew was gone, heading to Luca's home to bring him to his death.

Ivy went in the house and pulled a chair from the kitchen table placing it in front of the couch where Presley was sitting. After a moment of silence Ivy took a deep breath and said, "You know I wouldn't be doing this if they weren't planning to kill my brother."

"They wouldn't be planning to kill him if he hadn't already killed more than one innocent person," Presley retorted.

Ivy laughed, "Do you get jailed or killed every time you eat a burger? I mean humans kill all the time to survive. What's the difference?"

"He didn't have to kill to survive and that's the difference."

Ivy walked over to Presley sitting close enough to her that their legs touched. Placing her lips right next to Presley's ear she whispered, "Oh, sweet Presley, you're right he didn't kill them simply to survive." Running her sharp fingernail down Presley's neck over her artery she continued, "He enjoyed it, the taste of their blood, ripping their flesh from their necks. He's a vampire, that's what we do."

"You and you're brother are sick and twisted. I hope they kill you both," Presley said and then felt Ivy's grip on her neck tighten.

"You sure are a smart mouth little bitch, especially for one that's about to die."

"You may kill me but if you think for a moment I'm going to sit here and cry or beg for my life you're stupider than I thought."

As Presley spoke Ivy's eyes grew black and her fangs lengthened. "I'm beginning to feel a little hungry," she said leaning toward Presley and grabbing a fist full of her hair, pulling her head back to expose her neck. She slid her tongue over Presley's throat and Presley prepared herself for the pain she knew was coming. When Luca bit her it brought her nothing but pleasure but she knew that Ivy's bite would not. Just as Ivy's fangs where about to pierce Presley's skin the door to the cabin flew open and the entire doorway was blocked by Luca's massive body. Ivy's head snapped toward the door and a smiled crept across her face. Lifting Presley up by her hair she quickly and forcibly tossed her into the far corner of the room.

"You're early," she laughed as she made her way toward him.

Luca slammed the door with enough force to shake the walls of the small cabin. Presley watched with blurred vision as Luca's fangs grew longer then she had ever seen them and his eyes turned completely black. "I'm going to rip you apart!" Luca growled.

Ivy was laughing again. "No you won't," she said. "Not with her watching," she added running her fingertips over his well-defined chest. It was Luca's turn to laugh "Was that your big plan? She knows what I am."

"Oh, I'm sure she does. I bet she can't wait to see you sparkle. However, you know as well as I do if you kill me, if she sees what you truly are, what you are truly capable of that Twilight/Vampire Diaries induced haze she's living in will shatter." Her words had the effect on Luca she knew that they would. She saw the doubt in his eyes and when he broke eye contact with her she attacked, taking advantage of his distraction. Lunging forward with all her strength she took him to the floor. He struggled to move her off his body but she had her knees dug into his biceps with so much pressure he could almost hear his bones crack.

"I have been waiting for so long for this," she said with hatred thick in her words and burning in her eyes. Leaning down she pressed a rough kiss and his lips. When she pulled away from his mouth he spat at her. She simply laughed as she raised her hand above her head, rearing back ready to plunge it through his chest with all her vampire strength and remove his heart from his chest. With her arm up and ready to inflict the deadly blow she paused when she heard a blood curdling snarl coming from behind her. Slowly she turned her head to see what had made the terrifying noise. Her eyes widened and her arm fell to her side when her glare fell upon a very big, very pissed wolf. The white wolf had the front half of its body lowered in an attack position. Ivy stared stunned, her mind couldn't process what she saw. Luca used Ivy's distraction to toss her off of him. When her body hit the floor the wolf lunged, landing on top of her. She couldn't scream, she couldn't fight, she didn't have time... the wolf sank its teeth into her neck with a crushing force. With one swift shake of its giant head Ivy's head was removed from her body. Luca stood in awe for a moment watching the giant beast take down its prey with strength and grace. When the large beast raised it's head to let out a howl announcing its victory Luca darted to the far corner where Presley had been tossed. When he reached the corner it was empty. The only thing that remained was the tattered red fabric of Presley's prom dress. Luca bent down slowly picking up the dress. Looking from the dress then to the wolf standing across from him and back to the dress everything became clear. His mind went back to the first time he took her blood and the power it gave him, next it went to the way the wildlife in the woods behind his house reacted to her emotions, and then to the night she had her nightmare and the claw marks left on his sheets and on her skin. Slowly he broke his stare from the red material in his hand and looked where the powerful wolf had stood. In place of the glorious wolf who had saved his life was the beautiful girl who had saved his soul. She was curled up on the floor crying. He rushed to her side removing his shirt from his body and wrapping it around her trembling naked body. Lifting her face so he could look at her he pushed her blood stained blonde hair away from her tear stained face. "Oh Baby, are you..." he couldn't finish his question. Between her tears Presley choked out "Did I just...was I a wolf?"

"Yes Baby, and you are a beautiful wolf," he said as he lifted her into his arms. He pulled her close to his chest and began to carry her to the door. Before they could reach the door it flew open on its own and their three friends, every face showing concern, rushed over to them. **Oh god did they see? Do they know? Will they be afraid of me now?** With the fear of rejection running through her mind she searched her friend's faces looking for any trace of fear or disgust but all she saw was love and concern. ***They are your friends they love you. Don't worry they aren't going to reject you.*** Luca said to her through their newly developed bond.

"Presley, are you okay?" Kevin asked grabbing one of her legs that was dangling over the side of Luca's arm.

"I don't know right now," she said honestly.

As the group turned to leave their exit was blocked by Andrew. "What have you done?" he yelled as his eyes fell upon Ivy's headless body. His nostrils flared as he looked at Presley. Along with the scent of blood and death coming from Ivy's body he caught the distinctive smell of..."Wolf," he said as rage filled his eyes and his hands clenched into fists. Before anybody could respond he grabbed Stephanie by the hair and pulled her to him.

"Andrew, let her go." Luca demanded as the others froze in fear. Marcus lunged himself at Andrew. Andrew simply batted him to the side as if he was a mere fly.

"Let her go!" Luca repeated.

Tears streamed from Stephanie's eyes. She could feel Andrew's rage, she could feel that he wanted her dead, he wanted them all dead. "You killed her, or was it your little bitch?" Andrew asked through gritted teeth.

"It doesn't matter who did it. She was going to kill us. You didn't honestly think she would live through this did you?" Luca asked trying to remain calm. Andrew took a couple deep breaths as he stared helplessly at the body of the woman he loved lying lifeless on the floor.

"Neither will she," he said before plunging his sharp fangs into Stephanie's neck. Stephanie let out a loud sob when the pain of his fangs piercing skin and ripping her muscles hit her but her cries where over shadowed by the excruciating scream that came from behind her. Andrew threw her across the room. Grabbing his throat he fell to his knees still screaming. The group watched in horror as his mouth and throat began to melt and smoke came from his mouth. On hands and knees he crawled to Ivy's body laying down beside her. His screams quieted as his body disintegrated in front of them.

"What the hell was that?" Kevin asked unable to break his stare from the horrific scene in front of him. Luca was still staring at Stephanie who was sitting against the wall hugging her knees and staring at Andrew's body in shock.

"You're a witch," Luca said.

"What?" Marcus asked lowering himself to embrace Stephanie. As Marcus held her tightly she stared at Luca waiting on an explanation with her eyes laced with fear.

Still holding Presley tight against him he looked at Stephanie and began to explain. "You're a witch, that's why he's dead. A witch's blood is very powerful. People will kill for the power it holds. As a way to protect its self the witch's blood turns to acid when anybody or anything tries to take it in a violent matter or for an evil purpose. The only person who can take a witch's blood is her life mate."

"Her life mate, what's that?" Marcus asked.

"Her life mate is her......soul mate. He is born with the purpose of protecting her. I don't really know how it works. Given the sudden twist our lives have just taken I have a friend I'm going to call. She can help. She's a witch, Stephanie, she can help you." Stephanie, who still sat staring in utter shock over what had just happened, simply nodded.

"We need to get them out of here," Kevin said looking around the cabin trying not to look at the two bodies on the floor. He had already seen enough to haunt his nightmares for years to come.

"You're right, Marcus get Stephanie to the car. We'll take them to my house." Luca said. Following Luca's orders Marcus stood up, lifting Stephanie's stiff body into his arms and headed to the car.

"Um, what about this mess?" Kevin asked motioning toward Ivy and Andrew but refusing to look in that direction. Luca looked down at his two foes, "It'll take care of itself. In about 15 minutes their bodies and blood will disintegrate and there will be no trace of them," he said shrugging. Looking down at

Presley he kissed her forehead, "Everything is going to be okay Baby. I promise I'll do whatever it takes to ensure it."

"I love you," she whispered.

Kevin drove the Jeep to Luca's house while Luca and Marcus sat in the back seat both holding the girls they loved as close to them as they could. Kevin would occasionally steal glances through the rear view mirror. He had never been so worried about his friends. Both of the girls whom he had watch grow into strong capable women were now more like scared little girls, and it was breaking his heart. He wanted nothing more than to take away their fear and pain but he couldn't, not this time. This time he would have to sit by helplessly. When they arrived at the house Luca took Presley straight to his room and Marcus took Stephanie to his. Kevin made his way to the kitchen to start a pot of coffee, knowing they were all in for a long night. His heart broke for his friends a little more when he saw the romantic scene Marcus and Luca had set up in the dining room for their prom night dinner. Shaking his head he finished the task of making the coffee. He knew that coffee wasn't going to help anything but he had to do something besides sitting there helplessly.

Chapter Thirty Two

Luca gently placed Presley on his bed and was heading to the bathroom when she grabbed his arm, "Please don't leave." Her voice was shaking with fear. He sat on the bed next to her holding her hand, "I'm just going to run you a bath. I'm not going anywhere, I promise. Trust me you are stuck with me...as long as you'll have me," he said softly. Presley could hear the insecurity in his voice. "Then I'm stuck with you forever," she smiled. She was puzzled as to why he was feeling insecure. Luca kissed her softly then headed back to the bathroom. After he had filled the tub with warm water he turned to the bathroom door where Presley was already standing fidgeting with the bottom hem of the white button up dress shirt Luca had put on her earlier. "Am I a...um...um...?" She asked even though she already knew the answer but she seemed unable to convince herself it was true. He walked over to her, placing one hand on the side of her face. "Yes, and you are as beautiful in wolf form as you are in human form," he said with complete honesty.

"Does it bother you that I'm a...wh...what I am?"

"What you are is the woman I love. No it doesn't bother me that you're a werewolf. "

"Does this mean my biological father is...is a...wer...too?"

"Most likely. Honey, you need to say it."

"I can't. I don't know how to deal with this," she said as tears once again began to stream down her cheeks.

"You can and I have a friend I'm going to call to come help us figure out our next move, okay." he said trying to reassure her that everything would be okay.

"Wendy?" she growled and her blue eyes began to glow. Luca laughed at her reaction.

"Presley, Baby, she's a friend. I've always heard how possessive you wolves can be but I never knew how sexy you are when you're being possessive." Presley squinted her eyes, pursed her lips, laughed and then laid her head on his chest. Luca was caressing her hair as he ran his hand down the back of her head. "Take a bath, I'll go find you some clean clothes. I'm sure Stephanie has something." Presley smiled in agreement and once Luca left the bathroom closing the door behind him she submerged herself in the hot bath water.

Luca knocked lightly on Marcus' door. "Come on in," he heard Marcus say from the other side of the door. When Luca entered the room the first thing he noticed was that Stephanie wasn't there.

"Where's Steph?" Luca asked looking around the room.

"She's taking a hot bath," Marcus said pointing over his shoulder to the adjoining bathroom.

"Great minds think alike, my brother." Luca laughed.

"What's going to happen to them?" Marcus asked.

"It's going to be tough on them I'm not going to lie. There are things that are going to be brought to light that are going to be hard for both of them to take. So be prepared, she is going to need you more now than she ever has." Luca said shaking his head.

"Like what?" Kevin asked. Marcus and Luca both turned to see Kevin standing in the room holding two cups of coffee. "I thought they might want some coffee. I don't know, I had to do something." Kevin said.

"Good idea," Marcus smiled understanding his friend's need to do something, anything, to help. Both boys turned their attention to Luca and asked again what problems he was anticipating.

"Okay first with Stephanie there is a good chance her parents aren't her birth parents. There is no way any witch would not tell their child what they were because their magic can be triggered by highly emotional situations. Luckily, Stephanie is in more control of her emotions than any other teenager girl I have ever met. Wendy, will be able to help her learn to use and control her magic and her emotions. As far as Presley goes we need to find her father and her pack." Luca was interrupted when Marcus asked "Why do we need to go looking for a pack of werewolves?"

"Because I don't know anything about werewolves. I can't teach her to control it. Believe it or not things could have been much worst then they were."

"How could they possibly have been worst?" Kevin asked.

"If we had made it to prom and Becca, for instance, had gotten in Presley's face again and pissed her off enough it could have easily been Becca who lost her head tonight."

"Good point." Kevin said then added "What are we going to tell her mother? I mean her father had to be a werewolf right?"

"Yeah and I'm pretty sure her mother is, too."

"No, she would have told me," Presley said entering the room wrapped in an oversized towel.

"Where are your clothes?" Luca asked, not happy about the fact she was standing in the room with other males in only a towel. He mentally shook himself not understanding why he was bothered. These were her friends...his friends, but he was still insanely jealous of any male seeing her wearing so few clothes.

"I was coming to ask you the same question," she replied with a half-smile.

"Marcus, would you get her some clothes from Stephanie's stuff, please?" Luca asked never breaking eye contact with Presley.

"My mom is not a werewolf. She wouldn't lie to me about that." Presley said more hopeful, but not convinced, that what she was saying was true.

"Sweetheart, you shifted without trying you have to be pure blood," Luca said as he made his way toward her.

"You're wrong, she wouldn't!" Presley stopped when she realized she could be wrong. Her mother had lied to her about her father, maybe she was wolf. She began to tremble and weep, as tears fell her eyes began to glow and her canine teeth began to lengthen.

"Presley, you have to calm down. We will figure this out." As Luca lovingly covered her hands with his her anger subsided, her teeth and eyes returned to normal. "Go get dressed, please. You guys will all stay here tonight and tomorrow we will talk to your mother and make a plan okay." Luca said calmly. He gave her the pair of black leggings Marcus had handed him, and a cup of coffee. "Take these and get a shirt out of my dresser, okay?" Presley nodded and retreated back to Luca's room.

Luca returned his attention to the boys standing in the room with him, "Tonight let's just comfort them and try to keep them calm. Tomorrow when Wendy's here we can go into all the possible problems that may occur. Kevin, can you go make something for them to eat?"

"Yeah" Kevin said handing Marcus the cup of coffee he had made for Stephanie.

Just as Kevin left the room Stephanie entered the room with make-up on and fully clothed.

"Alright boys, what's the plan?" she asked completely calm and collected. Both boys stared in amazement at her attitude.

"We're just gonna hang tonight. Luca has a friend he's going to call to come help us tomorrow."

"Okay," she shrugged, "I'm starving." Both boys looked at her and then at each other. Both of them were trying to decide if she was really okay or if she was in shock.

"Why are you guys looking at me like that? Do I have a booger or something?"

"Are you sure you're okay?" Luca asked.

"No I'm not okay but freaking out isn't going to do anybody any good. Now if you don't mind please go take care of your girlfriend so my boyfriend can take care of me."

Luca smiled bowing his head slightly toward her then he left the room.

∞

After the group ate dinner, while trying the whole time to talk about anything but werewolves, witches and vampires, they all retreated to their rooms. Kevin took one of the guest rooms, Stephanie and Marcus went to his room and Luca and Presley went to his.

Presley laid her head on Luca's bare chest and drifted to sleep in a matter of minutes. The events that day had taken a toll on her both physically and mentally. Luca sat in silence for a while waiting until she was in a deep sleep before leaving the bed to call Wendy. He grabbed his cell phone and walked out onto the terrace connected to his bedroom.

Wendy answered the phone after the second ring, "Luca, what's wrong?"

"How do you know something's wrong?" he asked.

"Because it's after midnight and, well, I'm a witch I know everything."

"Well, it's something that's going to blow your mind."

"Tell me."

"I need you to come here."

"Why? What's going on?" Wendy asked unnerved by the tone of Luca's voice.

"For starters Ivy and Andrew are dead."

"That's good right? I mean you knew you were going to have to kill them."

"I didn't kill them."

"What? Who did?" Wendy asked.

"Stephanie, one of the kids I was telling you about, Andrew bit her and then he pretty much melted."

"She's a witch. Are you serious?"

"Yep."

"What happened to Ivy?"

"Presley bit her head off, literally."

"What?"

"She's a werewolf."

"What! Who's her alpha? Where's her pack? How did you not know this? I can't imagine any alpha being okay with one of their females dating a vampire."

"I don't know who her alpha is, she's not in a pack."

"What did you say her name is?"

"Presley Kluttz."

"What's her mother's name?" Wendy asked beginning to sound frantic.

"Brenda."

"Bloody hell, that's Silas Rushing's daughter. You're dating an alpha's granddaughter. "

"Oh there's more."

"Good God, what else?"

Luca took in a deep breath and looked over his shoulder at Presley's sleeping face.

"We can communicate through thought and in wolf form she's solid white."

"Shit! I'll be there in a few hours. Hey, Luca" she said trying to keep her voice calm.

"What?" he asked. She could hear the concern in his voice and she knew why it was there.

"Don't jump to worst case scenarios here. All of this happened for a reason… it's fate. It may seem twisted right now but it will all make sense later."

"We'll see," was all he said before ending the call.

Luca went back to his room and lay on his bed beside Presley. Now that he knew she was sleeping and wouldn't be able to read his thoughts he let himself feel his fear. He didn't know much about wolves but one thing he did know was that wolves have one true mate, one person who completes their soul, one person that they can't live without and he had never heard of that person being anything but wolf. He was sure he was going to lose the girl he loved but as long as he had her he would enjoy every precious second.

Book 2 of the
Twisted Series
Twisted Truths
Coming Soon

Follow me on:
Twitter @SBTwisted
&
Facebook

Printed in Great Britain
by Amazon